The *China House* recipe of spice, the supernatural, and suspense is blue-ribbon. It may become a classic

— *The Sacramento Star*

China House is the best of the gay gothics.

— *The Weekly News*, Miami

China House will appeal to readers who like a competently told tale whose main characters are unapologetically gay, embroiled in a mystery, and physically appealing, to boot.

— *L. I. Connection*

China House has one of the more intriguing plots of the genre. There are strange bumps in the night, unexplained faces at the windows and lights in the dark. All of this makes for an enjoyable read, indeed.

— *Bay Area Reporter*

Published as a trade paperback original by
Alyson Publications
40 Plympton Street
Boston, Mass. 02118.

Distributed in the U.K. by GMP Publishers,
PO Box 247, London, N17 9QR, England.

First U.S. edition: May, 1983
second printing: June, 1989

ISBN 0-932870-30-9

CHINA HOUSE

by Vincent Lardo

Boston • Alyson Publications

• I •

Dr. Howard Roth brought the Bentley to a stop at the end of Indiana Avenue and wondered, as he often did, if every seashore town in America named its streets after the states in the Union. He walked up the slatted ramp and onto the boardwalk, stopping to look at the ocean before he continued on to the Evans house. The sea was as blue and still as the cloudless October sky and as Howard inhaled the salty air his eyes scanned the horizon where sky and sea met in a thin and almost indistinguishable curving line.

The season had ended weeks ago and the beach at Sea-Air was void of people. The gulls had reclaimed what was rightfully theirs, and as Howard watched them hovering over the shoreline he suddenly thought of them as an airborne patrol whose mission was to guard their territory against yet another horde of human invaders. With wings spread wide the big birds soared effortlessly between sea and sky, screeching their own particular paean of victory but never ceasing to scan the calm water for a potential meal as they performed their guard duty. As he watched, one of the birds swooped down for a kill, pulling its victim from the ocean. With the fish caught between its lethal bill the gull shot upward, back into formation, one wing catching a glint of the setting sun as it cut through the air like the blade of a finely honed knife.

Howard smiled as he beheld nature's endless cycle of the large devouring the small, the strong the weak. He thought of the human mind and how it had learned to outwit nature. In the human jungle the smart could, and usually did, devour those larger and stronger.

Howard took a deep breath and at once felt exhilarated as the clean, fresh air filled his lungs. He turned from the ocean and headed south along the boardwalk. His wool blazer, which felt heavy and too warm a few blocks inland, was just right for the cool breeze which blew off the ocean and caused his hair and tie to rise and fall as he marched briskly toward the end of the stilted path. He passed one large, boarded-up house after another until finally at the very end of the row of beach-fronted houses, and set some distance apart from the others, the Evans house came into view.

It was not, like its neighbors, a gray Victorian beach house so popular with builders in the early nineteen hundreds. In fact it was a bastard form of architecture and one would be hard pressed to label its style. Two stories high, long and squat, it looked more like a windowed fort, guarding the shoreline, than a home constructed for the pleasure of sun and surf. But as Howard turned off the boardwalk and started across the slat-wood ramp which led directly to the house he realized it was indeed built for the pleasures of shore living.

The lower floor presented a row of windows, each a full ten feet high, facing the Atlantic and unencumbered by curtains or draperies. The second floor windows were actually glass doors, each leading to a mini-balcony where one could stand or sit and enjoy a commanding view of the beach and ocean. The patio ran the entire length of the house and Howard could tell at a glance that the flagstone structure could easily accommodate a hundred people. Howard knew the house was as old or older than its neighbors along the beach and marveled at how close to modern architecture its designer had come.

As he stepped onto the patio he asked himself, as he had done most of the day at the institute, why he had been asked to call at the Evans house directly after work. Howard had never met any of the family though he knew, as did all of Sea-Air, who they were. The Evanses were the town's celebrities and provided a constant source of gossip for the locals, although not more than a dozen residents could claim friendship with them. In New York they were society. Not the self-made variety so popular with the press but the kind that could trace its roots back to the arrival of the Mayflower and, one suspected, further, if necessary. They had married into other prominent families, keeping money and breed intact, until one could find them among the affluent in most of America's major cities. The house at Sea-Air was one of the lesser known of the Evans's residences. Others, certainly more impressive, were located in Southampton, Newport, Cape Cod and Palm Beach.

Like most of their ilk the Evanses were a generous people and the family foundation funded projects for the arts and sciences that could not exist without this help. The Sloan Research Institute was one such beneficiary. When the Institute's director had called Howard to inform him of the invitation to visit the Evans's home, his tone had left no doubt that Howard was expected to attend as requested.

Were Howard Roth an actor, Hollywood would have cast him in the exact role he had selected for himself in real life. The handsome professional was the star research psychologist at the Institute, although his intelligence was often underrated because of his boyish good looks. Slightly over six feet, with a full head of blond hair that was always roguishly in need of combing, Howard boasted a slim, muscular body which was the result of genetics rather than diet or exercise. He could pass for a man fifteen years younger than his forty-five years, a fact that was a hindrance in his chosen profession but that he secretly enjoyed.

Howard was startled when a figure suddenly appeared directly in front of him. The form stood before one of the large windows which reflected sea and sky and for a brief moment Howard was not sure if he beheld an actual person or an illusion created by the reflection in the glass.

"Dr. Roth, I'm so glad you could come. I hope I didn't put you out."

The illusion stepped forward and became a very real and very handsome young man in his early twenties. Reddish blond hair, long enough to be fashionable and short enough to be sensible, a row of perfect white teeth and big, brown eyes crowned a body dressed in tight, faded jeans and a loose fitting plaid shirt. The feet were bare.

"I'm Scott Evans."

His handshake was firm and Howard recalled dozens of fraternity brothers at Columbia who looked and spoke and shook hands exactly as did Scott Evans.

"My pleasure," Howard said, "and you didn't put me out at all."

They looked at each other, appraising, sizing up. The wind, colder now that the sun had dipped far into the west, blew off the water and kept their hair and clothing in constant motion. "I was going to tell you your father is expecting me," Howard finally said.

Scott laughed, tossing his head back and burying his hands deep into the front pockets of his jeans. Howard noticed that the young man's dark brown eyes were his brightest feature. "I'm not as young as I look, Dr. Roth."

"Don't knock it," Howard answered. "Perpetual youth is the new religion of our society."

"Not so new, I'm afraid," Scott said. "But the idea bores me. The very young, regardless of age, are tedious. Why don't we go inside, it's too windy to stand out here."

Howard followed Scott through the glass door which was almost indistinguishable from the oversized windows. Once inside he all but exclaimed aloud at the size of the room they entered. It ran almost the entire length and width of the house and was cleverly divided into a dozen separate sitting areas. One about the fireplace looked perfect for a winter evening; another obviously was devoted to games with chess, checkers and the inevitable backgammon table clearly visible; yet another faced the windows and afforded an unobstructed view of ocean and sky.

"Cozy, isn't it?" Scott commented as he watched Howard gaze about the room.

Howard smiled, unsure how to respond. The very rich, he remembered, are different than you and I. "I think it's breathtaking. Standing here and looking out is like being afloat in the middle of the ocean," he waved his arm about the room, "with all the comforts of home."

"My family is very big with things like oceans, Dr. Roth. Fishing, whaling, ship building, right up to the present off-shore drilling for oil." Scott looked out at the sea as he spoke. "We've always been involved with the ocean and the ocean, as you can see, has been very good to us."

A silence followed, compounded by the sudden quietness in the house after the constant roar of surf and wind on the patio. "Have you been here all summer?" Howard asked.

Scott nodded. "Since early June. Sitting on my ass and thinking; trying to get it all together. Sea-Air is a great place for contemplation, Doctor. Nothing. . . but nothing, to distract you."

"I know what you mean," Howard said, knowing only that he had no idea what the boy was talking about. Why would a young, rich and handsome lad like Scott Evans want to spend an entire summer sitting and contemplating? Howard's analytical mind shifted into high gear. Behind the boy's calm, sure exterior lay a troubled soul. Howard sensed this in the way Scott Evans's eyes darted constantly over Howard's person, moving from head to toe and resembling, Howard thought, a horse breeder at an auction. Are you truly a thoroughbred? Can you go the distance? How will you act under pressure? Scott, with his nervous glances, was trying to assay the inner man from his outward appearance. Howard sighed without making a sound.

The psychologist had wondered about the invitation to cocktails and now he was beginning to understand it. It was not going to be a social event. The boy was going to ask him a question. Howard was used to it. Lay people thought that psychologists or psychiatrists (few knew the difference) had the answer to every human problem and that all one had to do was ask in order to receive. And some of the questions he had been asked! The most personal, the most intimate. . . .

Howard shrugged without moving his shoulders and decided to enjoy his drink before the inevitable presented itself.

"What can I get you?" Scott asked, right on cue.

"Martini, if it's not too much trouble."

"Nothing could be easier. Dry?"

"Very, please," Howard answered, thanking the Gods the boy had not asked if Howard wanted gin or vodka. Howard firmly believed a martini was made with gin and that that other drink was vodka mixed with vermouth. The very rich know everything, Howard thought, and smiled to himself as if pleased that they did.

"Twist or olive?"

Howard came back to reality at the sound of the question and realized he was still ordering his drink. "Onion?"

"You've got it."

The boy started toward the bar, then suddenly stopped and turned to face Howard once again. Before Scott could ask Howard said, "On the rocks, please."

They both laughed aloud as Scott continued to the bar and started to mix the cocktails. "Asking people what they drink and how they like it mixed always makes me feel as if I'm getting personal. Everyone has a different idea of what the perfect cocktail should be. In fact these days it's easier to ask someone about their sex life."

So that's it, Howard thought. Sex. Carefully worked into the conversation even before the first sip of booze has been savoured by the summoned guru. I might have known, he continued, your average young man would go out and buy a book to find out what he wanted to know but the rich, by God, are different. They call in their own research institute. Howard sat in a comfortable chair and watched Scott approach with the drinks. Lost in his own thoughts he eyed the boy's ample crotch and decided there was certainly nothing wrong in that department. Howard's head jerked upward as the martini was placed under his nose and he saw a smiling Scott Evans looking down at him. Howard could feel the color rise on his cheeks.

"Cheers," Scott said, lifting his glass toward Howard.

Howard drank too quickly and almost choked when Scott asked, "Are you married, Dr. Roth?"

"I was. My wife is dead," Howard answered. Scott Evans was either a bitch or naive; at once he decided to settle on the former.

"I hope you don't mind the question. I've read all your papers and I'm curious about the man who wrote them."

Howard raised his glass in a mini-salute. "I'm flattered. In fact it's usually my son's writing that people read, very seldom mine."

"Your son? Is he in the field, too?"

Howard reached into his pocket for his cigarettes and stuck one between his lips. Before he could find his matches Scott had picked up a lighter from one of the small tables and moved the flame toward Howard. The Doctor leaned forward in his chair and accepted the light. "Thank you. No, Mr. Evans, he's not in the field. He writes romances, I believe they're called, and judging from the number that are sold I would say the public loves them."

"How interesting. Is Roth his pen name or does he use an alias?"

"Ken use an alias? Never. He would think he was being dishonest." Howard tried quickly to figure out how the conversation had swung from him to Ken in a matter of seconds. Before he realized that he was the culprit he plunged deeper into the subject of Ken and his writing. "He's Sea-Air's artist in residence and, next to members of your family, the most talked about person on the beach."

Scott laughed at Howard's candor and again Howard's attention was drawn to the lad's bright, honest eyes. It would be hard to dislike Scott Evans. No, the boy wasn't a bitch. He wasn't naive either. What he *was* Howard did not know, but after half a martini he was beginning to feel interested in learning.

"I know just how he feels," Scott said.

"No, you don't, Mr. Evans. You were born to it. Ken acquired it and, I fear, is loving it."

"Can we drop the Mr. Evans? My name is Scott."

"I can if you'll drop the doctor. It makes me feel so old."

"It's a bargain, Howard."

Another silence. The kind that always follows a sudden spurt of intimacy between strangers. *Where does one go from here?* they seemed to be thinking. Howard finished his drink and then noticed that Scott had hardly touched his.

"Can I get you another?" Scott asked, standing.

"I'm afraid I drank too quickly," Howard responded.

"Not at all. I drink too slowly. It's one of my more noticeable traits. I have to think about everything I do. Slow as whale shit at the bottom of the ocean is how friends and foes describe me."

Howard laughed at the colorful description. The young could always pinpoint a situation in a simple phrase with a dirty word thrown in for good measure. When Scott returned with the second martini Howard decided to sip the drink slowly and get to the point of the meeting quickly. He put out his cigarette in an exquisite crystal ashtray and at the same time spoke his mind.

"Now, Scott, before I get too far into this glass of gin can I know why you asked me here?"

The boy seemed surprised at the question. "I thought I told you. I've been reading your papers and find them very interesting. I wanted to meet you." Now it was Scott's turn to light a cigarette. "You don't believe me, do you?"

Howard got the feeling that Scott was playing with him and wondered again just what Scott Evans was all about. He shook his head. "No, I don't believe you. Lay people don't usually read psychological essays, especially the young who are too busy doing what we're writing about."

Scott sat far back in his chair which was framed by one of the huge windows and brought his bare foot up and atop the opposite knee. He wiggled his toes. "Well, it's half the truth," he said, sounding like a small boy caught in the cookie jar.

"And the other half?" For the first time since stepping into the house Howard felt he, and not Scott Evans, was in command.

The boy began slowly. "Things... some of the ideas you propose seem to apply directly to me."

Howard waited for Scott to continue and when the boy did not he said, "That's not unusual. I mean, we're all very similar, psychologically speaking, and most of us do see ourselves when reading the kind of stuff I write about. Some of us, the more sensitive, actually see more than is really there. I suspect that's the case with you."

"Do you think I'm sensitive?" Scott quickly asked and Howard, a trained interviewer, realized at once that Evans had jumped on that one word rather than on the meaning of what Howard had said.

Howard reached for a cigarette but this time had to provide his own light. Scott was too absorbed in himself and the true purpose of this meeting to any longer play the perfect host. "I used the word sensitive in the broadest possible meaning of the word. You interpreted it in a very specific way," Howard said.

The room had grown almost dark and Scott now uncrossed his legs and stood up. He walked about aimlessly, turning on lamps as he came to them. "I guess I did," he answered. "I took the word at its. . . ."

"Mystical," Howard broke in.

Scott was back in his seat. "You say that as a matter of fact."

Howard shrugged. "I'm used to it. The line of research I'm involved in is very often confused with the mystical. Mumbo-jumbo, Ken calls it." Again he had brought Ken into the conversation. Well, it was too late to retract the statement.

"Do you think it's mumbo-jumbo, Howard?"

"What? My work?"

Scott laughed, as he was supposed to, at Howard's attempt to lighten the conversation. "No. The mystical. I understand more and more scientists, serious men, are getting involved in the field. You even wrote that at the Rockefeller Institute in New York they're. . . ."

"Easy, easy," Howard held up his hand. "That's exactly the kind of image we're trying to shake off at Sloan and, I'm sure, at the Rockefeller, too. We are investigating the so-called mystic, but not to give it credence. We want to unmask it, separate fact from fiction and apply the facts to science. Use it to help humanity. I think the answer can be found within the human mind, a vast and still very unexplored area. But it's not mystical or a lot of mumbo-jumbo nonsense. Like electricity, it's there, ready to be understood and harnessed."

Was the boy listening? Howard was not sure. Scott's eyes were directed past Howard and toward the far wall of the vast room. When Scott spoke he did not shift his gaze to Howard but continued to stare across the room. "You wrote that thinking about something hard enough and long enough could cause the thought to become reality."

Before Howard could reply Scott leaned forward in his chair

and began to speak in a very soft voice, almost rapidly, like one who had rehearsed for a long time and is now ready for his audience.

"I had a twin brother. He died when we were five years old. I remember him, vaguely, like someone in a dream. They told me he had gone to heaven and I think, in my child's mind, I came to think of him as God. I would tell him what I wanted and wait for the favors to be granted. You'd be surprised how often they were." Scott paused but obviously not for a response. He looked upward, took a deep breath and, again sure of his lines, continued.

"In New York my parents hired a tutor-companion for me. Christ, how I hated that bastard. I asked Tom, my brother, to get rid of him. He was killed by a taxi while crossing Fifth Avenue." Now the speaker sipped from his glass. "At prep school I . . . I became involved with a teacher. It got to be messy and I was sorry it had ever started. The teacher died during the summer recess that same year. The small boat he owned capsized in Long Island Sound. No storm. The water was placid. The accident couldn't be explained."

For the first time since he had begun to unburden himself Scott turned and looked directly at Howard. "There were other incidents. Not as dramatic but, to me, just as convincing."

Howard smiled reassuringly. He wanted to reach out and pat the boy's arm. Console him in some way. When he answered it was in a tone one would use with a child who had expressed a fear of the dark.

"I think, Scott, you're the victim of a series of very unfortunate coincidences. That's all they are, believe me. Coincidences coupled with a lot of guilt. When you read my stuff you began to put two and two together and, I'm afraid, came up with five. When I wrote that thinking about something could cause it to happen I did not mean it would happen just like that." Howard snapped his fingers in the air. "I meant that when we dwell upon something we begin a series of actions, sometimes consciously, more often unconsciously, that cause the thought to become reality. Not by magic but by very real human effort. It seems to me that you did nothing physical to bring about the deaths of the people you mentioned."

"No. But I wished it and it happened."

"That's coincidence."

"How many times does a coincidence have to occur before it becomes more than a coincidence?"

"That's what I'm trying to find out, Scott."

"So am I, Doctor."

Scott opened the drawer of the small table next to his chair. He removed a photograph and passed it to Howard. "What do you see?" he asked.

Howard placed the photo under the lamp light and examined it carefully. It was a picture of the beach at Sea-Air. Specifically it showed the rock jetty that ran from the shore and straight out, about a hundred feet, into the ocean. A young man was standing on one of the rocks, close to the shore line.

"Do you recognize the person in the picture?"

Howard looked closely at the lone figure. "I think it's you," he replied.

"I think it is, too."

Howard was mildly surprised. "Don't you know?"

"Not for sure. You see, I took the picture."

"I don't understand," Howard said.

"Neither do I," Scott responded. "I took that picture and when I did there wasn't a living soul on that jetty."

"Are you trying to tell me that this is a photograph of your twin brother? Your dead twin brother?"

Scott took the photo from Howard and looked at it. "I'm not trying to tell you anything. I'm just showing you something."

"I'm sure it can be explained."

"Do you think I'm crazy?" Scott suddenly asked.

"Crazy people don't investigate their illusions. They believe them."

"Thanks for the vote of confidence. Will you help me?"

Howard did not know what to answer because he was not sure what Scott was asking of him. But the psychologist was rescued from the awkward situation when the room suddenly became ablaze with light and a voice boomed, "Is this a private funeral or can an outsider view the remains?"

Startled, Howard turned and saw a young man who had just descended the staircase at the far end of the room and now quickly walked toward where he and Scott were seated.

"It's not a funeral at all," Scott said. Howard was shocked at how animated he sounded compared to the sober, almost imploring tone he had used seconds before. "It's more of an exorcism. Let your hang-ups hang out and the good Doctor will lop 'em off."

The newcomer cupped his fly, almost lewdly, and looked at

Howard. "I only have one hang-up and I prefer to keep it hanging, thank you. Dr. Roth, I presume. I'm Michael Armstrong."

Howard, still confused by the sudden brightness — Michael had apparently flicked on a master switch to illuminate his entrance — and complete change in atmosphere of the room, stuck out his hand instinctively and had it pumped by an exuberant Mike Armstrong. "Nice to know you, Michael."

"You have to excuse Mike," Scott was saying. "He has a way of breaking into rooms and lives and making his presence in both known." He turned from Howard to Michael. "I thought we were going to read."

"We were, but we got lonely and thirsty." Mike started for the bar. "I'm behind, but don't worry, I'll catch up."

Howard watched and listened. Armstrong was the living image of the all-American boy that his name immediately brought to mind. Tall, slim and dressed in the inevitable faded jeans and polo shirt, his hair was straight and very black, his skin tanned and his eyes a bold blue. Mike Armstrong looked as if he would be at home peering at the world from the pages of a glossy magazine and imploring readers, with very little effort, to buy a particular brand of cigarettes or a fancy sports car.

"Make two gibsons while you're there, over ice," Scott called out.

"That's not fair," came the answer from the bar. "Then I'll never catch up."

Howard felt as if he were in the middle of a petty domestic quarrel. So Scott had not sat and contemplated in Sea-Air by himself. He had live-in company; clinical observation plus a sophistication that came from seven years at Columbia and ten years of living in New York told Howard that the young men's relationship went deeper than masculine friendship. "I think I've had enough," Howard said.

"Please," Scott begged, "just one more. Don't let Mike scare you off, he's really very civilized when he wants to be."

Mike returned to the conversation area carrying a tray and passed out the drinks. "I really am, Doctor. It's just when I get locked up that I start acting this way."

Howard accepted the drink and smiled at Mike. "I take it my visit prompted your exile. That wasn't necessary, Scott."

"When you get to know Michael better you'll understand the wisdom of my request."

"You just told me he was civilized and harmless," Howard answered.

"Oh, but he is. Just like a domesticated panther."

"Let's get off me and on to something interesting," Mike joined in.

Scott raised his glass. "Right on, brother," and tossed down half his drink. Once more Howard saw the change that had come over Scott since Michael Armstrong had arrived on the scene. Scott was trying to prevent himself from being overshadowed by the more extroverted Michael. And what a shame, Howard thought. Scott was obviously a more sensitive and more intelligent young man.

"This is really a beautiful house, Scott," Howard said. "I've seen it from the beach dozens of times and to tell you the truth it never impressed me. But being in it makes all the difference in the world."

Scott nodded. "I know. It wasn't meant to be viewed but to be lived in." He got up, drink in hand. "Come on, have a look around."

Howard and Mike both rose and followed Scott about the huge room as he pointed and explained. Michael joined in, playing host along with Scott, and gradually the tense atmosphere changed to domestic tranquility. Howard, helped along by the third martini, began to enjoy the company of the two young men. Like most heterosexual men in a situation like this his initial anxiety turned to interest once he was sure his manhood was not being threatened. If he had a fourth martini Howard was sure he would begin to act like a peacock and wonder why he wasn't being threatened.

They stopped before a large, antique desk and Scott was expounding on the piece but Howard's attention was drawn to a grouping of photographs on the wall above the desk. They were obviously family photos, many containing children, all neatly framed and arranged to form a large square. What had caught Howard's eye was a photograph of a house in the center of the square. It was a white, Greek revival mansion framed against a perfectly blue sky. Howard's mind quickly traveled back to a trip he and Ken had made to New England not a month before.

"I hope you're not going to ask me to tell you who they all are," Scott's voice brought Howard back to the present. "We're a very large family and that's only a small part of it."

"Actually I'm looking at the house," Howard answered, pointing to the picture. "My son and I were in New England last month and saw one exactly like it."

"New England is full of houses like that," Mike said. "I call that one Poseidon's Place."

"Why Poseidon?" Howard asked.

"Because it stands on a hill and faces the ocean."

"I told you, Howard," Scott added, "my family is very big with oceans."

"The house we looked at was in Salem," Howard responded.

Scott and Mike looked at each other and then Scott, turning to the picture, said to no one in particular, "China House is in Salem."

The hair on Howard's neck seemed to stand straight up and the feeling that he had lived this moment before came over him so strongly that he had to grip the top of the desk for support. Later he would wonder about this reaction but right now he was too caught up in it to think clearly.

"China House? Then it is the house Ken and I saw. We were told it was called China House."

"That is odd," Scott said, staring openly at Howard. "It's not in Salem proper. In fact it's quite off the usual tourist routes."

Howard nodded. "I know. I was going to Boston to attend a convention and following that my son and I were going to take a few days off and motor through New England. Just before we left I received a sort of travelogue brochure of the area in the mail. I take it the senders got my name from the convention roster. Anyway, a place called the Seaford Inn was depicted in the booklet and described as the oldest still-functioning inn in the Salem area. We had been thinking about driving to Salem and after reading about the inn decided to stay there." As he spoke Howard realized he was detailing these events as much for his own clarification as for Scott's and Michael's.

"The Seaford Inn is about halfway up the hill that China House stands on," Howard finished.

"You never told me about an inn," Mike said.

Scott shrugged. "I forgot about it, I guess."

"But why the picture of China House here?" Howard asked.

"Because he owns it," Mike answered as if it were a fact that Howard should have known.

"We were told it belonged to a family called Seaford."

Scott finished his drink and twirled the ice cubes about his empty glass. "My mother is a Seaford." He started back to where they had been sitting earlier and Howard and Mike followed.

"How strange," Howard thought aloud.

"Coincidence, Dr. Roth?"

Howard found his cigarettes where he had left them and put one in his mouth. This time Mike picked up the lighter and offered it to Howard. "Thank you. Yes. Yes, indeed. It is a coincidence."

"My life seems to abound in them," Scott said, again staring at Howard. "Some people collect stamps. Me? I collect coincidences."

It was night now and the big windows stood like black rectangles in the brightly lit room. Scott and Mike had lit cigarettes and the three men smoked in silence, all holding empty glasses and looking like the mourners Mike Armstrong had called them such a short time before. It was Mike who broke the silence and Howard was surprised at the soft, almost sympathetic quality of the young man's voice. Another sudden change in personality. The evening seemed to be full of them.

"China House is not a very pleasant subject for Scott," Mike explained. "He was born there and lived there until. . . ."

"My brother was killed in China House," Scott suddenly broke in. "He fell down the stairs and fractured his skull on the marble landing."

"I'm sorry," Howard said. What else could he say?

"Did Scott show you the picture?" Mike asked. "The one of the jetty."

"Yes. I saw it."

"And what do you think?"

Howard shook his head. "I don't know. I mean, there are any number of possibilities. It would have to be fully investigated before we could reach any conclusion, even to conclude that we can't explain it."

"Will you investigate it?" Mike asked.

Very neat, Howard thought. The request came from Mike Armstrong, not Scott. He could refuse Mike but he could not say no to Scott Evans. For some reason they wanted it to appear that they were getting a willing partner and not a hired hand. Mike's question also brought home the fact that Mike Armstrong was privy to Scott's troubled thoughts. "Am I being roped into some asinine charade by two rich kids who want to make a fool of me and my profession?" Howard wondered with a great deal of resentment. If he accepted, he would become the unwitting clown in whatever game they were playing at the expense of his professional integrity. If he refused, the Evans boy could make life hell for him at the Institute.

The psychologist, whose mind always worked along such lines, did not rule out the sexual implications of the proposed triumvirate.

"Let me have the photo," Howard said, feeling like a peacock whose feathers had been ruffled.

Again Scott removed the photo from the table drawer and handed it to Howard, who glanced at it quickly before putting it in the breast pocket of his blazer. "Are you in the habit of taking photos of desolate jettys?" Howard asked Scott, not trying to hide the note of sarcasm in his voice.

"I believe they're called seascapes," Mike quickly answered. "No, I'm the photographer. Or at least I'm trying to be. I've spent the summer practicing."

Scott seemed to withdraw from the conversation and now Howard was dealing directly with Michael Armstrong. "Could this be a picture you took?" Howard asked.

Mike shook his head slowly. "We're reasonably sure it's not. Scott took the camera to the beach one day and shot a roll of film. He says he took the used cartridge to the developer and picked it up himself."

Howard looked at Scott. "Is that true?"

"To the best of my knowledge it is," Scott answered.

In the silence that followed Howard tried to look interested and pensive. The professor deep in thought. He was sure he came off looking like the fool they were trying to make of him. He decided that he had allowed himself to stew for too long; it was time to leave before he boiled over.

"Can we get you another drink?" Scott made it sound more like a courtesy gesture than a genuine offer.

"No. I really must go now." Howard stood up.

Both young men rose, too quickly, as if having accomplished their mission they now wanted to discuss it between them and . . . and what? Plan their next move? They walked with Howard to the glass door. Mike stuck out his hand. "It was a pleasure, Howard."

"Thank you. You make a great martini." Howard looked into

Mike's blue eyes. He noted that they were the boy's darkest feature. Mike stared back at Howard, unblinking, a wide smile on his movie star face.

"We'll be hearing from you?" asked Scott.

"That you will."

Howard looked over his shoulder once as he made his way to the boardwalk. The big windows of the house were ablaze and Howard could easily see into the large salon he had just left. Scott had his arm about Mike's shoulder as the two walked across the room. Howard turned up the collar of his jacket against the sharp wind blowing off the ocean, put his hands in his pockets and began to walk back to his car. If he had been puzzled about his invitation to the Evans house earlier he was even more puzzled now that he had fulfilled the bid.

All that was certain was that he had allowed those two young men to talk him into 'investigating' a photograph of a full grown, living man purported to be the picture of a boy who had died at the age of five. He also had to listen to Scott talk about the dead five-year-old as if the child were his living brother's guardian angel. Howard grimaced. A somewhat diabolical guardian angel. Howard was also certain that he had been invited to view a carefully planned charade, the plot of which was to satirize his professional work.

"The two of them are probably having another drink, or smoking funny cigarettes, and having a good laugh at my expense," Howard mumbled into the wind. "But China House...." Again he felt his scalp tingle and he knew the sensation wasn't caused entirely by the cold ocean breeze.

A beam of light made a path on the black water. Its source was a big, full, orange moon.

All I need now, he thought, is to see the silhouette of a witch racing across the sky. He smiled at the idea but as he neared his car the smile left his face. He did indeed see a silhouette. Not in the sky but sitting in the front seat of his Bentley. The rash of crimes which plagued the big cities had not yet reached Sea-Air but Howard was taking no chances. He opened the car door very slowly. When the overhead light came on he saw Alice Miller, his assistant at the Institute, smiling up at him.

"I hope you don't mind. I was out walking and spotted your car, so I made myself comfortable and waited for a lift home."

"I don't mind at all," Howard said. "I'm delighted to see you."

• II •

The first time Howard Roth saw China House was toward the close of what had been a perfect September day. He and Ken, looking more like brothers than father and son, had driven and strolled through Salem, taking in as much of the historic town as their brief one-day visit allowed. They had been enchanted not only with the seaport, but even more with the feel of antiquity and history that Salem's inhabitants so diligently preserved.

After a late lunch of cold lobster, a freshly tossed salad and just enough white wine to make one at peace with the world, in a restaurant that seated no more than a dozen people, the sightseers felt pleasantly exhausted and anxious to get to the inn. It would be a long trip home in the morning. And on their way to the inn they could explore more of the Salem area which on this day rested under a late summer blue sky while buffered from the hot sun by a cool, fresh breeze that smelled of the sea and hinted at the promise of an early autumn.

Ken asked their host, an elegant man some years past his prime who would have looked more at home in a business suit on New York's Madison Avenue than in the too baggy jeans he wore in his tiny restaurant, if he could tell them the best route to the Seaford Inn and, without reservations, did he think they would have any trouble getting a room.

"The summer people are gone and it's too early for the leaf watchers' invasion," he answered, not sounding too kindly toward either group. "But to play it safe I'll call old Mr. Billingsly, he owns the place, and tell him to expect you."

"That's very kind of you," Howard said.

"Who should I tell him to expect?"

"Dr. Roth" and "Kenneth Roth" were ejaculated by father and son at the same time. The man ignored Howard and stared at Ken.

"Are you Kenneth Roth, the writer?"

Ken held up his hand. "Guilty."

"My pleasure. Ned. Ned Hartman." Ken held out his hand and Ned Hartman took it in his own and held it for a brief moment as if he were being introduced to royalty. "I thought I recognized you from the photo. The one on the back of *A Time To Remember.* I've read them all."

Ken beamed, his wide smile lighting up his pleasant face which was framed by straight blond hair that fell haphazardly across his forehead and over his ears. He looked very much like Howard except for his dark eyes and lanky frame which gave him the appearance of a young stallion not yet in control of his prowess. He was poured into a pair of jeans which were topped with a light blazer jacket and, like his father, gave the appearance of a man far younger than his twenty-five years.

"Thank you, Mr. Hartman. I'm glad you enjoyed the books."

During this exchange Howard smiled but his gesture lacked the warmth of Ken's and looked a little impatient, as if he had endured similar scenes many times before. Howard's expression and the fact that he was being totally ignored did not go unnoticed by his son. Ken quickly put out the cigarette he was holding and moved his chair back from the table.

"Perhaps you could tell Howard how to get to the inn, Mr. Hartman, while I use the men's room." He looked at Ned Hartman questioningly.

Hartman was looking at Ken like a movie fan who suddenly comes face to face with his favorite star and finds it hard to believe the idol is a living, breathing human being. The fact that he might actually have to use the toilet escaped the restaurateur to the point where Ken's words went unheard or else had no meaning for the man.

"The men's room, Mr. Hartman?" Howard prodded.

"What? Oh, yes, yes. Right that way, Mr. Roth, just to the left of the kitchen."

Howard looked at his watch. "How far is it to the Seaford Inn, Mr. Hartman?"

"Ned," came the reply.

Howard smiled his most insincere smile which Hartman took for the real thing. "Ned," Howard repeated and once again asked the distance to the inn. He was told to allow a good hour. Howard looked at his watch again. It was already three. If they wanted to get to the inn for an early supper and do some sightseeing along the way they would have to leave Salem proper immediately.

Ned Hartman disappeared up a flight of stairs but returned as soon as Ken emerged from the men's room. He carried a book with the back of the dust jacket facing up; it depicted a full face photo of the author. Ken saw Hartman approaching and tried to avoid him by heading straight for the door as he gave Howard a sign to follow. But the room was small and Hartman was very fast. He reached the door before Ken and all but shoved the copy of *A Time To Remember* under the young author's nose.

"Do you mind, Mr. Roth?"

"No, not at all." Ken answered, aware of Howard at his elbow as he took the offered book and pen. He quickly wrote his name under the photograph and handed book and pen back to Ned Hartman.

"Thank you, Mr. Roth," the man said.

"Thank you," Ken responded, "for a marvelous lunch."

"You will call the inn," Howard reminded Hartman.

"Sure thing, Howard. Right now. And here are the directions. I wrote them out with a little map you can follow."

"Really appreciate it," Howard said as he walked out the door which Ned Hartman held open for him and his son.

Hartman stood by the open door and watched Ken and Howard walk to their car. Not until the Bentley drove off did he close the door and return to his restaurant.

"He called you Mr. Roth and me Howard," the older man said as he drove the car a little too fast through the town. "Who did he think I was? Your footman?"

"Dad, please." He called Howard "Dad" when he wanted to pacify his father for any reason, a fact Howard knew but was powerless to stop.

Howard smiled and slowed the car to a saner speed. "I'm being a bitch, eh?"

"That you are."

"You don't have to agree with me."

"Oh, but I always agree with my father."

"You want to analyze that statement?"

"No," Ken said, rolling his eyes upward.

They both laughed and the tension passed.

It was almost six when they approached the inn, a few miles off the main road and halfway up a steep hill that was passable, by foot or car, over a winding dirt road. Just as Howard turned toward the old, gray-shingled building Ken touched his arm and exclaimed, "Howard, look!"

Directly in front of them and almost at the top of the hill stood the most impressive house either had ever seen. It was a mansion, really, and a perfect example of Greek Revival architecture. It faced east to the sea and now, with the sun setting behind it and nothing in view but sky and trees to mar its beauty, it looked like a newly built temple atop Mount Olympus. A white gleaming temple suspended between heaven and earth.

"Isn't it something?" Ken was awed by the sight.

Howard nodded. "It is. But cold. Christ, what a cold son-of-a-bitch."

"Yeah," Ken said slowly. "I know what you mean. There's nothing. . . human about it."

Howard looked at his son. "Houses are not human, Ken, remember? Only people are."

"You know what I mean," Ken told him. "Now that," he continued, pointing to the Seaford Inn, "is human."

"Well, I hope it has the human comforts. I'm thirsty, hungry and tired."

"Is that all?"

"No, my ass hurts, too."

"Howard, really."

Their apprehension about accommodations proved meaningless. Howard and Ken were the inn's only guests and old Mr. Billingsly, a thin-lipped New Englander who spoke only one syllable words, served them cocktails and a surprisingly good dinner.

"Nightcap?"

Ken nodded and Howard signaled to old Billingsly who now sat by the huge stone fireplace.

"I think we're keeping him up," Ken whispered.

"I doubt it," Howard answered. "I know these New Englanders. If he wanted us out of here he would say so in no uncertain terms." Howard lit a cigarette. "But I think we're keeping *you* up. You look like you're about to purr."

"I feel like purring. What a wonderful place. A real, honest-to-God, old-fashioned inn. If you removed a few items here and there we would actually be back in the nineteenth century."

Howard smiled. "I think you mean one item, Ken. Namely,

electricity. Take it away and there would be no ice for our booze, no lights to see your funny face by and, I'm sure, this cozy room is not the result of that fire or the two whiskies we had before dinner."

"Practical Howard. Where, oh where, is your sense of romance?"

"Between my legs. Et tu?"

Ken tapped his chest. "I'm all heart, father, all heart."

"Bull. Save it for your readers."

"Do you know why this place is empty?" Ken said quickly, cleverly avoiding the subject of readers and their counterparts, writers.

Howard nodded. "Those neon-lit motels we passed by the dozens on our way here."

"Exactly. And what a shame. This is what Salem is all about. And. . . I think we should act like nineteenth-century gentlemen while we're here."

"Nineteenth-century gentlemen weren't all heart either, my son, they screwed, too. If they didn't you and I wouldn't be sitting here with or without electricity."

"Touché, Howard, touché."

Mr. Billingsly was suddenly standing over their table, a drink in each hand. "One scotch, one rye," he said as he placed the former in front of Howard and the latter before Ken.

"Thank you, Mr. Billingsly," Howard said.

"Welcome, I'm sure," the old man answered.

"We'll be going upstairs as soon as we finish these," Howard pointed to the two fresh drinks on the table.

"Your room is the last one at the end of the hall. Your bags are already in it. Won't be able to show you up 'cause I'm turning in right now." The old man departed.

Howard smiled an I-told-you-so smile. "We'll find it, Mr. Billingsly. Thank you again."

"Mr. Billingsly," Ken called and the old man turned. "How old is this place? The inn, I mean."

Billingsly put a finger to his lip. "Hundred-fifty years. I'm seventy an' my father owned it before me."

"Very interesting." Ken held up a finger. "And one more question. When we drove up to the inn we saw a house, a beautiful white house on top of the hill. Who lives there?"

"That would be China House. Ain't nobody lived there for twenty years or more."

"China House? How did a Greek Revival mansion in the heart of New England get a name like that?"

"Because it's filled with Chinese furnishings, that's how," the old man answered.

"Who owns the house?" Ken asked.

"The Seafords," came the reply.

"Seaford? The same name as this inn."

Billingsly nodded. "That's right. Was a time, way back, when the Seaford family owned this whole hill an' more. The name stuck. Besides, never saw any reason to change it."

"And why the Chinese furnishings?" Ken continued to probe.

"They were a seafaring family. Commodore Seaford, one who built China House, owned a whole fleet of whaling boats. Story goes he made a dozen trips to China an' each time he came back he brought with him a shipload of furniture for his new house till he had the place looking like a Mandarin's palace."

"Where are the Seafords now, Mr. Billingsly?"

"Spread out, I guess. Some of them in New York, or so I've heard."

"And the house?"

The old man jerked his head backward. "The house is right up there."

Howard grinned at this and Ken gave his leg a not too gentle kick under the table.

"I mean do they ever live in the house? Summers or weekends?" The old man shook his head. "You mean," Ken continued, "in over twenty years none of the family has ever occupied the house?"

"Or been near it," Billingsly added.

"Have they put it on the market?" Billingsly looked a little uncertain and Ken quickly repeated, "Have they ever tried to sell it?"

"Never. Far as I know. Besides, no one 'round these parts would want it."

"A beautiful place like that?" Ken exclaimed.

Mr. Billingsly stretched his long neck and bent his head closer to the table. "It's haunted," he said in something of a stage whisper.

Howard rolled his eyes toward heaven. "Really, Ken, I think Mr. Billingsly wants to go to bed."

But neither Billingsly nor Ken seemed to hear him. The old man knew he had a willing listener in the young man and he was ready to make the most of it. Howard, from long experience, exchanged glasses with Ken, taking the rye and giving Ken the scotch. He drank and lit another cigarette.

"Haunted," Billingsly repeated for the effect.

"In what way?" Ken asked.

"Easy," Howard injected, "the Salem witches meet there every October 31st."

"Howard, please," Ken said.

"No witches," Billingsly told them. "Just lights."

"Lights?"

"Lights in the window," the inkeeper answered.

"You mean someone left a light on or turns the lights on in an empty house?" Howard joined in the questioning.

The old man shook his head. "Not what I mean at all. No one left a light on an' no one in the place to turn a light on or off. But after the Seafords left some people claimed they seen a light in one of the upstairs bedrooms."

"Was it investigated?" This from Howard.

Billingsly nodded. "Went myself with the sheriff an' his party. We checked it out all right. Basement to attic."

"And?" Howard asked.

"Nothing," Billingsly replied. "Nothing at all. Just a lot of rooms filled with expensive furniture an' no sign of life in the whole place."

"Someone was playing a joke on the town, Mr. Billingsly," Howard told the old man. "They could get in late at night and..."

"A joke? For over twenty years?"

"You mean it happened again... recently?" Ken asked.

"Last summer," Billingsly nodded triumphantly. "Some said they saw the light again just before the tourist season."

Ken looked at Howard but his usually verbose father remained silent while Billingsly looked ready to refute anything Howard might say.

"Has anyone tried pulling the plug?" Howard finally offered.

"He means was the electricity ever turned off," Ken quickly explained.

"Town wanted to. Contacted the family but they wouldn't hear of it. They pay the bill an' the power stays on."

"How fascinating..." Ken began.

"Thank you again, Mr. Billingsly," Howard broke in. "We'll be going up shortly."

The old man nodded, turned, and walked slowly from the

room. Howard and Ken watched him make his way out of the small dining area, their eyes not leaving his back until he disappeared down the dark hall passage beyond the stairs that led up to the second floor.

The room was suddenly quiet. The log which had been burning steadily in the huge stone fireplace collapsed, giving off a burst of sparks, then settled down to its smoldering death. The late September wind, inaudible till now, began to stir the trees and bushes that surrounded the inn. Ken lifted his glass and took a long sip of scotch. He shivered as the liquor went down his throat.

"Do you think he was serious?" Ken asked Howard in a tone usually reserved for talking in church.

"He was serious all right. It's called local color and not having a Chamber of Commerce the color is painted on by bartenders and innkeepers."

Ken sighed. "Where's your imagination? Why, I could take that story and. . ."

"Write another book?"

Ken bit his lower lip and pushed the blond hair from his forehead. The exposed nerve had been touched for the second time in one day. It had been a good week. It had been Howard's week and now, at the very end of their holiday, it was ruined by the one sore spot in their otherwise peaceful relationship: Ken's writing. It was an old story, five years old, but if one wanted to date it from its origin it could be traced back to the day Kenneth Roth was born.

Howard's first and only child was going to be a doctor. Hopefully a psychiatrist but the proud father was ready to settle for any branch of the science so long as the initials M.D. appeared after the name Kenneth Roth. The psychologist used a subtle but firm approach in guiding the boy toward this goal and when Kenneth, at age two, played doctor the term "play therapy" took on a completely new meaning. By the time the boy started school his direction, which he thought entirely his own, was perfectly clear. Howard's wife died suddenly and unexpectedly when Ken was ten, and father and son were drawn even closer together in their mutual grief than they had during their ten year romance of mutual admiration.

The change in their relationship was more nuance than observable fact. Ken, then attending a good private school in New York, adamantly refused Howard's suggestion to hire a housekeeper to take charge of their comfortable apartment. Howard knew the boy's reaction was more indignation at the idea of a stranger taking his mother's place than a desire to take over a multitude of chores he had never before tackled. What Howard didn't know, or chose to ignore, was that he allowed Ken's emotional motivation in this matter to influence his father's approach to their new lifestyle.

Remarrying was out of the question until Ken was mature enough to accept a new mate for Howard. Fifteen years later Howard still used this theme, though it varied as Ken grew to manhood, as a reason for remaining single.

Once he had recovered from the loss of a loving wife and devoted mother, Howard's sex life consisted of brief affairs with an endless array of nurses who worked for the large metropolitan hospital where the psychologist was also employed. Howard, handsome and bright, had no trouble attracting the opposite sex. The rules, Howard's rules, which governed these liaisons were strictly adhered to. Never did he take his current favorite to his apartment, never did he introduce them to his son, and always, when the young ladies became serious, Howard broke off the relationship. And Howard never knew if Ken, fast maturing, believed his father was abstaining from sex; by mutual and unspoken consent the subject never arose.

They were parent and child, teacher and student, friends, roommates and survivors of the single parent syndrome, inhabiting a totally masculine and sexless world within the confines of their private milieu. But sex, as it will, reared its head in the classical fashion. Howard, home from the hospital earlier than usual, walked into his son's room and found the boy masturbating. The scene, like a photograph, took a second to expose but once developed would become a permanent part of the beholder's psyche. The open window, the balmy afternoon breeze and the sound of traffic coming out from the street below, the discarded jeans and jockey shorts, the thirteen-year-old body, slim and practically hairless, half reclining on the carefully made-up bed, the blond head slightly bent, the hand caressing a startlingly mature penis while the dark eyes beheld a vision visible only to the dreamer. One brief second.

"I beg your pardon... I mean... I'm sorry." And Howard retreated.

How many books had he read, lectures had he heard and parents had he counselled on the subject? Howard laughed, hysterically, at this thought. One psychiatrist, a female, even suggested that fathers should immediately take part in the ritual in order to allay the youngster's sense of guilt. Howard recoiled from the idea as well as from the pleasant sensation that persisted in the area of his groin.

Ken, slightly flushed, his dark eyes bright, appeared moments later.

"Is it a bad thing to do?"

Howard wondered if the boy was wearing his underpants under his jeans. What an incredible, insane thought.

"No," Howard assured the boy. "It's perfectly normal and a very good release for... for sex. I shouldn't have entered your room without knocking first."

"Why? You've never knocked before."

And so they entered upon a new phase in their relationship, the world of masculine friendships where outwardly everything is open, back-slapping fun as long as the sacrosanct areas of thought, feel and emotion are never violated. Ken's evening hello kiss was replaced with a rousing, "Hi, how's it going." No longer did they sit, Howard's arm around the boy and the boy's head resting on the man's shoulder, watching television or pondering over an exceptionally tough equation. The lock on the bathroom door was used. Bathrobes, long forgotten except on cold winter nights, became standard morning attire. Those nights when they shared Howard's bed for no other reason than the unspoken need for the warmth and companionship each was able to give the other were forever gone.

"Do you dream, Dad?"

"Sometimes."

"What do you dream about?"

"Being operated on by my son."

Giggle.

"Do you dream, Ken?"

"Sometimes."

"What do dream about?"

"Funny things."

"Nightmares?"

"No. Just funny things."

Just about the time Ken was ready for college Howard received an offer for a position at the Sloan Research Institute. Howard was delighted. He had long wanted to get into research, Sloan was a prestigious organization, and both he and Ken would be embarking upon a new life at the same time. Howard accepted the offer, bought a house in the small New Jersey shore town where Sloan was located and sent Ken on his way to a degree in medicine.

His first summer home from college Ken brought with him his roommate, Kevin Roberts. Was Howard jealous? Naturally. He had had Ken to himself for so long it would be unnatural not to be jealous. But the feeling waned as he watched the two handsome men bask in the glory of their youth, the summer sun and the attention of every teen-age girl on the beach at Sea-Air. Howard even refrained from complaining when the boys went into New York on Saturday evenings and didn't return until Sunday afternoon. They were men, and that's what men do. But Howard did voice his opinion when Ken announced he was going to spend the second half of his vacation at Kevin's home in an Ohio town that Howard refused to believe existed outside of a television soap opera.

"Christ, Ken, we just have the summer. You've been with Kev all year and you'll be with him another three."

"Well. . . if you want me to stay. . . ."

"No. No. I'm just getting old and tiresome. Go on. Go to mudville and enjoy yourself."

"Loveville, Howard, it's Loveville, Ohio."

A week before graduation Ken arrived home unexpectedly and announced, "Kevin is going to be married in June."

"That's great," Howard responded.

"Is it?"

And that was about the extent of what Ken had to offer in the way of conversation that weekend. Howard didn't push. He knew better. Ken had four more years of school ahead of him. Kevin was free to start a career and family. The psychologist knew what his son was feeling.

"You'll be Kev's best man?"

"No."

Howard was shocked. "Why not?"

"Because it would be a fucking sham, that's why not."

Ken managed to lace that sentence with more anguish than four more years of schooling warranted.

That summer Ken told Howard that he was not going to Med school. Howard didn't panic. He knew better. "What do you plan to do?"

"I think I would like to write."

Howard breathed an inward sigh of relief. What intelligent, well-educated young man didn't want to write? The desire would pass before Christmas. "Why not give it a try? Take a year off. You're young. There's plenty of time to decide what you want to do."

When an agent in New York accepted Ken's first effort Howard was surprised. When a publisher bought it Howard was shocked. When the book sold well, surprise and shock turned to chagrin and open hostility. "Now that you've got it out of your system and you've proved that you can do it, how about getting on with your lifelong ambition."

"Your lifelong ambition, Howard, not mine."

War was declared.

"The publishers want another book. They've given me a hefty advance."

Howard could not believe the contract. The hefty advance was almost as much money as Howard made in a year. And for nothing but the outline of an idea Ken had submitted to the publishing company. The second book was an even bigger success than the first. It drew the kind of reviews that read, "A successful first novel always makes one wonder if the author can sustain; especially when the author is just twenty-one years old. Kenneth Roth, happily, not only sustains but improves with his second work..."

The war was over but the skirmishes continued.

When Ken was asked to lecture at a writer's conference the young man asked his father what he should talk about. "How about 'a funny thing happened on my way to medical school,'" came the helpful reply.

"It's like pulling teeth to get ten cents out of the general public for scientific research, but they're ready to make you a millionaire in return for glossed over jack-off fodder," was another of Howard's favorite comments. He was awed by the money Ken was making but refused to share in the comforts it could buy. The house was run on Howard's salary and what Ken did with his own money was his own business... except for the Bentley. It was a birthday gift that Howard found parked in their car-port when he arrived home that evening. He was too thrilled to be angry and too excited to even mention the extravagance of the gift.

"Like a little boy at Christmas time," Ken thought and that night wrote in his journal, 'the father becomes the son, and the son becomes the father.'

Five Kenneth Roth books stood on the mantel, neatly held up by a miniature Rodin's The Thinker on one end and Michelangelo's David at the other end. "The progeny of a damn good education," Howard commented on the arrangement.

"What are you doing to The Thinker?" Ken asked.

"I'm going to break his arms. He's not supposed to have arms, is he?"

"He is, Howard. Venus is armless. And if you do I'll circumcise David."

"I find that remark very interesting. Very interesting, indeed. Would you like to analyze it?"

"As a matter of fact, no, I would not."

"Let's, anyway. If I cut off The Thinker's arms..."

"He could no longer write," Ken finished the thought.

"Aren't you bright? Exactly. My attack on The Thinker was direct and to the point. But you didn't want to castrate David. Or kill him. You just wanted to trim him down, so to speak."

"So?"

"So maybe that's what you want to do to me. Not cut me off, no. But you would like to trim me down."

"Howard, if I thought you should be circumcised I would tell you so and not beat around David's bush."

"That dammit, is NOT what I meant and you know it."

When Howard was invited to be the star speaker at a psychology seminar in Boston it marked the first real indication that he was beginning to make a name for himself in his field. Howard was delighted and Ken did his best to keep his father's ego inflated. "I want to come with you and we can take a few extra days and bum around New England."

"You'd be bored," Howard said.

"No, Dad. I'll be proud. Very proud."

And so Howard's week had arrived, with Ken playing the role of devoted son to the hilt. The boy thanked all the Gods that not once did a member of the convention say, "Are you Kenneth Roth, the writer?" For three entire days he was Dr. Roth's son, nothing more and nothing less. The world of psychology did not know, or did not care, about romantic-adventure novels. Ken thought this interesting and mentioned it to Howard.

"We deal in reality," Howard told him.

"So do I."

"Romance, Ken, is a state of mind. Don't think about it and it'll go away."

"Really? You'll have to explain that to my pecker the next time it starts nagging me."

Howard laughed and Ken felt the week had gone extremely well. He didn't want it to end on a sour note. He took another sip of his drink and sighed, "I feel so good, Howard. Content, is what I really mean. I wish we could spend more time here at the inn and do some exploring and shopping."

Howard agreed. "I was thinking the same thing. Let's come back for a three-day weekend before Thanksgiving."

"Or even after. I bet it's beautiful in December. Snow and pine trees and fireplaces that work. The whole area is like a page out of a child's storybook."

"Typically Ken. Always trying to turn reality into fantasy."

"Imagination is the only reality," Ken said.

"Oh, you've been listening to my lectures."

"No, reading de Sade."

"You naughty boy."

"Spicier than your Playboy."

"I'll bet. Did de Sade really say that?"

Ken nodded. "He did. And it does sort of sum up your theory on the human mind, doesn't it?"

Howard frowned. "I've been misquoted, misinterpreted and compared to everyone from Satan to Christ but never. . . never with the infamous de Sade. And you know what? I think I like it." Howard winked suggestively.

"On that note I think we'll turn in. Can we take these with us?" Ken indicated the two unfinished drinks.

"I don't see why not. We can offer them to the ghost if he makes an appearance."

Ken picked up both glasses. "The ghost, Howard, doesn't live here. He lives in the big house on top of the hill."

"Well, you can never tell about ghosts. They're apt to stray." They climbed the stairs. "Christ, it's dark up here. Can you see?"

"I'm okay," Ken replied.

There was one small light on in the long, narrow upstairs hall. Again the wind rattled the window panes. The ice in the glasses Ken carried also rattled. "I'm cold," Ken whispered.

"It is cold up here. I hope the room is heated. Last door he said, eh? This must be the place."

Howard opened the door and Ken went in ahead of him, carrying a drink in each hand. Both of them stood just inside the doorway, silently staring, completely enchanted by the room. "Even a lit fireplace," Ken said at last.

Howard marched to the fireplace and examined it. "Gas," he announced. "Gas jets burning under artificial logs."

Ken sighed audibly."It's still beautiful."

"It is," Howard admitted. "And warm, thank God." He began to undress as Ken opened an overnight bag. "It looks like a room they always picture in American history books. Remember those paintings? GEORGE WASHINGTON AND HIS MOTHER."

"I wonder if they're all real," Howard thought aloud, indicating the highboy and rocker and commode.

"They look real enough for a Madison Avenue dealer to blow his mind over," Ken replied. He removed his jacket and started to unbutton his shirt. Howard, already down to his shorts and T-shirt, looked at the two doors opposite the room's entrance. "I would guess that one," Ken said, pointing to the door at the right.

Howard opened it and looked in. "The bathroom. You had a fifty-fifty chance and you won."

Ken unzipped his fly and his pants fell about his feet. "Not at all, Holmes, that's an outside wall, baths usually have a window and for windows you need an outside wall."

"Oh, shut up."

When Howard came out of the bathroom two things registered in his mind simultaneously. One was that a large double bed was the only one in the room; the other was that his son stood by the fireplace clad only in his jockey shorts, his back to Howard and his slim, muscular body haloed by the dancing flames. Howard went to the fireplace and stood next to Ken, taking his own drink from the mantle.

"You smell good," Ken said.

"Thank you. It's called soap and water."

"I must remember to get you a large supply for Christmas."

They drank in silence, enjoying the warmth of the fire and each other's company, both lost in his own thoughts. Howard put his hand on the boy's shoulder and Ken shivered. "Are you still cold?"

"No, but your hand is."

"Cold hands, warm heart."

"Cold hands from holding cold glass."

"Say that in public and they'll expel you from the writer's union."

Ken laughed. "I had a good week, Dad. A very good week."

"So did I, son. Come on, let's get into bed before our behinds freeze. Fireplaces can only warm one side at a time."

Howard turned down the bed covers as Ken looked for the gas feed and closed it tightly. Then the boy went to the window and looked out.

"See any witches on broom sticks?"

"No, but the sky is so bright with stars I can just about make out China House on top of the hill."

"Check for lights."

"Sorry, not a light on in the place."

"Good. Now come to bed."

Ken slipped in beside his father and Howard pulled the heavy quilt over both of them. "Howard, do you really believe that imagination is the only reality?"

"Tricky question. You see, Ken, there are ways of defining such a statement that make it impossible to refute."

"Explain."

Howard sighed. "Now?"

"Now, Howard, please."

"Well," Howard began, "you're on the phone with a friend. You have a nice chat and when it's over you hang up. A minute later your friend drops dead. Are you upset?"

"No. I don't know he's dead."

"Exactly. You think, or imagine if you will, that he's alive. In reality he's dead. You're not upset because your imagination is your reality."

"That's like saying what you don't know won't hurt you."

"Correct. Now there's another meaning which, as any of my critics will tell you, is very refutable. You go to the doctor and he tells you you have an incurable disease. In reality it's not true. He's made a mistake, read someone else's work-up or something like that. The mistake is never discovered and in six months you're dead."

Ken nodded. "I've heard of such cases."

"Oh, it's fact. Documented fact. But it doesn't always happen."

"So it's not scientific."

"So it's not scientific," Howard repeated. "It can't be repeated in a controlled situation. Our learned scientists shrug it off as coincidence or one of those things that can't be explained and is not worth investigation."

"But you think it is."

"Definitely. And I'm not alone. Some fine men in the field think that in the near future medical science will be replaced by mind science. Treat the mind and the body will cure itself."

"Right now though it falls into the realm of mysticism. Mumbo-jumbo and stuff like that."

"Oh, no," Howard protested. "Sure a lot of kooks are connected with these ideas, always have been, that's why they never got the attention they deserved. But every day more and more respected men in research are looking to the human mind in search of answers to the unanswerable."

"ESP, kinetics, clairvoyance. . . is that all part of it?"

"It's all part of it and one day they will be as explainable and acceptable as electricity or the jet plane."

"Do you think the light in China House could be scientifically explained?"

"You little imp. All that interest in my work was just research for the next Kenneth Roth novel." Howard pounced on his son and began to tickle the boy under his arms.

"Stop it," Ken yelled, laughing and struggling to free himself. "Stop it. You know I can't stand that."

"That's exactly why I'm doing it." Howard pressed himself against the squirming body.

"I'm sorry, Howard," Ken laughed and moaned. "I'm sorry. Uncle. Uncle."

"Shut up, you'll wake the dead. . . ."

"Jesus, what a hell of a thing to say here." Ken put his arms around Howard and drew him closer in an effort to stop Howard's probing fingers.

"Or Mr. Billingsly," Howard continued.

"He'll think I'm not your son and send us to a neon-lit motel."

Howard suddenly let go of the boy and they rested, panting, in each other's arms. The match had ended and the wrestlers were painfully aware of their proximity to each other. Moments ago a thumb grazed across a masculine nipple, a knee prodded a crotch, a nose nestled in a mass of unruly hair. They had been transformed from flesh to stone, an ancient Greek statue recalling a dim past. Ken moved his leg. Howard shifted his weight.

"I always manage to say the wrong thing," Ken whispered.

"I don't know what you're talking about."

"Dad, please. . . I want to tell you. . . ."

"That your next book will be called China House."

Ken turned his back on his bed partner and squirreled under the blankets. "Yeah... isn't that a great title."

Ken opened his eyes to the eerie gray light of pre-dawn. For a few seconds he didn't know where he was and thought perhaps he was dreaming. Then he remembered. Howard was still fast asleep, his head buried in the pillow under him and his blond hair almost glowing in the strange light. Ken was cold. Icy cold. He remembered a sweat-shirt in his overnight bag and got out of bed, shivering, to get it. He pulled it over his head and down his chest. Better, but not much. Christ, could the temperature really have dropped that much so quickly? He went to the window half expecting to see snow or an icy rain, but the night was clear. White stars filled the sky and the trees moved restlessly in a steady wind. He looked up the hill.

China House was clearly visible. The boy's eyes opened wide as a shiver of fear, not cold, raced up his spine and invaded his scalp. A light was on in China House. An upper floor window was ablaze, like a beacon facing the sea. As the sun's first rays touched earth the light went out. Ken tore himself away from the window and dove into the warm bed.

"Howard. Dad. Wake up. Jesus... wake up."

• III •

Dinner over and the kitchen cleared, they sat by the fire, the first of the season, in their comfortable living room, Howard with the evening newspaper and Ken with a crossword puzzle. Howard was not reading and Ken was not working his puzzle. They both stared into the fire, watching the burning log and listening to its comforting crackle as outside a cold wind announced the end of autumn.

"What are you thinking about?" Howard asked.

Ken shook his head. "Your meeting with Scott Evans."

"And?"

Ken moved the crossword puzzle from his lap and reached for a cigarette. "And nothing. It's all very interesting but none of it makes any sense."

"You're right and I think that's just what it is. Nonsense."

"Do you really think they're playing a game? Scott and his friend, Michael, I mean."

"What else?"

"Maybe he's serious. You said Scott struck you as a sensitive and intelligent man. It could be true."

"Ken, you're beginning to believe what you write. Do you really think that picture is of Scott's twin brother who died when he was five years old? We've all heard tales of the dead reappearing, but never growing, chronologically, as we mortals do."

"But why? For what purpose?" Ken asked.

Howard shrugged. "It's Halloween time and the rich kids are having fun. They're going to pull off the most macabre Halloween trick ever conceived."

"Somehow I just can't believe it."

"I can," came Howard's quick reply. "Look, they spent the summer in Sea-Air contemplating and getting it all together, whatever the hell that's supposed to mean, and they read my papers. The Institute sends everything it prints to the Evans house. So, bored, maybe even with each other, they decided to have a little fun and yours truly was selected for the role of clown. Ken, that photo is of Scott Evans standing on the jetty and it was taken by his buddy, Mike Armstrong."

"For someone who is supposed to be an objective observer you sound a wee bit too emotionally involved."

Leave it to Ken to find the wound and rub in the salt, Howard thought. "Sorry, but I just don't like the idea of being played for a fool, especially when it concerns my work."

"Then why did you take the photo and tell them you would investigate. . . what?"

Howard laughed. "I haven't the faintest idea. That's what makes it such a lot of bull. Besides, how could I refuse? His family just about supports the Institute single-handedly."

"Let me see the photo, Howard."

"It's upstairs in my jacket. I'll show it to you before bed. I'm too comfortable to move right now."

Ken picked up his crossword puzzle and stared, meaninglessly, at the black and white squares. "You're leaving out one important fact that has nothing to do with Halloween or practical jokes."

"Namely?"

"Namely, China House."

"China House? What's that got to do with what we're talking about?"

"Everything. Don't you see, it's the link. A link between us and them. We came upon China House by accident. I saw a light in the window, exactly as Mr. Billingsly described it. You get asked to Scott Evans's for a drink and what do you see? A picture of China House and Scott Evans owns it, no less. Howard, those two guys couldn't have planned that."

Howard sighed, his entire torso moving with the sound. "Ken, I will say it once more and I hope for the last time. You did not see a light in the window of China House. What you saw was the sun reflected on the glass."

"The sun wasn't up yet."

"But it came up a minute later. The house is on a hill. The

rising sun would hit there first, then down where we were. It's all very simple and very logical."

It was Ken's turn to sigh. "Okay, I didn't see a light. But what about the house itself and the way it links up with Scott Evans and his friend Michael Armstrong?"

Howard rubbed his chin. He always rubbed his chin when he had to do or say something he did not want to do or say. "Coincidence?" Then he smiled his little boy smile.

Ken laughed with him. "I think I'm on Scott's side. Too many coincidences. There has to be more to it."

"So far, son, we have only one coincidence. The house. The rest is just hearsay. Hearsay, I might add, fed to me by the person involved, not an objective observer."

"So," Ken said, "we do some research. I was going into New York anyway."

Kenneth Roth made frequent trips to New York, sometimes spending the day, sometimes staying overnight or for an entire weekend and occasionally even longer. Howard never questioned these excursions, accepting Ken's off-handed references to seeing his agent or publisher or taking in a Broadway show or art exhibit. The father, recalling his nurses, respected his son's privacy as the boy had once respected Howard's. Ken often went to the city unprepared to stay but arrived home the next day looking fresh and clean-shaven. Howard suspected the boy kept an apartment in his old hometown but refused to pry. Ken could well afford it, and what he did with his own money was his own business.

Howard's social life was peopled with psychologists and psychiatrists, their wives or husbands and others connected with Sloan. Their cocktail parties, bridge and golf games or days spent lolling on the beach were little more than extensions of their days at the Institute. They also idolized Ken, made a fuss over him and constantly asked about his writing and fame. Ken avoided them like the plague.

Sea-Air itself lacked any social life of its own. In the summer it was overrun with upper-middle-class, very straight-laced families. In fact, Ken often referred to Sea-Air as the Bible Belt of the North; in the winter most of the population went to Florida. Howard secretly blessed the fact that Sea-Air was only two hours away, by bus or train, from the city. Their arrangement worked. Howard was hurt because Ken never brought any friends home but didn't press the point. Ken had brought Kevin Roberts home, many times, and Howard had certainly been civil to his son's roommate. When the friendship ended in disaster — Ken didn't even attend the wedding — Howard had elected to ignore Ken's depression and obvious boyish 'crush' on the now lost roommate. The rapport father and son had always shared evaporated along with Ken's youth and desire to go on to medical school. Howard, who should have known better, placed the blame for all of this on Kevin.

Now Howard counted aloud as he checked off the points Ken should look into. "The twin brother. If he existed and how he died. The tutor. The teacher. The picture."

"The picture is your department," Ken cut in. "What will you do with it?"

"What can I do? Give it to our lab man to go over. Make sure it's real and not some pasted together bit of trickery. But even that's foolish. It has to be authentic. Mike took the picture of Scott. No witnesses to prove it false or true."

"Check it out anyway and I'll go to New York and do my research."

"So you've started a new book. About China House, I take it." Ken looked surprised. "Come on, Ken, this rushing off to research the Evans family is not strictly on my behalf."

"Yeah, I've started a new book but that doesn't mean I don't want to help you. The two projects just happen to coincide." Ken's tone was stronger than he intended it to be.

"You're putting words in my mouth."

"I have to because you never say anything." Ken stood up, his long legs trembling slightly, and went to the fireplace. He knelt and began to prod the burning log with a poker. "Every time I reach out you turn your back," Ken said to the fire.

"Reach out? You never tell me anything."

"You never ask me anything."

Silence.

Ken returned to his chair and puzzle.

"Truce?" Howard offered.

Ken grinned and pushed his hair from his forehead. "I'm sorry, Howard."

"I think China House has us all rattled. Now tell me about the new book..." Ken began to protest with a wave of his arms... "no, I insist. I want to know."

"Just some notes. Nothing definite."

"I guess the sea captain is your hero. The one who keeps going to China and returning with another load of furniture for his house."

"And a Chinese mistress," the young man laughed.

"Oh, dear, what does his puritan New England wife say about that?"

"Plenty."

They both laughed and Ken suddenly felt very good and very expansive. "Let's have a cocktail party, Howard."

"Okay. The usual group?"

"Oh, no. I want Scott Evans and Michael Armstrong. You should reciprocate, don't you think?"

"Ken, what are you up to?"

"Nothing, really. Just a small cocktail party and to add some spice we'll ask Alice Miller."

Howard inspected the ceiling and spoke to it. "Trying to fix up Alice?"

"Are you kidding? But living in this town she could certainly use some help... and don't say fix-up, when people say that they always mean...."

"Getting fucked? Yes, they do."

"Howard, really."

"Why do you always say 'Howard, really' whenever I make a point?"

"I say it when you use dirty words like a little boy."

"Fuck is a good Anglo-Saxon word."

"So is bastard."

Howard roared. "The writer's instinct. I must remember never to match wits with you. Okay, we'll invite Alice for all the good it will do her. I told you Scott and Mike are only interested in each other."

"Just speculation on your part, Howard."

"No, Ken, it's clinical observation and I'm a professional, remember? Besides, I have a feeling for things like that."

Ken opened his eyes very wide. "Really?"

Howard blushed. "Excuse the expression but you're hitting below the belt." They were now both laughing openly. "We seem to be traveling in the lower regions of the male ego and anatomy."

"I can think of worse places," Ken said.

"Oh?"

Ken felt good. Except for the one flare-up earlier he and

Howard were actually communicating. In a way he could not explain, Ken felt that China House was responsible for bringing them closer together than they had been in years. The trip to Salem, when they had discovered China House, had been almost ideal. True, there had been a few moments in that bed... Shit, what had Howard thought? Did he think Ken wanted to...?"

Too much or too little. When was it going to be just right again?

But it *had* been just right, after Ken had seen the light and woke his father. It had been the way it used to be. Howard had not laughed, or worse, been annoyed. "Just a dream, Kenny. People can dream even when they're walking about." And he had rubbed Ken's back, his hand under the sweatshirt, slowly and gently. "I used to do this when you were a little boy and it always put you to sleep." And it did just that once again.

Now China House, in the person of its owner, had brought them close once again. They were partners in what was probably some foolish game, ready to outwit their opponents against all odds.

"When should we have our party?" Ken asked.

"When?" Howard seemed surprised. "October 31st, naturally."

Ken went up to bed while Howard remained downstairs, saying he would follow as soon as the fire had burned itself out. Alone, he went into the kitchen and made himself a weak rye and water, remembering that he had had more than his usual share with Scott and Michael. Then he stepped out the back door for some fresh air; he needed to think clearly about the events of the day.

The wind had died down somewhat but the night was still cold and Howard hunched his shoulders as he breathed in the chilly ocean air. The moon, high now, was yellow and smaller than when Howard had seen it rising over the ocean, but still bright enough to light the tree tops and make them shimmer in the mild breeze. The sound of the surf in the still night brought back Scott Evan's words. "My family is very big with oceans, Dr. Roth."

Howard wondered what was happening at the big house on the ocean. Perhaps they were in bed now. No, he didn't want to think about that. Nor did he want to think about the picture Scott had given him or the true reason he had been invited to the Evans house. He wanted to think about his strange reaction to the fact that Scott Evans owned China House. Even now, hours later, Howard could recall all too clearly the flash of horror or, even stranger, a precognition of horror, that had engulfed his mind when Scott had spoken the words, "China House is in Salem."

Howard had immediately dismissed old man Billingsly's tale that China House was haunted, and he was still convinced that Scott Evans had been less than truthful about the purpose of their meeting. He was too intelligent to be superstitious and as a well-trained psychologist he understood that what he had experienced was significant and peculiar to him and not, as Ken thought, connected with a supposedly haunted house. One's emotions are not evoked by outside stimuli but rather by one's reactions to the stimulus. Howard was not afraid of old empty houses or of ghosts, so the feeling of déjà vu and fear he had experienced at Scott's house was triggered by something within his own mind, some thought deep within his subconscious. A thought so frightening that he could not, or would not, allow it to surface. A thought that was in some way connected not with China House but with the evening he and Ken had spent at the Seaford Inn.

He knew that the more he tried to reason it out and bring it into his conscious the more it would evade him. So, still troubled, he went back to the warmth of his kitchen and placed his drink, hardly touched, in the sink.

All that remained of the fire was a heap of smoldering, gray ashes. Sure that it could be left alone, Howard began turning off the lamps and as the house grew dark his thoughts turned from things unknown to the universal and very real subject of romance. Alice Miller. He had been surprised to find her waiting for him in his car. Surprised, but not angry as he knew he should have been by her impetuousness. He had made it clear to her several months ago that their affair was over; and even clearer that it never should have started in the first place.

It had begun on a rainy autumn afternoon just about the time Howard's ego was feeling the first smarting blows of Ken's success, on the couch in Howard's office. His young, pretty assistant was just the balm his masculine pride needed at that time. He was intrigued and delighted with the clandestine air of their romance which continued on and off for two years under the noses, as it were, of the entire Sloan Research Institute. The rude awakening came, as usual, when Howard realized that Alice

Miller was in love with him. He was not and could not be unkind. Alice was only a few years older than Ken, and Howard had no intentions of marrying her. They had no future together. Howard felt that he had taken advantage of Alice, although she had never even pretended to discourage him, but refused to allow his poor judgment to ruin her young life.

When he decided to end the affair he did so gently but firmly. Until tonight he had thought Alice had gotten over her infatuation. But her boldness this evening made it obvious that Howard had been more gentle than firm in ending the relationship.

Now, as he climbed the stairs, he found himself physically aroused, a reminder that he was only flesh and blood and a fact he had been repeating to himself since leaving Alice Miller at her doorstep. He went into his bedroom and undressed quickly, the bulge under his briefs a memento of his thoughts of Alice Miller. Why had he refused her invitation to go in for a drink? She was, after all, a grown woman who now knew the score. He touched himself and remembered that he had not shown Ken the photo Scott had given him. He patted the bulge, "You can wait," and went to the closet for his blazer. Might as well put the photo on his dresser now so he would remember it in the morning. He reached into the breast pocket of his jacket.

The pocket was empty.

His hand went through the jacket's two side pockets. He found his key chain in one and some loose change in the other. He went through his pants and even his shirt pocket knowing it was too small to hold the picture. They were all empty.

Howard began to sweat. The pleasant stiffness in his groin turned to limp fear. *Ken.* Of course. Ken took the photo to have a look at it. Without worrying about disturbing his son he marched into Ken's room, turned on the ceiling light and searched the dresser and night table. Ken slept peacefully. The photo was nowhere in sight. "What the hell could he have done with it?" But even as he spoke the words he knew Ken had not taken the picture. It was not like the boy to go through his father's pockets. No, Ken would never do that.

He would ask Ken about it in the morning just to make sure. No, he wouldn't. If he didn't take it, and Howard was sure he did not, how would he explain the fact that it was missing?

For the second time that day Howard Roth felt genuine fear. What made it worse was that he did not know what he was afraid of.

· IV ·

The big house on the ocean was dark except for one light in a corner room on the second floor. Inside the room Scott Evans, stark naked, stood by the window gazing out at the black ocean. A moment later Mike Armstrong, also naked, entered the room from the adjoining bath. He walked with long, masculine strides, so sure of his beauty he appeared just as confident naked as he did fully clothed.

"Nothing to see out there, buddy, but the cold, dark night."

Scott turned his head and took in all of Mike Armstrong. "Nothing to see in here, either."

"Ouch. But I refuse to believe you. There are more interesting sights within than without." Mike leaned his tall, firm body against Scott's back and encircled his friend's bare chest with both arms.

"I can feel one of them on my butt; do I have to look, too?"

Mike's hand moved down Scott's chest and belly until it encountered the tangled mass of soft hair. "Sex demands the attention of all the senses, including sight."

"On a scale of one to ten where do you rate sight?" Scott asked, allowing Mike's fingers to explore wherever they chose to wander.

"Number ten."

"You would," Scott laughed.

"Where would you rate it?"

"Second to feel."

"Like this?" Mike whispered.

Scott inhaled deeply. "Yeah, just like that." He was now fully aroused.

Mike pulled Scott away from the window and gently pushed

him down on one of the room's twin beds. "I just want to look at you."

Scott stretched himself out, one hand rubbing his chest. The reddish-blond hair there, an almost invisible narrow line between his breasts, moved downward in a continuous line, over his flat belly, then branched out to a generous pubic area. His long masculine legs were perfectly matched and covered with the same sandy down. Scott walked his fingers down to his groin and encircled his erection. "You're a voyeur, Armstrong."

"Yeah, ain't it nice." Mike joined in the ritual.

"At prep school we used to call this a circle jerk."

"Funny, we called it the same thing at Hemstead Junior High. It's nice to know the rich don't have an exclusive on sharing it with a friend."

"Christ, you're big."

"That's not a pee-pée you're holding." Mike knelt between Scott's spread legs. "Little boy time is over, now the adults show you how it should be done."

Scott raised his knees. "Put something on it. I can't—"

"You said feel was number ten and I want you to feel... me... all of me."

"Christ, Mike... Oh, Christ."

"You feel me?"

"Yes."

"All of me?"

"Yes. Shit, yes."

"You love me?"

"Michael... Oh, Michael... Michael... Michael."

Mike propped up his pillow and leaned back on it as he reached for his cigarettes. He lit one and blew a cloud of smoke into the air. From the other bed Scott was saying, "Wasn't that a gas about the house? China House, I mean. What do you make of it?"

"You've asked me that a dozen times since Roth left and all I can tell you is—"

"You don't know."

"Well, I don't. But you obviously do."

"I think I do, but I'm not sure. What I am sure of is Dr. Howard Roth. Good choice, eh?" Scott reached out and Mike automatically put his cigarette between Scott's fingers.

Mike shook his head. "I don't know what to make of it. He'd actually been to China House."

"Well, he's not been in it but he's seen it and is aware of it. Something, isn't it?"

"It's something, all right," Mike agreed. "What do you think he'll do with the photograph?"

"I don't know, but we'll soon find out." Scott took a final drag on the cigarette and handed it back to Mike before turning off the bedside lamp. The sound of the surf entered the room as the light left it.

"Scott?" Mike's voice was little more than a whisper.

"Yes?"

"Do you think Roth believed you?"

"According to his theory he won't believe or not believe. He'll investigate."

"And that's what you want?"

"That's what I want," Scott answered.

"I'm afraid, Scott."

"Of me?"

"No, buddy, of China House."

"Why, because he died there?"

"No, because he lives there."

"You believe me, Mike, don't you?"

"I believe in you."

"Thank you," Scott whispered. "I have to go, Michael."

"I know you do. And I have to go with you."

Scott's hand reached out between the two beds and Mike's did the same. Their fingers touched and clasped.

"Which hand am I holding, Scotty, your left or your right?"

"My left, why?"

"Where's your other hand?"

"On my belly. Why?"

The silence that followed was made painfully acute by the pounding sound of the ocean which filled the dark room with a menacing roar. But in spite of the din Scott could clearly hear Mike's deep, erratic breathing.

"Why, Mike, why?" Scott pleaded.

Mike felt Scott's hand grow limp and damp as he gripped it with an urgency that caused Scott to whimper. But still Mike Armstrong did not reply.

"Good Christ, Michael, why?" Scott shouted in a shrill, hysterical voice that momentarily reduced the ocean's majestic roar to an insignificant hum.

"I feel two hands, Scott. Two."

The surf picked up the timbre of Scott's sobbing moan and hurled it back into the dark bedroom again and again.

• V •

Ken returned from New York with a briefcase full of notes and a new pair of jeans from Bloomingdale's. He held the jeans up for Howard's inspection.

"What do you think? Complete with some guy's name stitched on the ass and don't ask how much they cost, you'd faint if you knew."

"They look kind of narrow, are you sure they'll fit?"

"They're supposed to be tight, Howard, and I did try them on." Ken began to fold the pants. "I mean if you've got it, flaunt it."

Howard looked at his son's long legs and laughed. "I think you've got more than your share."

"I should have been a dancer."

Howard winced. "You should have been a doctor." Ken took a deep breath and let the air out of his lungs very slowly. "I'm sorry," Howard quickly added. "It's been a long day."

Ken passed behind his father's chair and as he did so he patted Howard's shoulder, then stared for a moment at Howard's blond hair which was still thick and silky. Most men Ken knew who were Howard's age had hair that was beginning to thin. He thought of Dorian Gray and wondered if there was an oil of Howard in the attic. Laughing to himself he headed for the kitchen.

"Ready for a drink?" Ken called out.

"I'm overdue. Need any help?"

"Stay right where you are, I'll get them. Did you do anything about dinner?"

"Nothing," Howard said. "I thought we would go out."

"Good thought," Ken shouted over the sound of ice being freed from the tray.

He returned with a scotch for himself and a rye for Howard. "Cheers. Hummm, that tastes good. Now if you'll give me a cigarette I'll tell all."

"I take it your snooping proved rewarding."

"Please. . . it's called research and it was most rewarding."

"Well, let's have it."

"One. Jeremiah Evans, Scott's father, did indeed marry a Seaford of Salem. Abigail."

Howard laughed aloud. "Jeremiah and Abigail. I don't believe it. Are you sure you weren't reading Hawthorne?"

Ken nodded. "These people are the real thing. Their ancestors are who Hawthorne wrote about. Now, where was I? Yes, China House. They own it all right."

"Is it really known as China House?"

Ken nodded and sipped from his drink at the same time. "It is. I found it in *A History of Salem*. The house was built by Commodore Seaford. . . remember him?. . . in the eighteen thirties. And those Chinese furnishings that he filled the house with include some of the finest oriental antiques in America. Or in China, for that matter. The Chinese government, I don't know which one, tried to get them back and for all we know is still trying. Now, remember that Chinese mistress I was going to invent?"

"He didn't," Howard said.

"He most certainly did. But he surpassed even my very fertile imagination. He brought home a whole shipload of them."

"Where did he keep them?"

"One guess."

"China House."

"Bingo."

"My God, Ken, he had a harem in puritanical New England."

"I guess you could call it a harem."

"Guess? What would you call it? He was running a glorified whore house with him as the only customer. Some man, the Commodore."

"You don't know the half of it." Ken reached for another cigarette. "Listen to this. The girls, no one knows how many there were, were definitely brought to China House, but they were never seen or heard of again. It's one of Salem's famous mysteries."

"How many famous mysteries does Salem have?"

"The book, father, is very thick."

"Was the Commodore married?"

"Would you believe Mildred?"

"I would believe," Howard said. "Are you ready for another?" he asked, pointing at Ken's glass.

"Not now, but you go ahead."

Howard stood up and headed for the kitchen. "Well, what did Mildred think of all this?"

"That is not known. But I don't think wives commented on such things a hundred and fifty years ago."

"Here's to wives a hundred and fifty years ago."

"Very funny."

Howard returned to his seat. "Did anyone say anything? Like the police for instance."

"These were very respectable people, Howard, and the Commodore just about owned the town. If there were any questions to be asked he asked them."

"So the oriental beauties went in but never came out."

"That's about it."

"But the local gossips had some ideas on the subject?"

"You know it," Ken answered. "Everything from plain old orgies to devil worship to deflowering of virgins to human sacrifices and you name it. Lights burning in the wee hours of the morning, strange sounds, oh, and no visitors."

"Not ever?"

"That's what it said."

"What about children? They must have had children if Abigail appeared a hundred years later."

"Two," Ken answered. "A boy and a girl. The boy, as they say, was fruitful and multiplied. The girl—"

"Yes?"

"No one seems to know. She was born in 1840. Her name, Abigail again, was recorded in the family bible and she was seen in the town as a little girl, then . . ." Ken opened his arms wide, "she was never seen or heard of again after about age nine or ten."

"Ken, how much of this is actual fact? Salem, as you noted, is full of mysteries and most of them I'm sure are strictly imaginary. They had witches there too, remember?"

Ken shook his head. "I don't know, Howard. I'm not editorializing, I'm reporting."

Howard nodded. "And we'll never know, I'm sure. There is a

house, it contains a lot of good, Chinese antiques, it was built by Commodore Seaford and he was married to Mildred. They had two children. Those are the facts. So much for the house. Now what about my friend, Scott Evans?"

"Plenty. The family is well documented. What you can't find in *Who's Who* you can find in the newspapers—" Ken wagged a finger at Howard, "—if you know the dates, and that's where I had trouble."

"I know, we don't have any dates," Howard answered.

Ken opened his briefcase and took out the notes he'd taken. "Well... I got most of it. I told you Jeremiah Evans married Abigail Seaford. They did indeed have twin sons. Scott and Thomas, born twenty-six years ago. You told me Thomas died at age five so I checked the newspapers of twenty-one years ago."

"Very good, Watson. Very good, indeed."

Ken ignored the jibe and continued. "Thomas's death was recorded in the *New York Times* and the *Boston Globe*. The child fell down a flight of stairs in the family home located just outside of Salem and died instantly, unquote."

"Any follow-up stories?"

"In the *Times*, no. But in the *Globe*, yes, and most interesting."

"How so?"

"The funeral was held in the house and the boy was laid to rest in the family cemetary on the grounds of the estate."

"Along with the Commodore and a dozen Chinese mistresses," came Howard's response.

"One would imagine. But get this. At the funeral a reporter asked Jeremiah Evans if there was any truth to a rumor that the local coroner had asked for an inquest concerning the accident."

Howard sat forward in his chair. "That is interesting. What did Jeremiah say?"

"Absolutely untrue," Ken answered, reading from his notes.

Howard shrugged. "What else would he say? But that clan is big enough to put the lid on a small town coroner, or even a doctor."

"Or the police," Ken added.

"Anything else?"

"Nothing. Just a note in the same issue of the *Globe* saying the family was closing the house and going on an extended trip to Europe with no immediate plans to return to China House."

"And twenty-one years later their plans remain unchanged. You know what I find most interesting about all of this?" Howard pointed at Ken's notes.

"The rumor about the inquest?"

"No, Watson, what I find most interesting is your friend Mr. Billingsly."

"Billingsly?"

"Doesn't it strike you as odd that our inkeeper who was so hot to tell us about strange lights and haunted houses said not one word about the fact that the Seaford girl had married an Evans of the Evans clan; Christ, they're as well known as the Rockefellers. Nor did he say one word about the boy's death. An accidental death in a very prominent family which took place right under his nose and not one peep about it from the old man. Forget the Commodore and his China dolls. That was a long time ago and maybe Billingsly never read *A History of Salem*, but the boy's death. . .?"

Ken looked amazed. "You know, Howard, you're right. He said the family had gone away but never said why. I just took it for granted he didn't know."

"It gets curiouser and curiouser. More?"

"More. Scott went to Ryder Prep."

"Naturally."

"Naturally. For people like the Evans family it's the only place to prep. I got hold of the yearbooks for the four years Scott was at the school. In the book for year number three there's an obit for one John Summers, English teacher. He drowned in a boating accident the previous year. No details."

"Did you check the newspapers?"

"Impossible without an exact date. It would not be a front page story like the boy's accident. And ditto for Scott's tutor. Impossible to check. We don't even know his name and the accident isn't reported in anything I read on the family."

"You did a great job, son. I'm surprised you got as much as you did."

"I learned enough to prove that Scott was telling the truth."

"Oh, I never doubted him for a minute. He's too smart a young man to lie about what could be disproved. It's what he implied about these accidents that concerns us. Look, little boys do fall down flights of stairs and die. Only God knows how many people have been hit by cabs while crossing Fifth Avenue and dozens of boat accidents happen every summer on Long Island Sound. So, what do we do now?"

Ken stood up. "We go to Jimmy Brown's, that's what we do."

Jimmy Brown's, Sea-Air's only restaurant, was a five minute drive from the Roth house. Strictly informal and with a menu that never varied the restaurant was surprisingly good and, compared to similar New York establishments, modest in cost. During the summer months it was packed but now, late in October, Ken and Howard had their pick of a half dozen tables.

Howard waved to Jimmy who was behind the bar and a waitress who knew the Roths by name took their order. Jimmy himself carried their cocktails to the table and exchanged a few words with the pair before returning to his few customers who seemed more interested in watching the television screen than in chatting with the bartender or each other.

"What about the photo, Howard?" Ken asked. "I almost forgot all about it."

Howard looked as if he, too, would like to forget about the photo and quickly raised his glass to his lips in order to hide the consternation Ken's question had provoked. In moments his entire horrific day at the Institute flashed through his mind.

Howard had been relieved when Ken did not ask to see the picture the morning after he discovered it missing. He had spent a restless night, waking often and each time his mind immediately began to dwell on the photo. How could he have lost it? He left the house early that morning, pretending to be in a hurry, purposely to divert Ken's mind from the photo and the ruse had worked. He kept telling himself that he didn't want Ken to know about the disappearing picture because Ken was already making too much of China House and Scott Evans. This new kink would only add fuel to his son's overworked imagination. The true reason he wanted to keep it a secret, and Howard knew it, was that he could find no logical explanation for the mystery.

He felt certain it was all a trick conjured up by Scott and Michael but how they had worked it Howard had no idea. This fact didn't bother Howard. Since researching in the field of parapsychology he had come across the most uncanny of charlatans. The disappearing photo would be considered amateur when compared to the 'mysteries' pulled off by professional con-artists Howard had read about and even interviewed personally.

What did annoy Howard was that he had fallen for the trick and was the butt of the joke. Driving to his office he decided that no one was to know the photo was missing, especially not the perpetrators of the trick. Two could play at any game and Howard was ready. He would pretend he had the photo and was having it investigated as promised. He wondered how the Messrs. Evans and Armstrong would react to that. If they were trying to drive him balmy they had picked the wrong man. Howard would have both those boys in a state of hysterics before this game ended.

Having arrived at a positive plan of action Howard felt better as he pulled the Bentley into his parking space. But the mystery of the photo had not been resolved. In fact, it had only just begun.

Howard devoted the morning to a little research of his own. From the Institute's well stocked library he selected several tomes devoted to magic, especially disappearing tricks. By lunch time his efforts had proved to be in vain. All the references were to disappearing acts performed on a stage or in some other confined area. The more elaborate required an accomplice. He was fascinated to learn that by slightly changing the position of a few properly placed mirrors an elephant could be made to vanish from a stage before a thousand eyes.

But nowhere could he find an example of an object disappearing from the person of a non-participant after he or she had left the stage or confined area. Howard closed the final volume with an audible thud. That settled it. The photo had been removed from his jacket before he left the Evans house. But how?

"Shit," he said aloud and thereby summed up his four hours of researching into the magical arts.

He dialed Alice's extension and was reminded by the woman who shared Alice's tiny office that it was Friday and on Friday Alice spent the entire day with the rabbits in the lab. Howard lunched alone and returned to his office immediately after eating. He had work to do and it wasn't going to disappear by magic, real or imagined.

Seated behind his desk he opened its big center drawer and found himself staring at the photograph Scott Evans had given him the night before. Shock, clashing with a multitude of thoughts which flooded his brain at the same time, caused Howard's nervous system to short circuit and for a split second he actually felt as if he were losing control of his mind. The moment passed, his eyes focused on the picture and when they did he saw, not Scott Evans, but a grinning child looking up at him from the glossy frame. With a cry of anguish he pushed himself away from the desk, toppled his chair and fled to the door of his office. By the time he reached it he was once again in control and feeling like a fool. He stood with his back to the door and repeated to himself.

"I am in my office. The sun is shining through the windows. Because of that goddamned photo I had a sleepless night. I am tired and overwrought. I hallucinated. It could happen to anybody. Even me."

He returned to his desk, righted the chair, sat and once again opened the desk drawer. The little boy was still there, still grinning at Howard from the jetty on the beach. The psychologist took a deep breath and reached into the drawer. The skin on his hand reacted as if he were sticking it inside the cage of a wild beast. Quickly he picked the photo out of the drawer.

Was it the same photo Scott had given him? The boy was standing in what appeared to be the same spot Scott had stood in the original but without the other to compare it was impossible to be sure. Howard's stomach was still shaking but he was getting calmer. He was able to think clearly and he did not like what he was thinking. He heard his own voice saying:

"We've all heard tales of the dead reappearing but never growing, chronologically, as we mortals."

Could the picture have heard him last night and altered itself to make it more convincing? Howard replaced the photo and closed the desk drawer.

Logic. All his schooling, all his training, the very essence of his profession forced him to focus on the that one word: Logic.

He went out to the reception desk at the end of the hall. "Was anybody in my office while I was out to lunch?"

The girl looked starteled. "No, Dr. Roth. Is something wrong?"

"No. Nothing. Did you see anyone at all in this area?"

"Well... naturally... I saw Dr. Baxter and Dr. Maletti and Ann..."

Howard rubbed his chin. "Of course you did. I'm sorry, Joan. Just forget it, please."

He took the elevator down to the security room and spoke to Neil Harris, head of security for the Institute. No unauthorized person, or anyone for that matter, had been in the Institute last night. The cleaning people had arrived at six and left at midnight, as usual.

Three visitors had signed in so far today and all were known to persons in the Institute.

"Is there something wrong, Dr. Roth?"

Yes, there was something wrong. There was something very wrong. "No, Neil. I was just curious. Forget it."

On the way back to his office Howard knew what he was going to do. He would take the photo to the lab and have them go over it. He didn't know why he was going to do this but it was a positive move and doing something was better than doing nothing. Once in his office he went directly to his desk and pulled open the center drawer.

The photo was not there.

A wave of nausea overwhelmed him and he ran blindly to the private bathroom adjoining his office. When it was over he stood leaning against the tile wall, shaken and ashen, and realized for the first time that he was dealing with professionals, not amateurs. But professional what? He looked into the small mirror over the sink and spoke to the pale image reflected there. "Who is going to be in hysterics before this game is over?"

Howard slowly put down his glass and answered Ken. "No word yet. I only gave it to the lab people today. And I wish you would forget that photo, it's just a load of crap."

Ken shrugged. "Did you extend your invitations today?"

"I did and they were accepted by one and all. When I called Scott he was deep into a Kenneth Roth novel and seemed to be enjoying it."

"Your're kidding," Ken answered just as the waitress arrived with their steaks and salad.

"I'm not. Didn't I tell you I mentioned your work to Scott when I called on him?" Ken, his mouth full at the moment, shook his head. "Well I did and at the time he didn't seem very interested but he obviously was. Said he bought all your books and wanted me to tell you how much he was enjoying them."

Ken grinned, displaying a row of white teeth, and his dark eyes danced with merriment. "Smart man Mr. Scott Evans."

"You can tell a lot about people by what they read," Howard said as he casually waved his fork in the air.

Ken cut into his steak. "But not always by what they write."

• VI •

Cocktail parties are an aspect of modern society that are tolerated by many, shunned by some and enjoyed by very few. Thanks to Ken's expertise in such matters the Halloween bash, as Howard called it, proved to be a success.

Ken had the ability to make people feel completely at ease as soon as they entered his home. Even more important for these functions he could keep a conversation going without appearing to dominate or push the situation. As it turned out he had to rely heavily on these attributes when, because of bad timing, Scott and Michael arrived minutes after Howard had left in the Bentley to pick up Alice Miller.

"Scott Evans and Michael Armstrong," Ken smiled and held out his hand first to Michael whose handshake was a bit too firm and then to Scott whose eyes locked onto Ken's for a fraction of a second too long as he took the offered hand.

"You can put your coats in the hall closet, right there. My father will be with us shortly."

"You're safe with us," Mike said. "We'll be as good as acolytes in church."

"I'd be safe even if you were bad," Ken shot back and dispelled at once the implication that he was a teenager playing the host in his father's absence.

Mike paused, looked at Ken and grinned.

Ken Roth grinned right back and Scott Evans looked amused.

"How nice it all looks," Scott said as all three entered the living room. And indeed it did. Ken had done the room with just the right amount of 'we're having a party' touches. A fire in the fireplace, a pumpkin sitting on the hearth and a cluster of freshly cut fall flowers that bespoke taste and not frivolity. The weather, cold, clear and windy, cooperated in making the room even more cheerful.

"Nice jeans, Ken." This from Mike. "Who made them?"

Bastard, Ken thought, but undaunted he raised his jacket and turned his behind to Michael as he pointed to the name on the pant pocket. "He does all my stuff."

"Really? They fit so well I thought they were made for you." Mike didn't add 'like mine are' but he didn't have to, his tone made his meaning clear.

"They fit," Scott said, "because they're made for people with bodies like that." He pointed directly at Ken's belly.

Ken blushed. Holy shit, he thought, this is supposed to be a nice family party, but nonetheless enjoyed the compliment and supported Scott's opinion. "That's what the salesman at Bloomingdale's said."

Scott, now warming his hands at the fireplace, said to no one in particular, "That's what Bloomingdale's salesmen always say." Ken felt betrayed and didn't know why.

"I think we're now supposed to call them salespersons, no?" Mike offered.

"I think so," Ken said, "but I'm wondering if one is supposed to offer drinks before all the guests are assembled."

"Emily Post says no but I say yes," Mike answered.

"I agree with Michael," was Scott's response.

"So do I. That's three against one and Emily loses again. What can I get you?"

"Let me do it," Mike said. "I like to make myself useful." Scott grinned broadly at his friend's remark. "Just point the way to the bar."

"It's the same direction as the kitchen. Matter of fact they're one and the same place but you'll find it all set up on the table. I'd like a scotch over ice with a splash of water."

"Scotty?" Mike said.

Scott winced slightly and answered, "The same as Ken but make it bourbon."

When Mike left the room Ken joined Scott by the fireplace. "I just learned that you don't like to be called Scotty."

Scott shrugged his shoulders. He was about an inch shorter than Ken and wore gray flannels with a tweed jacket under which he had donned a soft wool crew-necked sweater. He looked exactly like what he was; a rich and good-looking young man. "I don't mind it when we're alone but he only calls me that in public when he feels threatened."

Ken blushed, again, and tried not to stare into Scott's brown eyes. "With a face like that I doubt if Mike has ever felt threatened in his life."

"You don't know Michael."

"No, and I don't know you either."

"That can be easily remedied."

"Don't flirt, Scott, it's not becoming and I'm not the Doctor's little boy, I'm a man."

Scott Evans laughed. "You're a very honest person, Kenneth Roth. I like that."

"Good. So do I."

"And I like your books. Did Howard tell you I read them?"

"He did, and it was very kind of you but not necessary," Ken answered.

"Oh, I know that. I bought one just to see what it was like. Then I bought the others."

"I take it you approve of Kenneth Roth the writer."

Scott nodded. "And Kenneth Roth the person—"

"I'll drink to that," Mike announced as he entered the room carrying their drinks on a tray.

"Did he startle you?" Scott asked Ken. "He has a way of bursting into rooms like the vice squad raiding a massage parlor. You know, Mike, one day you're going to walk into a conversation whose subject is you."

"But I have," Mike said.

"And what did you learn?" Ken asked.

"Nothing I didn't already know."

They laughed as they took their drinks from the tray. "To Ken Roth, writer and person," Scott toasted.

The three sipped and then Mike added to the toast. "And to witches and spooks and things unknown."

"Especially to things unknown," Ken said.

"Why that?" Scott, suddenly very tense, asked.

"Because it's the stuff my novels are made of. That unknown quantity in life that brings people together seemingly by chance but always with an ulterior motive."

"Does Howard believe in that unknown quantity?" Scott asked.

"Howard?" Ken laughed, but not unkindly. "Hardly. To

Howard most things are known and what isn't soon will be. He reduces it all to electricity. It's always been around only we didn't know about it till very recently."

Scott and MIke laughed at this like two school boys sharing a joke about a teacher. "Can I quote you?" Scott said.

"Fuck off," Ken answered.

"By the way, where is the good Doctor?" Mike asked. "Does he come down the chimney or out of the pumpkin at midnight?"

"He should be coming through the door at any minute with Alice." Ken reached for a cigarette from the coffee table and Scott struck a match and held the flame for him.

"Alice? The unknown quantity for our Halloween gathering."

"No, you two are the unknown quantity. Alice Miller is Howard's assistant at the Institute. A charming girl, let me add."

"Ah-ha," Mike said. "The unknown quantities have just discovered the ulterior motive. A single girl and two available bachelors."

"Who said she was single?" Ken asked.

"You did when you said she was charming," Scott spoke up. "If she were married she would be lots of fun. Divorced, she would be interesting. But single, they are always charming."

"You should have been a writer, Scott. Yes, she is single and charming, I repeat. Alice has lived in Sea-Air all her life and I feel she's never had a chance to. . ." Ken hesitated.

"Swing?" Mike completed the thought.

"Not likely," Ken said. "Alice is not the swinging kind."

"Don't be too sure of that. I knew a gal once who—"

"Mike, I don't think Ken is interested in one of your horny stories," Scott interrupted.

"Like hell I'm not."

Mike smiled triumphantly and was about to continue when the front doorbell sounded. "Saved by the bell," Scott said.

"Only a reprieve," Ken said to Mike. "I'll see you later."

Alice Miller entered the room followed by Howard who was running his fingers through his hair in an attempt to straighten what the wind had dislodged. With their arrival the small party suddenly burst into life with a gush of conversation.

"We voted aginst Emily Post and started drinking without you. Alice Miller, I want you to meet Scott Evans and Michael Armstrong."

"I'm in favor of headscarfs for men. Alice's hair is where it belongs and mine is everyplace but. Scott, Mike, good to see you again."

"Have you ever thought of a hat, Howard?"

"Hats are for old men."

"And headscarfs are for ladies."

"It's my fault we're late. I wasn't ready when Howard arrived."

"You arrived just in time to save us from one of Michael's dirty stories."

"Oh, I want to hear it."

"See, what did I tell you?"

"Michael, shut up."

"Would you make three more while you're out there, Howard? One scotch and two bourbons. I'm afraid we'll be one up on you."

No you won't. I had one at Alice's."

"New jeans, Ken? Very nice."

"That's what the salesperson at Bloomingdale's told him."

"Two bourbons, one scotch and two ryes."

"Here's to the unknown."

"Oh, dear, we're being esoteric."

"Well it is Halloween."

When the wave of euphoria had passed Ken found himself once again near the fireplace with Scott Evans. "David and The Thinker holding up the complete works of Kenneth Roth. Is there some hidden meaning to it?"

Ken shook his head. "Frankly I don't even remember how the arrangement came about but it certainly is a conversation piece."

"Are you working on a new book?"

"I am," Ken blurted out and then recalling the book's theme and research he had done he cut himself short. "But I'm always working on a new book. If first chapters were novels, the mantle would be crowded." Ken looked at Alice who was seated next to Howard; both were listening intently to what Mike Armstrong was saying. Scott followed Ken's gaze.

"Brown hair, brown eyes, nice figure, petite I guess you would call her and, yes, charming." Scott ended with a bow to Ken.

"Christ, you make her sound so dull."

"Not at all. There's a lot of passion in that charming lady."

"Really? How can you tell?"

"I have a feel for things like that."

Ken groaned. "You sound just like Howard."

"Did Howard tell you about me?"

"He said you were a very good-looking young man."

"Bull. You know what I mean. Did he tell you why I asked him to visit me last week?"

"Well, he told me it wasn't exactly a social call, if that's what you mean." Ken was now on his guard.

"And what do you think?" Scott asked.

"I'm not a professional," Ken answered. "I don't know what to think."

"I understand you saw China House."

Ken felt a shiver go right up his spine and marveled at the strange effect those two words seemed to have on all of them. China House. Party conversation had come to an end and the game of cat and mouse had begun. Ken recalled that this, in a way, was the true purpose of the Halloween bash. Us against them. Had Scott purposely steered him from the group for his own clandestine reasons? Right now Ken could not remember how he and Scott had gotten separated from the others.

"I did and Howard told me it belonged to your family. What a beautiful place it is, Scott."

"I haven't been there since I was a little boy but I remember it. You know, childhood memories, highly distorted I'm sure." A sudden burst of laughter came from the other side of the room. "Don't look now but I think Michael is out-charming Alice."

Ken laughed, mostly from relief, happy that their conversation was back on a more general footing. "I think Michael could charm a cobra out of a basket without benefit of music."

"I'm sure you're right."

"Have you known him long?" Ken asked.

"Most of my life. His father was the family chauffeur for years. We were very close as boys, then went our separate ways and saw each other only occasionally. Mike was out in Hollywood for a while. He wanted to be a movie star."

"I would imagine he would do very well at that," Ken commented.

"He would," Scott nodded, "or at anything else he set his mind to for that matter. But Mike has one very large problem. He's the laziest son-of-a-bitch in the world. He won't work at anything."

"How does he support himself?" Ken wanted to bite his tongue even before the words were out of his mouth.

Scott grinned. "Don't be embarrassed," he reassured Ken,

"we're all adults. Right now he's my traveling companion. Does that make you feel better?"

"Me? It doesn't make me feel anything. Does it make you feel better, that's what counts."

"You're not only honest, you're smart," Scott replied. "And I really would like to get to know you better."

Ken responded to this like a teenager. He felt elated and his cheeks flushed. He hadn't felt this way since his college days and the feeling was not unpleasant. "I would like that."

"Why don't you two join the party," Howard called out. Scott and Ken moved away from the fireplace and toward the others. Alice was speaking as they approached.

"Mike was just telling the most interesting stories about Hollywood. He was actually in a film."

"Two films," Scott said, " and if you blinked slowly you would have missed his performance in both."

"I think it's time for some food," Ken announced.

Alice stood up. "Can I help?"

"You most certainly can. Howard, would you check the drinks?"

"Another?" Howard asked Scott and Mike.

"Just freshen this if you would," Mike answered and Scott went along with his friend's request.

"What do you think?" Ken asked Alice when they were alone in the kitchen.

"Charming, both of them." Alice answered.

Ken wrinkled his nose. That word was becoming the kiss of death. "Mike is the extrovert but I like Scott better." He tried to sound disinterested as he piled sandwiches on a tray.

"He's also richer," Alice stated.

"Now that you mention it, yes."

Howard came into the kitchen. "Just a splash of booze and some ice is all I need. It looks good, Ken. Where did you learn to do all of that?"

"In the yellow pages under caterer."

"What this house needs is a woman," Alice told them.

Howard looked embarassed and fled with his drinks. Ken looked like he wanted to say something but didn't. Alice continued working on her tray.

"Do you think they're, you know, what Howard told me . . . gay?"

Fuck Howard, Ken thought, "I don't judge people by their sex or their sex lives," Ken said. "Besides, maybe they're just good friends."

"No, Howard said they were lovers and he ought to know."

Ken suppressed a smile. He didn't know what was funnier, what Alice had intimated or the fact that she had no idea what she had intimated. Thank God she's not a blonde, Ken thought.

As Howard handed Scott and Mike their drinks Scott asked, "Any news on the photo, Howard?"

Howard rubbed his chin with the back of his thumb. "Didn't get it back from the lab yet." He felt like an actor repeating a line by rote whenever given the proper cue. "We have priorities at the Institute, Scott, and frankly I didn't think the picture important enough to be put on top of the list."

"I guess you think I'm playing games with you," Scott said, a slight edge to his voice.

"I don't think anything of the sort," Howard lied.

"Scotty, you are so damned sensitive." Mike joined the conversation in an effort to keep it from becoming an argument.

"What do you think of all this, Mike?" Howard turned to the other man.

"I think my boy has a very vivid imagination, Doctor. He always did. But now he's getting carried away by it and I think the sooner he gets his ass in gear and on to other things the better off he'll be."

"Can we talk about it some other time, Howard? In private?" Scott said, ignoring Mike's remark.

"Sure, any time. Do you want me to set something up at the office or. . . ."

"No. No. I'll make the arrangements."

The three men turned as Ken and Alice came into the living room, each carrying a tray loaded with things to eat. "Clear the coffee table, Howard, please. Now I want everyone to help themselves. There's another tray in the kitchen with all the accessories we'll need."

"I'll get it," Mike volunteered.

"It all looks so good."

"Scott, stop dreaming and help yourself."

"Everybody want wine?"

"Is it midnight yet?"

"What happens at midnight?"

"Scott strips down to his jockey shorts and dances under the full moon."

"Interesting. I might join him braless."

"If you try it tonight you'll freeze your. . . ."

"Howard, really."

Mike poured the wine and when he had filed all the glasses he picked up his and gestured toward Howard. "A toast to the nicest Halloween party I've ever been to."

"Thank you."

Before any one had a chance to drink Scott added, "And when shall we all meet again?"

"That's sounds like an invitation," Ken said.

"It is," Scott answered, a big smile on his handsome face. "I'm inviting you all to China House for a week of fun and games."

They all stared at Scott Evans. The grandfather clock in the hall was suddenly audible as was the wind which had begun to blow up a storm outside the house. Even the logs burning in the fireplace made themselves heard. Howard, Ken, Scott and Michael all stood perfectly still, their wine glasses raised, like store window mannequins posed for a party scene. The partners eyed each other.

Alice finally broke the spell. "China House? What's that?"

· VII ·

Alice's preparation for retiring was a series of long rituals learned from dozens of magazine articles on the subject. She brushed her hair a hundred strokes but more often than not lost count as her mind wandered from the task at hand. She removed her make-up with a cream and followed that with a light astringent gently applied to cheeks, forehead and chin. A moisturizer, upward strokes only, completed the job.

As she performed she thought over the events of the day. As usual, that included Howard. She so seldom enjoyed a late night there was never any reason to skip the routine or the thoughts which accompanied it.

Though it was late when Scott and Mike dropped her off after the Roth's party, close to two, and more from habit than desire, Alice brushed her hair and applied her lotions as usual. As she thought of Howard she compared him to the two young men who had driven her home. There was no doubt in her mind that Howard was far superior to either Scott Evans or Michael Armstrong. How silly and frivolous the younger men seemed next to Howard. Handsome? Well they certainly were that.

In spite of the party atmosphere and both Howard's and Ken's glib manner, Alice had detected a certain tension in the air. Was trouble brewing between father and son? Well, one could only hope. There was no question in Alice Miller's mind that Kenneth Roth blocked the aisle that led to the altar. "They've been together so long they've come to depend on each other like a husband and wife."

And had she been convincing when she said she wasn't ready when Howard called for her? Actually she had been ready hours before Howard arrived... well, ready for her purposes anyway. She had met him at the door dressed in a robe and nothing else. Oh, he had been reluctant but it was so easy to sway a man, especially a man like Howard who liked his sex fast and spiced with the danger of being caught at it.

"It's all over Alice, let sleeping dogs lie."

Alice smiled at her reflection in the mirror. The dog had woken up the minute she removed her robe. Then the smile faded from her face. "I love him and I'm going to have him... permanently," she and her reflection said in unison and then nodded at each other.

China House. They were to leave next weekend and for a whole week. With Ken there it would be impossible for her and Howard to... Alice smiled again. "I'll find a way."

Scott drove the car through the dark and deserted streets of Sea-Air. It was still windy and now a fine icy rain had begun to fall. "Nice night for a killing," Scott commented.

"Want me to drive?" Mike asked.

"No. I'm fine."

"Tired?"

Scott shook his head. "More excited than tired."

Mike had not intended to discuss the evening but Scott's remark caused him to plunge right in. "Leave it to Scotty to drop a bomb right in the middle of a nice, friendly party."

"I thought it was pretty clever myself. Mike, I told you I want to go back to China House and I want Howard Roth to go with me. Well, I accomplished my goal."

"I think you're going to get more than you bargained for. Did you also intend for his son and girlfriend to be part of your soul searching?"

"Girlfriend?"

"The charming Alice Miller."

"You're nuts," Scott answered.

"Am I? Then I guess Howard Roth does a lousy job of applying his lip rouge."

"What the hell are you talking about?" Scott asked.

"Scotty, didn't you notice? When he came into the house he had traces of lipstick on his mouth. Wiped off to be sure but enough still there to be seen."

"Holy shit. You don't miss a trick, do you?"

Mike put his hand on Scott's knee. "You learn a lot when you have to live by your wits. I wasn't born an Evans you know."

"Christ, don't start that."

"I won't, but tell me something. The house has been closed for years, how do you expect to entertain the group?" Mike jerked his thumb over his shoulder to emphasize his last word.

"I called the caretaker days ago and told him to get the place ready." Scott smiled. "You see, I was born an Evans."

"So you had it planned all along."

"Opening the house, yes. Tonight, no. The perfect opportunity just happened to present itself."

"The unknown quantity, seemingly accidental but always with an ulterior motive. What's your motive, Scott?"

"I'm not sure. Are you?"

"No. But I guess we'll find out."

"Do you really think Howard and Alice are having an affair?" Scott questioned.

"I don't know if they're having an affair but I do think he knocked off a quickie before the party."

"You are a bastard, Mike."

Mike's hand moved up Scott's leg. "I know. That's why you keep me around."

"Ken, you of all people should be delighted with the invitation. Living in China House for a whole week. My God, your book could be more a documentary than a novel."

The conversation between Howard and Ken which had started downstairs while the two emptied ashtrays and stacked the dishwasher now continued in Howard's bedroom.

"I know, Howard, and I want to go to China House. Not only because of the book but just to see what it's like inside. I felt that way the minute I saw it, and after reading about it I'm twice as fascinated."

Howard had taken off his suit and stood in shirt and shorts as he carefully hung his pants and jacket in his closet. "Then what's the problem?"

"There is no problem." Ken sat on his father's bed. "It's just that it all happened so fast and so neatly, if you know what I mean."

"No, I don't know." Howard pulled off his shirt.

"Look, to come upon a house quite by accident, hundreds of

miles from home and then become involved with the person who owns the house and get invited to the house is certainly odd, to say the least. What do you think the chances are of it ever happening again?"

"One in a million, I guess." Howard had removed his T-shirt.

"More like one in a billion." Ken began to undo his tie.

"What do you think of Scott?" Howard asked.

Ken avoided looking at his father. "Nice guy."

"You don't think he's strange?" Howard slipped his shorts down his legs and stepped out of them.

Ken shrugged. "Maybe I have a thing for strange people. I'm a writer." He watched his father light a cigarette. (What did the Bible say about a son looking upon his naked father? Or was it the other way around?) "Do you know what Scott said about Alice?"

"I'm all ears."

"He said she was a passionate young lady."

Howard let out a sound which was a cross between a snide laugh and a groan. "He is strange. Whatever gave him that idea, and about Alice of all people?"

"He said he could tell."

"Ha," Howard exclaimed, exhaling smoke. "Some authority."

"Don't be a bitch, Howard, and while we're on the subject why did you tell Alice you think Scott and Mike are gay?"

"I don't think, I know, and I told Alice because I didn't want her to take a fancy to one of them and make a sad mistake."

"Let her make her own mistakes, sad or otherwise, she just might enjoy it. Do you have a thing against gay people, Dad?"

Howard shook his head. "Certainly not. You bring your bag and you do your thing, that's how I feel."

"I was thinking of doing a book on the subject. Homosexuality, I mean." Ken pulled his tie from under his shirt collar and began to roll it into a ball.

"You're going to ruin that tie, Ken. How would you research the book. . . on homosexuality I mean."

I've been around and—"

"Yes?"

"Nothing. . . . You know, Howard, I think Scott wants your help," Ken spoke very rapidly. "Whatever is troubling him has to do with China House and his dead brother and he's reaching out for some professional guidance."

"I know that, Ken," Howard said very softly.

"I guess you do. And I also think Scott and Mike are truly interested in your work."

"This is the only thing those two are interested in." Howard cupped himself lewdly. "Now get your tail out of here, I want to go to bed."

"You're a dirty old man, Dr. Roth, that's what you are," Ken said laughing as he started out of his father's bedroom. "Be good, I'm going to inspect your sheets for peter tracks in the morning."

"That's your department, sonny."

Ken felt his father's eyes on his back as he retreated.

Howard put out his cigarette and turned off the bedside lamp. He got into bed and stared at the black ceiling. The wind blew the icy rain against the bedroom window in a steady tattoo and with a force that made it sound as if the house were being pelted by a barrage of tiny stones.

Howard thought everything connected with Scott Evans and China House was strange but he was not about to admit it to Ken or anyone else. He was going to appear totally unaffected by anything Scott and Mike did or said. To do otherwise would be playing right into their hands which, Howard still thought, was what the pair wanted. He had watched Scott carefully when reporting that the photo was still with the lab people, but had not noticed a trace of surprise, or anything else, on Scott's face. The boy was either a skilled actor or so emotionally disturbed that nothing could alter that faraway, dreamy look which seemed to be Scott's perpetual countenance. Howard would get to the bottom of it. There was nothing like a challenge, especially a duel of minds, to excite the psychologist; the disappearing and reappearing photograph had been more than sufficient bait to hook Howard.

His eyes looked about the dark bedroom. The furniture, solid and familiar, looked ethereal and strange. Every object took on the shape of a small boy standing on a mossy rock while the sound of rain driven by a steady wind helped to complete the picture of dark water rippling over the child's bare feet.

"Imagination," Howard sighed and forced his mind to go blank.

In the adjoining bedroom Dr. Roth's son was also having difficulty falling asleep. The sound of rain, while he was snug in his bed, usually lulled Ken to sleep in minutes but tonight it acted as a stimulant to his already keyed-up state. He was sexually aroused and ordinarily would have masturbated and in the after-glow of his relief drift off into a dreamless sleep. But on this evening he recoiled from the erotic images that paraded across his mind and refused to touch the erected flesh that would not concede to his inhibitions.

Scott Evans. Scott and Mike were tight and Ken wasn't going to be the bastard to come between them. He knew how fragile such relationships were and having been burned himself didn't wish the experience on anyone else. But Christ, Scott had come on strong. "I really do want to get to know you better." Was he hinting at a three-way scene? Ken didn't go for that but. . . .

And Howard kept talking about Scott being strange, whatever the hell that meant. Maybe Scott was demented. . . . No, Ken could not believe that. Scott was upset and Ken wanted so much to help him. But Scott had Mike and. . . shit, Mike was a handsome bastard.

Howard. Was that lipstick Ken had seen on Howard's face when his father and Alice walked into the house or was it just Howard's reaction to the cold wind? Cold wind, hell. It was lipstick. Howard and Alice? Could it be? "Why doesn't he ever tell me anything?"

Ken twisted and turned but the thoughts and images remained fixed in his brain. Scott. . . Michael, Howard and Alice. . . Howard nude, "This is the only thing those two are interested in. . . . " Kevin Roberts. . . "Why Kev? Oh, Christ why?"

"I'm getting married becasue I'm not going to spend the rest of my life as a second-class citizen."

"We don't have to be second-class anything, Kev, we can make it."

"Bullshit. The world is not a college dorm."

"You made your mind up so keep your hands off me."

"One more time, Ken, for old times sake. Come on, for Kev, one more time. . . . "

"Is it wrong, Dad?"

"No, son, I was wrong coming into your room without knocking."

"Do you do it?"

"Sure I do it. . . . "

"I really would like to get to know you better."

"What happens at midnight?"

"Scott strips down to his jockey shorts and dances under the full moon."

Ken's fist became as uninhibited as the flesh it now caressed.

· VIII ·

Morning soon came, and with it a new perspective for Ken Roth. It was funny how several drinks and a few words could set one's mind off on the most bizarre tangents. Scott Evans was being friendly, nothing more and nothing less. Howard and Alice? Ken almost laughed aloud as he moved about, putting the house to rights. God, he thought, imagination is the only reality. An idea planted in the mind and watered with booze could make one see all sorts of things that weren't there. What had Howard said? If the thought persisted one would begin acting to make it a reality. Ken thought of Scott Evans and grinned. "Maybe I'll try it."

Once the house was in order he went into the den to organize his notes and thoughts for the new book. He made a mental note to discuss it with his publisher — China House existed and so did libel laws. Next he began to work on the main character of the book: Commodore Seaford, henceforth to be known as Jason Jerome, captain of a fleet of whaling vessels and founder of the Jerome dynasty. As Ken constructed the character he kept in his mind the physical appearance of Scott Evans, endowed with the personality of Mike Armstrong. He liked the final result. Here was a man any woman could fall in love with and, most important, love enough to tolerate his idiosyncrasies.

Idiosyncrasies. The word brought to mind Scott Evans. Was Scott strange? Ken still didn't think so but he had the feeling Scott was playing a game whose object and rules were known only to Scott Evans. Yes, Ken could understand why Howard felt Scott and Mike were up to no good.

"But why Howard?" Ken reached for a cigarette.

And then there was Michael Armstrong. Just as it was easy for Ken to imagine Scott brooding over the past, it was hard for him to accept Mike Armstrong's complicity in the drama. Mike was too rooted in reality, too much of a here-and-now person. Ken knew that the brain working behind those dark blue eyes did not dwell on the past or contemplate the future. "Or am I just putting him down for the obvious reason?" Ken thought. But it was perfectly clear; Mike liked the good, rich life and Scott gave it to him so Mike went along with whatever Scott wanted. But what the hell did Scott Evans want?

Ken expressed his thoughts to Howard that evening. "I think Scott is your nemesis and Mike a reluctant partner."

"So do I but what made you come to that conclusion?"

"At the risk of sounding Victorian, I would say that Mike is a kept boy and as such he does what Scott wants him to do. I don't think Mike cares about the dead even when they pose for snaps on the beach. I'm sure at this time of year Michael Armstrong would much rather be in Palm Beach or Aspen or staying at the Evans's Park Avenue aparment where the New York season is in full swing." Ken shrugged his wide shoulders. "So, that leaves Scott as the problem-maker."

Howard clapped his hands without making a sound. "Not bad, Watson, and on the surface rather logical."

"And under the surface?" Ken questioned.

"The psychological composition of the two men. What you say is true and I'm firmly convinced that Scott Evans is after something that has nothing to do with Mike Armstrong, but Mike is a much stronger personality than Scott and you don't have to be a professional to see that obvious fact." Ken, somewhat reluctantly, nodded his agreement. "It would be easy for Mike to sway Scott away from some silly scheme, if there is a scheme, and toward Palm Beach or Aspen or New York." Howard began to use his finger as a pointer. "Mike is not only a stronger personality he is also a very. . . what's the word for sexy when you're talking about a man?"

"Sexy," Ken said.

"Very sexy guy and I think Scott would follow Armstrong anywhere."

"Scott is not exactly Quasimodo," Ken cut in.

"I didn't say he was," Howard answered and raised an eyebrow at his son.

"Sorry." Ken forced himself not to light a cigarette.

"So I think," Howard continued, "Mike is going along with Scott because he wants to."

"Wants to, or has to?"

"Wants to. It suits his purpose."

"Which is?" Ken asked.

Howard held up his hands in a sign of despair. "I have no idea. In fact, Ken, I'm not even sure what in God's name we're talking about. I wonder if we're beginning to see things that aren't there."

"Maybe. But there are facts that can't be denied, like Scott's twin brother and the photograph."

Howard relieved Ken's frustration by lighting a cigarette. Ken immediately did the same thing. "I'm beginning to believe my meeting with Scott was a spur of the moment idea on his part. He's a sensitive man and I'm sure the incidents he told me about are the cause of a lot of guilt. That type blame themselves for everything, even things they have no control over. He must have been feeling exceptionally depressed and called me to get it off his chest and relieve the anxiety in much the same way a person unloads to a therapist."

"But you told me he wanted to discuss the matter further with you."

Howard nodded. "True. But I think, and this is just supposition on my part, that Scott is now being more realistic. I mean he wants professional help in alleviating the guilt and strange notions that are beginning to go along with it."

"That's what I said last night."

Howard laughed. "I know. We seem to be going around in circles. By the way I gave Alice a little background info to prepare her for our visit to Salem."

Ken felt a pang of jealousy. This was *their* game: Ken and Howard opposite Scott and Mike. Why the hell had he brought Alice into it? "Did you?" Ken said.

"I thought it only fair," Howard answered. "Naturally she asked me about China House and if we're all going to be there for a week I thought I owed it to her to tell her as much as I knew about the house and its present owner."

"Was that wise? Alice can sometimes be a bit silly and she might say the wrong thing or even start imagining things." Error, Ken thought as he spoke the words; what the hell do I care if Alice knows or not?

"Ken, I'm surprised at you. I've never heard you say anything about Alice being silly."

"Me? I'm her biggest fan." Another error. "But she can be silly at times and I guess you've never noticed it."

"No, I never did. She's a very competent assistant and the truth is I thought it would be helpful to have another trained observer on the scene."

"What am I, stupid?"

Howard didn't like his son's tone or the direction their conversation was taking. In a minute they would be arguing. And over what? Alice Miller? Did Ken suspect the truth about Howard's relationship with Alice? If he did, why didn't he just come out and say so? Why don't I? Howard added to the thought.

"I didn't say or imply that you were stupid, Ken, and what the hell is bothering you?"

"Nothing. I'm sorry."

"You're always tense when you begin a new book." Howard touched the rawest of nerves and knew it.

"Fuck off, Howard." Ken started out of the room then stopped abruptly. "Scott Evans consulted you in confidence."

"I told you about it."

"I'm your son."

"And Alice is my professional assistant. It would be more logical and more ethical to discuss Scott Evans with her than with you."

Three strikes and I'm out, Ken thought, as he went into the kitchen and began to prepare dinner. Howard was left to speculate once again about the cause of his son's sudden animosity toward Alice Miller. Ken had never even hinted at knowing that his father and Alice were more than just professional associates and last night was no different from any other night Howard and Alice had spent with Ken — except for the presence of Scott and Mike. Howard shook his head. All roads seemed to lead to those two young men. What had Scott said to Ken? Something about Alice being a very passionate woman. Why the hell had they been discussing Alice Miller? Howard opened his newspaper. Well, it was about damn time Ken realized that his father had a sex life. Howard tried to read the evening news but a feeling of guilt kept him from concentrating on the bold black print.

Ken moved about the kitchen, pouting, and hating himself for his immature reaction to Alice's being privy to the enigma of China House and Scott Evans. Was he sore because he felt Howard had betrayed him by revealing what Ken considered to be their secret? Or was he upset because telling Alice seemed a betrayal of Scott Evans?

A few days ago Ken thought the beautiful white house in

Salem had brought him and his father as close together as they had been before Ken gave up a medical career in favor of writing. Now he wondered. A line from Ken's favorite poem came to mind. "A thing of beauty is a joy forever." In the case of China House forever had been very short lived.

The week preceding the trip to Salem flew by. Howard took great delight in telling Ken that the Institute could not spare Howard for the unexpected time off until they learned where he was going and with whom. Then, it seemed, they could not only spare him but offered to distribute his workload and even, Howard added, help him pack his bags if need be.

Ken noticed that Howard's seemingly casual interest in Scott Evans and China House and his constant demeaning of "those two young men" was more pretense than a reflection of Howard's true feelings. Often during the week Ken caught his father staring into space, his eyes clouded and a puzzled look on his handsome face. Howard seemed not only apprehensive but afraid. But of what? A haunted house?

Alice called to find out what Ken thought she should take with her in the way of clothing. "Take your standard objective observer outfit," Ken wanted to answer but he just promised to check with Scott and call her back. As it turned out, Scott called Ken to thank him for the party and to announce that he had arranged transportation and would pick them all up early Saturday morning.

"By the way," Scott added, "if I look out my window about eight in the morning I see a tall, lanky guy jogging up the boardwalk in a blue sweat suit. Do you happen to know him?"

"Does that sweat suit have a yellow stripe down the pant leg?"

"No, white," Scott answered.

"Then I guess it's me," Ken said.

"Why don't you jog up the path and knock. We serve coffee and cake about that time."

"I just might do that," Ken replied, feeling delighted and trying his best to sound as off-handed as did Scott Evans.

Ken thought about the invitation all day and most of the night. He would stop at Scott's. No, he wouldn't. Why should he? Why shouldn't he? The next morning dawned bright, winter seemed to have retreated momentarily and the tepid air smelled of salt water and freshly cut grass. "I won't have to wear my long-johns under the running suit today," Ken thought. He pulled a pair of jockey shorts out of his dresser and pulled them up his long legs. He paused, pulled the shorts off and reached for his jockstrap. As he stepped into the jockstrap he paused again. . . . "What the hell am I doing? I'm not going to stop at Scott's and even if I were what difference would it make what I wore under my suit?" He grinned as several possible answers to that question formed in his mind. He pulled off the jockstrap and once again donned the shorts.

Running was more than exercise for Ken. It was a release for a myriad of pent-up emotions, a bath for brains and lungs and a form of communing with a remarkable body he too often took for granted. As a boy, especially as a teenager, Ken had thought himself awkward and doubted he would ever grow into his long legs and arms. This self-image persisted long after his body had matured into an enviable physique. But when he ran he felt himself to be the sleek animal he was, every muscle coordinated and every forward sprint a reminder of his masculine grace and strength.

The morning sun had turned the ocean a sparkling green and the east wind, carried on the sea's waves, brought with it a heady aroma. The sand had been washed to a brilliant white and reflected, like diamonds, the almost microscopic bits of colored stones meshed into the grit. The gulls kept their vigil and screeched high above the head of the lonely runner.

Ken ran, acutely aware of the world around him, his heart pounding not only from exhaustion but also from the realization that he was a part of the miracle. Everything fell into place. Even his blond hair rode the wind in an intricate pattern of studied disarray.

He spotted the Evans house and a moment later saw the solitary figure sitting on a public bench, facing the ocean. He knew it was Scott long before he was close enough to distinguish the form. Scott turned his head as if he had heard Ken think his name and stared at the approaching runner until Ken was a few feet from the bench.

"I didn't know what color the stripe was," Scott said, continuing their telephone conversation of yesterday as if time and place held no meaning for him. "I just guessed."

Ken kept jogging in place. "Why did you pick white?" he panted.

"Virginal?" Scott grinned.

"If that's a compliment, thank you; if it's a dig, go screw yourself."

"Will you stop jumping up and down?"

"Can't. Break the stride, the timing, the mileage."

"Well jog up to the house and I'll pour you a cup of coffee."

"Don't drink coffee."

"Why not?"

"Caffeine."

"Orange juice?"

Ken shook his head as he bounced. "Bad sugar content. Quick energy but dissipates in minutes."

"Just what I need, a health freak. Would you buy grapefruit juice?"

"Sold."

Scott rose and started for the house as Ken paced himself down to a walk. "If I wasn't sitting out there would you have stopped at the house?" Scott asked.

"Nope."

"Why not?"

"Don't want to lose my famous virginity."

"You're safe with me," Scott answered.

"Then I would be disappointed."

They both laughed as Scott opened the front door and allowed Ken to enter first. The room was just as Howard had described it to his son and Ken felt on familiar ground. "I like it," he announced, "All of it."

"Glad you approve. Now wait right here and I'll get your juice." As Scott disappeared into the kitchen, Ken's eyes spotted the grouping of photographs arranged over the antique desk. When Scott returned he found Ken looking up at China House.

"Thank you." Ken took the glass from Scott. "I saw China House, you know."

Scott nodded. "Howard told me. What did you think of it?"

"A dream. I can't wait to get in it."

"I'm anxious, too," Scott said. "It's been a long time." Scott looked at the picture of China House and a peculiar expression formed on his face, as if he were shutting out the rest of the world to focus in on what he alone could see.

"Mike still asleep?" Ken asked, more to distract Scott than out of any interest in Mike Armstrong's whereabouts.

"Matter of fact, no. He took the commuter's bus to New York over an hour ago. Wednesday matinee."

"The early morning bus to catch a matinee?"

"Sure. That gives him all morning to raid the men's botiques and better department stores."

"And he'll look great in whatever he buys," Ken said with a resigned look on his face.

"Thank you, I won't tell him that."

"You don't have to tell him . . . he knows it."

Scott laughed. "That, I'll tell him."

They stood a few feet apart and looked at each other in silence.

Ken felt Scott's eyes bore into his own and he forced himself to turn away, embarrassed, to contemplate the empty juice glass still in his hand.

"Can I get you a refill?" Scott's voice came from a million miles away.

"No, really, I have to go." Ken handed the glass to Scott and their fingers touched. When Scott made no attempt to withdraw his hand Ken's fingers enclosed Scott's wrist as he slowly leaned his head forward. Scott met him halfway, their lips just touching, not pressing, their bodies strained by the effort of keeping themselves rigidly apart.

"I'm sorry," Ken whispered. "I shouldn't have done that. You and Mike—"

"Don't be sorry. I asked for it and you know it. And it isn't just Michael, it's me. Right now I'm all fucked up."

Ken shook his head. "Don't say that . . . you're not." He put his hand on Scott's shoulder. "What about you and Mike?"

"Mike and I are friends and brothers and lovers and everything and nothing. Do you understand?"

"No," Ken said. "I don't. And I don't want to break up any partnership. That's not my style. What I want is an honest answer from you. Do you want me in your life or out of it?"

"Both."

Ken groaned. "Jesus, Scotty, you have a way of complicating everything that touches you."

"And you think a simple yes or no can solve all life's problems."

Ken searched his shirt and pants for non-existent pockets. "There are cigarettes on the coffee table," Scott offered.

"I don't want one."

Scott forced a smile. "Yes you do, but like a true romantic you want your suffering to be complete. I find that charming."

"Don't toy with me, Scott."

"I'm not. Look, Kenny, right now I have something on my mind that's as important to me as life itself." Scott's brown eyes looked at Ken without seeing him. "As a matter of fact it *is* my life and until it's settled, one way or another, I can't cope with anything else. I'm sorry."

"You're talking about China House and your dead brother." Ken felt a damp chill move up his spine as he recalled the light he had seen in the window of China House.

"Something like that," Scott was saying. "You wouldn't understand."

"But you think Howard does?"

"Your father is a professional in the field of parapsychology and I think he can help me."

"And Mike?"

"Mike understands me, Ken."

Ken made a slight bowing motion toward Scott. "Then I guess you've got everything you need, Mr. Evans." He started for the door then stopped abruptly and turned. "What do you expect to find at China House, Scott?"

"Myself," was Scott's very uncomplicated answer.

The sun was high now, the ocean black and menacing looking, the sand dank and littered with debris left behind by a retreating tide. The air smelled of rotting clams and the gulls looked like hideous vultures. Ken knew it was his perception, not the world, that had changed. "We make the magic," he thought.

The runner walked home, his wide shoulders slightly stooped.

• IX •

The alarm went off at six a.m. — an unusual occurrence on Saturday morning in the Roth household but one that heralded the start of a most unusual week for Howard and his son. The pair awoke to a dark and cold winter morning which gave no promise that the sun would show itself that day. They showered, shaved and packed what they hadn't organized the night before. Breakfast consisted of juice and toast and conversation was limited to words rather than sentences, spoken in voices more asleep than awake.

Alice arrived promptly at eight and the three of them waited for their host, trying to get into a party mood but all wondering why they had consented to drive to Salem on this bleak November morning. Then the sound of a car horn moved them into action and coats and scarves and gloves were donned, luggage picked up and the front door locked all in one swirl of activity.

Scott Evans had indeed arranged transportation and the sought-after party mood came over the three guests as they got into the back seat of the long black limousine which held Scott in the driver's seat and Michael next to him.

"All the comforts of home," Mike said by way of greeting.

"Home was never like this," Ken answered.

The spacious car contained a portable bar, a telephone, a tiny television set, three mink leg warmers and, for this occasion, the morning newspapers and a deep hamper from which the smell of hot coffee and sweet rolls mingled delightfully with the chilly morning air.

"And if you bore me I can do this," Scott announced. As he pressed a button, a glass partition rose between the front and back seats and locked into place. No sound could pass between the two halves of the limousine.

Ken quickly found the corresponding button on the door panel next to his seat and pressed it. The glass wall began to melt away. "Two can play that game," Ken said.

"And it's always more fun with two," Alice added.

"Or three," Mike joined in but was discouraged from continuing when Scott put the car in gear and started it going with a jerky forward thrust. "How about the coffee?" Mike sounded like an airline steward confronting a group of nervous passengers. "It won't stay hot forever."

Scott headed the car toward the ocean, then swung north, following the shoreline as far as possible before getting onto the Parkway to begin the long ride to Salem. The ocean looked cold and black, its color broken only by the white waves which crawled rather than pounded along the long stretch of empty beach. The November sky hung heavy and low over the colorless landscape.

The dreary surroundings made the car with its comforts and hot coffee and rolls even more inviting to its five passengers. Conversation was amiable. Would it snow? Did anyone know what the weather was like in New England? What route would they take, what time would they arrive and when should they make their first stop?

Howard, who took no part in the question and answer game, sat between Ken and Alice reading his newspaper and sipping his coffee as if born to it all and above the general banter which exploded around him. However, when the last question was posed he looked up and announced, "Let's stop soon. I have to go."

"Howard. We just entered New York."

"Cross your legs."

"Suffer. It's good for the soul."

"You're all a bunch of sadists," Howard told them and once again buried his face in the sport page.

They stopped for lunch at the halfway point of their journey, settling for a roadside restaurant where the Bloody Marys proved to be extremely good and the hamburgers extremely bad. Scott saw to refilling the big car's gas tank as Howard and Mike headed straight for the men's room, leaving Alice and Ken to select a table. The moment they sat Alice exploded, "Did Howard tell you he told me all about Scott and China House?"

Ken winced, unnoticeably he hoped, and nodded. "Yes. What do you make of it?"

Alice shrugged. "Scott doesn't look depressed and certainly he's not hysterical, but just between you and me I'm more than a little afraid."

"Afraid? But why?"

"Ken, in my line of work I do a lot of reading. Case histories, I mean. I'm sure you've read about the more sensational cases."

Ken was amazed, not only by what Alice seemed to be intimating but even more by her cool, clinical approach to the subject. He had never seen Alice in this role and was impressed. What other aspects of Alice's personality had evaded Ken? He looked closely at the color of her lipstick and tried to recall Howard's rosy lips that windy night his father and Alice had entered the house together. Could be, he thought, and suppressed a nervous giggle. Was Alice really a passionate young lady?

"Alice, I hope you're not talking about mass murder."

"You said it, Ken, not me. But that is exactly what I mean and you've obviously been entertaining the same thoughts but not allowing them to surface to the point of making them verbal."

Ken felt suddenly bored with psychological bullshit and its special language. "Alice, I verbalized it because you hinted at it and not because it was on my mind or anyplace else on my person. Scott and Mike are two healthy men and not characters in one of your case histories. Scott might have a problem but he's smart enough to be aware of it and is seeking help and Mike couldn't kill a fly if his life depended on it."

"Don't underestimate the psychotic mind, Ken. They are often undetectable, even by professionals, and sometimes hide behind the most innocent faces. Besides, does anything about this trip make sense to you?"

"No, but we're a part of it."

"Meaning?"

"Meaning that if there's anything irrational about Scott's invitation there is the same degree, or more, of the irrational in the acceptance."

Alice clammed up and Ken, feeling triumphant, hailed the waiter.

Mike stepped up to one of the two urinals in the tiny men's room as Howard hesitated by the door. "Nothing to fear, I don't bite."

Howard colored slightly and made his way alongside the younger man. "I'm not afraid. . . of anything."

"You don't like me, do you, Doctor?"

Howard inspected the white tiled wall. "Not true. I reserve that emotion for people I know. I hardly know you."

"I don't mean me, personally. Me, collectively." Mike moved back as he zipped up his fly.

"You, collectively, is none of my business."

Mike ran water over his hands then moved aside to allow Howard access to the sink. "Three cheers for liberation. Look Howard, it's going to be a rough week and I'll need all the help I can get." He stuck out his hand toward Howard, who was now facing him in the small room. "A truce?"

Howard grinned. "I didn't know there was a war."

"Let's say it's to avert a war." Mike smiled and Howard was actually awed by the man's beauty.

"You are an irresistible bastard," Howard said as he shook the offered hand.

"Too bad you can't afford me."

"Even if I could I doubt I would be interested."

Mike Armstrong shrugged. "Just trying, Doctor, just trying."

"I know." Howard answered.

The second half of the trip was quieter. Mike took the wheel and Scott sat silently at his side. Ken nodded, actually going off to sleep several times until a bump in the road or a sudden turn jerked him awake. Howard tried the television and, to his surprise, found that it really worked. Alice looked out the window, daydreaming, as they drove thorugh town after town, each complete with pretty houses and picket fences.

Late in the afternoon they reached Salem and Howard, from memory, directed Mike to the winding dirt road that would take them to China House. Just as they began to climb the hill snow began to fall. Big white flakes suddenly swirled about the car, quickly coating its front window and outlining the bare trees to form a picture from a child's coloring book.

"There's the inn," Ken pointed. "The one Howard and I stayed at."

They all looked at the gray building which seemed deserted but both Howard and Ken knew that old man Billingsly was sitting inside, by the fire, awaiting their arrival. Or Scott's arrival, for the old man would have no way of knowing that the Roth's were part of Scott's party. Neither Howard nor Ken doubted that Billingsly would be the first to know that China House was being readied for the young Mr. Evans's visit.

"And that," Scott said, leaning forward in his seat, "is China House."

Mike had turned on the windshield wipers and all five passengers stared at the majestic mansion that came into view as the blades cleared the window only to be lost again in a sea of snow and then reappear like an object in a crystal ball.

"It's breathtaking," Alice whispered.

"I'm home," Scott said as the car made is way toward one of Salem's famous mysteries.

• X •

They watched the house grow larger and larger as they approached it until finally all they could see from within the car were the bases of the enormous doric columns and the lower half of the windows and front door which were set back a good distance because of the great width of the snowy portico.

The car came to a halt and almost at once its occupants emerged from all four doors, their shoulders raised and their heads held down in a futile effort to keep the snow out of their faces. Scott opened the trunk, bags were quickly pulled out and soon all the luggage had been brought out. From a distance both car and people resembled miniature cardboard representations, blown about by the blizzard before a grossly oversized doll house.

Scott opened the front door and stood aside, allowing his guests to enter before him. They stepped in, one after the other, each carrying one or two bags, faces red and hair and coats covered with snow. The door closed behind them and they stood in a semi-circle in the sudden quietness and warmth of China House.

The entrance hall, like everything else about China House, was vast. The expanse of marble floor was broken only by several teak chairs, a long table polished to the point of brilliance and a tall grandfather clock, its ivory face inlaid with Chinese etchings. The marble floor and white walls gave the impression one had entered a temple or church, a holy place which commanded respect and reverence.

At the far end of the hall were the stairs to the second floor. The staircase was wide enough to accommodate a half dozen people, ascending or descending six abreast, and the steps were covered with a plush green carpet. The passageway beyond the stairs was unlit.

They stood like worshippers, silent, as if awaiting the arrival of the keeper of the temple and not daring to move without instructions lest they perform a forbidden act and anger the God within. The snow which had covered them melted, leaving them unadorned, wet and looking pathetically vulnerable. It was as if the house was forcing them to declare its superiority before allowing them to occupy its being.

Howard lowered his two bags to the floor and took off his wet topcoat. "I think my entire house could fit inside this hall," he said. His tone implied respect rather than comparison.

Now that Howard had made a move and broke the silence the others became animated, putting down what they carried and removing their outer garments.

"I'm awed," Ken said as he walked to the clock and stood on his toes, trying to get a closer look at its majestic face.

"So am I," Alice agreed, "and this is just the entrance hall."

"You ain't seen nothing yet," Mike commented as he ran his fingers through his straight black hair.

"I don't remember the stairs being carpeted," Scott said. "I thought they were marble like the floor." He was the only one who had not yet moved since entering the house; he stood with his back to the door and his eyes directly on the staircase that loomed before them. His eyes moved up and down the plush covered steps, over and over again. As soon as he spoke everyone turned to look at him and once again an eerie silence pervaded the hall of China House. It was Mike who broke the almost hypnotic mood as he stepped between Scott and the staircase, obliterating Scott's view as he took the valise from their host's hand as one would relieve a child of a burden.

"We have company. Wet company. Let's get them comfortable," Mike stage-whispered.

Scott sprang into action and the tension, real or imagined, was dispelled as he flung open a closet door and told everyone to hang their coats in it. Next he marched to one set of sliding doors and with some effort pulled them apart. "The main salon," he said with a flourish of his arms. He spoke the words in jest but none of his guests laughed or even smiled. They could only stare.

What they saw was a room which dwarfed the hall in size and overwhelmed it with its opulent decor. An array of American and Chinese antiques, not clashing but blending so that teak and pine, ivory, jade, silk screen and hooked rugs, captain's lamps and bird cage tables came together and presented a picture of rich taste and comfort. A marble fireplace dominated the far wall and was flanked by tall windows, unobstructed, allowing the viewers a picture postcard scene of the snow that now whirled about with blinding rapidity.

As they looked at the salon Scott crossed the hall and opened the opposite set of doors. "The dining room is here and behind it the sun room and kitchen. As I remember you can get to the kitchen from the sun room or straight past the stairs." Scott turned and pointed toward the dark passage. The smile faded from his face and was replaced with a look of pure terror. He staggered backward, his arm still extended, his finger pointing. "Christ. Holy Christ."

The others, rooted to where they stood, could only follow the line of the pointing finger. A small boy emerged from the shadowed passageway and walked slowly toward them. His silky blond hair cast an eerie glow in the dim afternoon light. He wore a parka and yellow rubber boots. When he saw Scott's reaction to his appearance and noted the others staring at him he stopped walking and stood as still as a statue.

"It's him," Scott whispered. "Mike, it's him." The arm pointing at the child trembled spastically.

Mike moved to Scott's side and put his arm around his friend's shoulders. "Who are you?" Mike asked the boy, his voice calm and steady. Gently he pulled Scott's arm downward until the finger, still pointing, was aimed at the marble floor. "Who are you? Mike repeated.

The boy remained silent, staring at them as they stared at him.

Ken looked at Howard. His father's eyes were fixed on the small boy. A thin film of sweat covered Howard's forehead. Ken's hand reached for Howard's elbow and he felt Howard respond to the touch as one would respond to a more than small charge of electric current. Alice's gaze was directed at Mike Armstrong.

"We won't hurt you," Mike said as he took a step forward and placed himself between the boy and Scott Evans.

Footsteps echoed along the dark recess of the passageway and now all eyes were raised above the child's head as a man appeared and halted directly behind the boy. "Hello. I thought I would be gone before you arrived. I hope Billy wasn't making a pest of himself."

The man's friendly smile and normal, matter-of-fact conversation were so incongrous to the atmosphere in the hall it caused the new arrivals to look upon the man more oddly than they had looked upon the boy. The man waited for a response and when he was sure none was forthcoming his eyes darted from one unsmiling face to another as he tried to comprehend the stony silence which greeted his arrival. Less sure of himself he nonetheless tried once again to make contact.

"I just delivered the last of the supplies you ordered. Put 'em in the kitchen. Like I said, I thought I would be done before you arrived but I got stuck in town." The man put his hands on the boy's shoulders either to protect him from the five strange people confronting them or merely to touch something friendly and familiar.

The group relaxed and exhaled in unison, and one by one began to move about aimlessly and smile nervously at each other. All except Scott Evans. He continued to stare at the little boy. It was Mike who finally responded to the man in a civilized manner.

"I'm afraid the boy startled us. We didn't see your car out front."

"My truck is parked out back," the man answered, still a little uncertain of the strangers.

"Well, thank you very much," Mike said.

"No problem." The man shifted his weight from one foot to the other. "I'll be getting back now. I hope you have a nice visit in spite of the weather. It looks like a real bad storm. The first and last of the season are always the worst they say."

The man took the child's hand and pulled him back down the passageway. The boy turned his head once and looked at Scott, then both man and child were gone.

"Well," Mike exhaled deeply as he spoke the word, "nothing like a good scare to start off a week of fun and games."

"It was only a child," Alice said. "I wasn't afraid."

Mike poked Scott in the ribs. "Come on, Scotty, we got people to settle and feed."

To everyone's relief Scott smiled as he nodded at Mike Armstrong. Clearly the appearance of the little boy had not only upset Scott but had made a deep impression on his already fragile mental condition. He seemed surprised to hear the sound of his own voice as he spoke. "I'm sorry. I'm just not thinking."

"The house is beautiful, Scott," Ken said, hoping to restore the proud-host mood Scott had displayed only a short time before.

"Thank you." His smile told Ken that he appreciated the support. "And there's a lot more to see. I'll show you to your rooms and then we'll meet in the salon for cocktails and to start organizing dinner. The kitchen, as we now all know, is well stocked."

"Alice and I will see to dinner," Ken responded.

"I hope you don't mind," Scott said as once again they all picked up their luggage and began to climb the stairs. "I didn't engage any help. When you do, you have to live by their schedule and I wanted this week to be completely at ease."

"I don't mind at all," Ken said. "In fact I think it would be fun if we all pitched in with the cooking."

"You won't think it's fun when you taste my contribution," Mike told them.

"Or mine," Howard added.

"I think it boils down to us in the kitchen and them behind the bar," Ken said to Alice.

"I'll help in the kitchen," Scott said, "and so will Michael."

"I'm always Michael, never Mike, when he offers my services."

"Sorry about that, Michael," Howard said. "That leaves me behind the bar."

"And with the dirty dishes," Ken and Mike said at the same time and burst out laughing.

On the second floor an oriental carpet of exquisite color and design covered the floor. "When I made the arrangements to open the house I didn't know how many we'd be so I had them prepare four bedrooms. I thought Howard and Ken could double up if that's okay."

"No problem at all, Scott," Howard answered.

Scott pointed to a door to the right and opposite the stairs. "That's for you and Ken, Howard. Alice, you're right across the hall from them." Now Scott pointed to the left. "I'm there and Mike is opposite me."

Ken caught Mike's surprised reaction to the fact that he was not to share a room with Scott. Ken was delighted with the arrangements and hated himself for being so. Mike quickly walked to the door of his room and opened it. "I'm going to shower and change. Last one in the salon helps Howard with the dishes."

"Take your time," Scott told the others. "It's just five. We'll meet for drinks at seven."

With that they all disappeared behind a closed door, each person glad for the chance to be alone to wonder about their strange, elegant surroundings and the young man who had brought them all to Salem on a stormy winter day.

Howard carried their bags into the room as Ken closed the door and then turned to inspect their accommodations. "What was it Mr. Billingsly said? Something about a Mandarin's palace. Well, he was right, but God, it's beautiful."

Howard nodded, his mind far from furniture or classical architecture. "Did you see his reaction to the kid?" he exclaimed.

"Yeah," Ken answered. "And I saw yours."

"Christ, what did you expect? Ken, it was eerie. It was one hell of a. . . ."

"Coincidence?" Ken finished, his tone more humorous than sarcastic.

Howard shrugged and smiled. "I'm getting so I believe Scott. Too damn many coincidences. And what did you think of Mike? Doesn't anything bother that guy? Cool as ice, he was."

"Mike was the only one of us who acted with any sense," Ken said. "The guy with the movie star face is no fool, pop, and don't you ever forget it."

"I won't." Howard sat on one of the twin beds and sighed. "It's as comfortable as it looks — or am I just so beat that anything softer than the floor feels good?" He got up and walked to the window.

"I'll shower and then you can take a hot tub. That should make you feel better." Ken began opening his luggage.

"Just look at that storm. If it keeps up we'll be snowbound in China House."

"I can't think of a better place to be snowbound," Ken replied as he joined Howard by the window. "Look, see that gray building? That's the Seaford Inn."

Howard nodded. "It must be. No other buildings in the area."

"Howard, this is the east side of China House. The side we could see from the inn. When I saw the light it came from this side of the house. One of the bedrooms facing east. It could have come from this very room."

"You're not going to start that again, I hope. We're going to have enough on our hands this week without you adding fuel to the fire."

Howard turned from the window and Ken followed. Both began to unpack.

"You mean Scott," Ken said. "He *is* acting stranger."

"By the minute. Even before the kid arrived he looked a little out of it. Did you see him staring at the staircase? Mike had to actually shake him back to reality. Christ, I hope he doesn't pick this week to crack up."

Ken looked concerned and a bit frightened. "Maybe that's why he came here, Howard. To face the nightmare he's been living with all these years. His brother's death. A sort of exorcism, if you know what I mean."

"You could be right, Ken." Howard sat on the bed again and lit a cigarette. "You just reminded me of a paper I wrote several years ago on fear. Nothing unusual." He began to use his cigarette as a pointer, delivering a lecture to a class of one.

"If we face our fears, verbalize them and investigate their source, more often than not we learn to see them for the charlatans they are and in time they disappear or, at the very least, we learn to live with them and not allow them to stop us from functioning normally. But if we flee from fear we give it power; unchecked, fear grows all out of proportion to reality and dominates our lives. Sometimes we even forget what the original fear was and the vicious cycle begins." Howard made small smoky circles in the air with his cigarette. "We fear the very feeling of fear which causes us to be constantly afraid until—"

"We crack up?" Ken concluded.

"Or we end it, once and for all." Howard drew his finger across his throat.

"You think Scott read that paper?"

"I'm sure of it. That's why he gave me all that background information and that's why I'm in China House."

"To see him through it?" Ken said hopefully. "To help him dispel the fear? That's a good sign, Howard, isn't it?"

"If that's the reason, yes."

"But you're not sure, is that it?"

Howard found an ashtray and killed his cigarette with a series of hard jabs. "I don't know what to think. And do you realize we're doing it again. Speculating and coming to conclusions based on the speculation. All meaningless. Now why don't you take your shower so I can soak in the tub before we all assemble."

Howard stretched out on the bed and Ken cautioned him against falling asleep. "It'll only make you bitchy when I have to wake you up." Ken stripped down to his shorts and located the bathroom door on the first try. "It's enormous," he cried. "Like a palace."

Howard grunted a reply.

"Do you think every bedroom has one?" Ken shouted.

"Has what?"

"A bath like this."

Howard closed his eyes and began to drift into a limbo between sleep and consciousness. He heard the sound of the shower and the ticking of a clock but both sounds came to him from some distant place or perhaps he didn't hear them at all because they were not real but a piece of the past he was recalling.

He could not hear the snow falling but he could feel it. Big white flakes being pushed and shoved about by a cold wind, the endless cascade covering the hill and the inn and China House itself, burying them all under a cold wet blanket.

Howard shivered and his body sank deeper into the warmth of the soft bed. And then he was naked, his hands clasped behind his head, his legs spread and his penis full and throbbing. Alice stood over him and removed her kimono as Howard watched. She was naked beneath it. Her face was painted like a doll's and when she smiled at Howard her red lips parted and the tip of her tongue became visible. His groin ached with longing as he extended his arms, imploring her to come to him and she did, mounting him like a wanton whore she guided him between her legs and laughed wildly but no sound came from her ruby mouth.

Now Ken appeared. Howard ordered his son from the room but Ken refused to leave. The young man stood by the bed, arms folded across his chest and stared down at the very point where Alice and Howard coupled until Howard lost his hardness and shrank, not to normalcy but to the size of a prepubescent boy.

Alice, enraged, tossed back her head as if to shout but still no sound came from her throat. Ken laughed, filling the room with his hysterical outburst. Howard pulled the cord that dangled from the ceiling. He pulled it again and again until it fell and covered the bed like a thick silk snake.

Two Scotts entered the room, identical in every way and both naked, exhibiting erections so large they appeared as comic representations of the male phallus. Howard covered his tiny penis with one hand as he tossed the silk cord to the two youths and pointed at Ken. Ken stopped laughing and began to scream in terror as the two Scotts tied the cord around his neck and began to pull, one from each end, tighter and tighter. "No, Howard, no. No, Howard, no. Howard. . . ."

"Howard. Howard."

He awoke with a start, jerking himself to a sitting position, his body drenched with sweat, his hands and lips trembling.

"Howard, are you all right?" Ken asked. "I tried to wake you but you kept pushing me away so I let you sleep while I dressed. Then you started yelling and waving your arms in the air and... Howard, you look awful."

Howard shook his head and brushed the hair out of his eyes. "I'm okay. Just a nightmare. Do you have a cigarette?"

"There, on the night table. Do you remember the dream?"

Howard's hands trembled as he struck a match. "No," he lied. He looked around the room. "It's this damn house. It's beginning to get to me."

"Now just stop that. It's a beautiful house and we're going to have a good week. Let's be positive. I'm going to ask Scott if they keep skis here. We have the weather for it and it would be fun."

Howard got off the bed and began to undress. "Not a bad idea. Get us all out of the house if nothing else."

"I'm ready," Ken announced. "I'll get Alice and we'll go down to the kitchen and get things started."

Howard felt his cheeks flush at the mention of Alice and almost tripped over his pants as he stepped out of them.

"Are you sure you're all right?" Ken asked again.

"Fine. Still a little out of it from the nap. You go ahead, I'll be down as soon as I wash."

When Howard was alone, and for a reason not even he could explain, he began to search the bedroom for a clock. There was none. He went into the bath and looked at himself in the wall mirror. He looked pale and afraid. Howard recalled the day he had looked at himself in the mirror of the tiny wash room adjoining his office. He had looked pale and afraid then, too.

"They can make pictures appear and disappear," he said to his reflection, "but they can't get inside my head. Only I can do that."

He ran water into the tub, making it as hot as he thought he could stand it. "Do I really want to kill Ken?" Finally, having verbalized the thought he began to calm down. For a brief moment he even felt a flood of relief and was able to laugh at his own foolishness. The bath was as warm and comforting as a womb and, while the icy storm raged outside, he relaxed completely and was himself again.

Coming out of the bath Howard pulled on his robe and jumped backward when he saw Scott Evans standing in the center of the room.

"I'm sorry. I didn't mean to startle you. I knocked but you didn't answer. I guess you were in the bath."

"Yes," Howard answered. "I was." Anxiety began to replace serenity and for one horrible moment Howard actually imagined Scott would walk to the bell pull and rip it from its mounting.

"I just wanted to see if you were comfortable and had everything you needed." Scott appeared timid, as if he were meeting Howard for the first time.

"To say it was as comfortable as my own home would be a lie. It's that and much, much more. Ken and I have everything we need and we're looking forward to an enjoyable week."

At the mention of Ken, Scott looked about the room. Howard explained. "He and Alice went down to the kitchen to see about dinner."

"I'll go down and see if they have what they need. It's so seldom we have guests at China House." He smiled at Howard and left the room as quietly as he had entered.

Howard stood looking at the door which had just closed on Scott Evans. "So seldom we have guests at China House? What the fuck is he talking about?"

The kitchen was at the end of the main hall and down a short flight of steps. It was a large, old-fashioned kitchen; one could easily imagine it filled with servants working diligently to turn out well-planned meals for the members of the household.

"It sure is well stocked," Ken was saying. "Everything including the kitchen sink."

"Look, Ken," Alice pointed, "bells. I bet there's one for every room in the house. See, they're all labeled. Salon, sun room, dining room, master bedroom. . . and Ken, look, twins' bedroom."

Ken was standing next to Alice. "Yeah, I see. Twins' bedroom. It makes me feel. . . ."

"Can I help you?"

At the sound of his voice the two jumped and turned quickly from the call bells. "We were just starting dinner," Alice said.

"We have everything we need, Scott," Ken added. "Your man really put in supplies. There's enough here to feed twenty people for a month."

"And drinks," Alice said. "Beer, wine, soda, just name your poison."

"Good. I'm sure there's plenty of liquor in the salon. Can I help?"

"We're doing just fine," Ken told him. "How does roast beef sound for tonight?"

"Perfect. I'm going to change for dinner. Welcome to China House."

When he left Ken and Alice exchanged questioning looks. "Welcome to China House?" Ken said.

"What a strange young man," Alice commented.

"Alice, you're not still thinking about you know what."

Alice smiled. "What we talked about this afternoon? I'm trying not to but I'm not letting down my guard either."

"Your guard? You're being dramatic, Alice."

"Perhaps, but I'm keeping my eyes and ears open nonetheless. Scott Evans is mentally disturbed. Howard thinks so and so do I."

"But he's reaching out for help and I think it's us he's counting on to help him."

"There are more conventional ways of asking for help, Ken."

Ken shoved the roast into the oven. Alice, he thought, had a very unromantic soul. She would make a good psychologist but would she ever catch a man? Ken paused. . . maybe she already had.

Howard and Mike were in the salon when Ken and Alice entered the grand room. A fire blazed in the fireplace and outside one could see the snow falling by the light of the tall, majestic windows. The two men were inspecting the liquor contents of a portable bar wagon.

"What's for dinner?" Howard asked.

"Wait and be surprised," Ken answered.

"Two ryes, one scotch and one bourbon," Mike announced.

"The fire is heaven," Alice said, warming her hands over the blaze. Her head was lower than the top of the mantle making her appear even smaller than she actually was.

"Where's Scott?" Ken asked, taking his drink from Michael.

"When last viewed our host was sound asleep," Mike answered as he carried a drink to Alice.

"That must have been a while ago," Alice said. "He was with us in the kitchen and said he was just going up to change."

Mike looked at Alice as if what she had just said was completely absurd. "I don't think Scott has left his room since he tucked us all in."

"No I haven't and I want to apologize." A strikingly handsome Scott Evans announced as he entered the grand salon.

• XI •

Ken and Alice looked at each other, both at a loss for words. Mike began to fill a glass with ice, his usual complacency obviously rattled. Howard sipped his rye and never took his eyes off Scott Evans.

"Thank you," Scott said, taking the offered drink. "Why is everyone so quiet? I feel like the proverbial fifth wheel."

"Because we're a bit confused, Scott." Howard spoke slowly and the tone of his voice indicated a confrontation was at hand. The others physically withdrew, leaving a clear path between Howard and Scott. The great clock in the hall struck the half hour.

"I don't understand," Scott said.

"Then let me explain," Howard answered. "You just told us you never left your room but you most certainly did. You came to my room not a half hour ago and Alice just told us you visited her and Ken in the kitchen."

"I never left my room. I swear it."

"Scott, you don't have to swear to anything. You're not being accused of anything. You had a slight lapse of memory and we're filling you in, that's all." Howard was being most solicitous.

"Mike?" Scott sounded like a little boy calling for help.

Mike shrugged his shoulders and shook his head. "I went to Scott's room a few minutes after you had all closed your doors." He looked at the Roths and Alice. "He said he was going to rest awhile. I went back after my shower and he was sound asleep. I lay down myself for an hour or so and then I knocked on Scott's door and woke him just before I came downstairs."

"This is silly," Ken exploded. "No one is on trial. It's cocktail time, remember, the happy hour. Besides, what difference does it all make?"

"It was him," Scott said.

"Stop that, Scotty. Right now, stop it." Mike's voice was strong and commanding.

"Who was it, Scott?" Howard asked. It was the question Ken had been praying his father would not ask.

"Tom. My brother. It was him you all saw and spoke to. Not me."

"Come off it, Scott," Mike demanded once again.

"Why? Are you afraid, Michael? Are you, Dr. Roth? Don't be. I'm not. Tom is here with us in China House. He showed himself and he will again." Scott paced the room as he spoke, looking where no one stood as if expecting a sixth person to materialize before his eyes.

"No one is amused, Scotty." Mike took a long swallow from his glass and walked to the bar where he began to help himself to another.

Ken and Alice stood by the fire, their shoulders hunched in spite of the flames which danced wildly in the hearth. Scott ignored Mike and turned to Ken and Alice.

"I'm not hysterical, please believe that," he began. "Was I in the kitchen with you this evening?" He spoke with a calm and steady voice, the tension replaced with a plea for understanding. "Was I?"

Alice nodded very slowly as if not wanting to commit herself to what she knew to be the truth.

"Was he?" Howard asked loud and clear. The psychologist was determined to end the nonsense and, if necessary, shock Scott Evans out of his hysteria. "Alice? Ken? Answer Scott."

"We inspected the kitchen and decided on a roast for dinner," Ken began. He sipped from his glass. Howard produced a pack of cigarettes and offered one to Scott. The atmosphere became less charged. Everyone was determined to be polite and civil. Mike looked out the window at the falling snow but listened carefully to what was being said.

"We were looking at the call bells," this from Alice. "And had just discovered one marked twins' bedroom. . . ." She paused and looked at Howard. He nodded his encouragement. "That's when we heard your voice. Ken and I. We turned around and there you were, just entering the kitchen."

"I spoke to you?" Scott asked.

"Yes, you did," Ken answered. "You asked us if we had

everything we needed and you said there would be plenty of liquor in the salon. In here."

"Then you said you were going to change for dinner and would join us shortly." Alice finished.

Scott sank into a chair. "And I came to your room?" he asked Howard.

"You did. Just as I came out of my bath. In fact it was I who told you Ken and Alice had gone down to the kitchen."

"I don't remember a thing," Scott moaned. "Not a fucking thing."

Everyone had had their say and now they looked at each other, each hoping someone would say something to end the morbid silence. Ken saved the moment by announcing that he had made up a tray of snacks to go with their drinks and now would be a good time to serve them. "And not a moment too soon," Mike aptly put it and then offered to get the tray.

"Howard, why don't you make us all a fresh round," Mike asked as he started for the door. "Scotty, drink up, it will do you good."

"Mike?" Scott called. "You're not afraid to go to the kitchen alone, are you?"

Mike paused and faced the group. "As a matter of fact, I am," he said in his usual straightforward manner. "But so is Ken and being the co-host I did the honorable thing."

"I'll go with you," Ken quickly said.

"Ken, stay where you are. This is ridiculous." Once again Howard took charge. "Mike, get the tray."

Mike clicked his heels together, saluted Howard in Nazi fashion with one arm raised, turned and left the room.

"Now," Howard said, "let's all sit and relax and talk like the sensible people we are. Are you ready, Scott?"

They all took places around the fire. Cigarettes were lit and Ken, in an effort to divert Howard, commented on the weather. He received a reply from Alice and was ignored by his father and Scott.

"Let's have it, Scott. All of it," was Howard's blunt opening.

"I feel like a fool," Scott replied.

"That, my boy, is an understatement after what you pulled around here a few minutes ago."

"Howard," Ken tried to intercede on Scott's behalf but was put off by Howard with a wave of his hand.

"I told Ken and Alice everything you told me at our first meeting," Howard said to Scott.

"I was sure you had. In fact I'm glad you did. It suits my purpose."

"Good. I'm glad to know there *is* a purpose in all of this." Howard's arm indicated all of them and the house in one gesture. "I think it's time you told us what that purpose is, especially since we all seem to be a part of it."

Scott leaned forward in his chair. "I want to prove that my brother, my twin brother, never left me. That he's been with me all my life and is with me now."

Mike reentered the room but no one saw or heard him until he joined the group and placed the tray he carried on the low, brightly lacquered tea table about which they were seated. No one reached for the canapés except Michael himself who took a caviar-covered bit of toast before sitting on the arm of Scott's chair.

"And you think he'll show himself here, in China House?" Howard asked.

"I think he already has," Scott answered timidly.

Ken shivered and tried to think rationally at the same time. He got up and walked to the fireplace.

"And we," Howard said, "are to bear witness to this. . . this phenomenon?"

"Especially you, Howard." Scott was excited and appeared almost feverish as he spoke. "A professional. Interested and trained in the field of the extra sensory. I would be laughed at if I stated my case. But you! They would have to listen to you."

Howard shook his head as Scott spoke. When he answered his face was flushed with anger. "I told you, young man, and at the time I made it very clear, I am not interested or trained in any kind of superstitious nonsense. And certainly not in anything as bizarre and absurd as the dead returning to walk the earth. If you think your little charade earlier this evening has fooled me, or any of us, you're sadly mistaken."

"I never left my room," Scott said flatly.

"You did, only you don't know it. Why? Because you don't want to know it. The human mind can block out anything in order to make itself believe what is reassuring and comforting. It's a defense mechanism. A form of self-preservation." Howard stopped suddenly when he realized he was expounding to an uninterested audience.

"What would it take to convince you?" Scott asked.

"Surely not what you told me in Sea-Air. A man hit by a taxi. A man drowned in a boating accident. Everyday occurrences, Scott, everyday occurences."

"The photo?" Scott put in quickly.

Howard's face reddened. He turned to Mike Armstrong as he answered. "I think Mike might be able to tell us something about that."

Mike opened his mouth to speak but before he could Scott again posed his question to Howard. "What would it take to convince you?"

"Seeing you and Tom together, at the same time and in the same place." As the words echoed in the room a picture of Tom and Scott, naked, entering his room and reaching for the silk cord filled Howard's mind. The glass he held in his hand trembled until the remaining pieces of ice it held became audible.

Ken moved away from the hearth and stood behind his father's chair. He touched Howard's shoulder in an effort to calm him. Mike put his hand on Scott's arm and squeezed it reassuringly. Alice sat apart and alone and stared into her glass as if it contained the answer for all of them.

At that moment the dinner bell sounded. A soft, pealing chime, coming from the empty room across the hall. The five of them turned to the wide opening where the sliding doors had been pulled apart and then, shyly, looked at each other.

"I think dinner is being announced," Mike said in a voice that lacked the intended bravado.

"Who's announcing it, Doctor?" Scott asked and without waiting for a reply began to march triumphantly out of the salon.

• XII •

Ken entered the sun room and found Mike Armstrong curled up in a comfortable chair, reading. He looked up as Ken approached.

"Good morning," Ken said cheerfully.

"What's good about it?" Mike shot back.

"Well, it stopped snowing," Ken answered as he sat.

"But not for long."

"Did you have breakfast?"

"Juice and coffee is all I take."

"I just have juice," Ken said. Mike, obviously, couldn't care less what Ken took for breakfast. "What are you reading?" Ken tried again.

"A tale of blood, sweat and tears by one Kenneth Roth. I think I prefer porn."

Ken smiled indulgently. "I get it. Michael was reprimanded last night for being a bad boy and this morning he's going to be nasty to all the adults."

"Fuck you, Roth." Mike closed his book with a bang and sunk deeper into the chair, extending his legs across the floor. The tight jeans he wore accentuated his masculinity and Ken tried desperately to avoid looking at the spot.

"What you did was not very funny," Ken said.

"At the time I thought it was. Shit, how was I to know the scene in the salon had gotten so heavy. I thought Scotty would be back to normal and everyone ready for a good joke."

"At any other time, or place I might add, it might have been very funny, indeed. But at that particular moment it was. . . well, almost goulish. How did you do it, Mike?"

The handsome man grinned in spite of the mood of the conversation. A bright grin lit up his blue eyes and was instantly infectious. "It was the stove timer. You know, one of those gadgets you set ahead to go off when the stew is cooked. I saw it in the kitchen when I went for the tray of goodies and tried it. It didn't buzz or ring but pealed like chimes or a dinner bell. That's when I got the idea."

Mike was smiling openly now and Ken tried not to join in the belated amusement of Mike's little joke.

"So you set the timer ahead for a half hour or so and put it in the dining room before coming into the salon." Ken finished Mike's story.

"Did you see Howard's face?" Mike laughed aloud, tossing back his head and slapping his hip. "I thought he would wet his pants."

"Mike, really." But Ken was laughing along with Mike as he recalled the events of the previous evening when the dinner bell had so mysteriously summoned the group in the salon. "And Alice," Ken laughed. "Did you see Alice? She stood up, sat down and, my God, stood up again. And the look on her face—"

"And you," Mike roared. "You were standing next to Howard's chair and you know what you did? You ran behind it."

"I did not."

"You did, Ken, you did."

The two of them started to laugh again and the merry scene greeted Howard who at that moment entered the sun room. "Well, I'm happy to see that some of us are having a good time. Let me in on it, I could use a good laugh."

"We were talking about last night," Ken told his father.

"The dinner bell," Mike elaborated. "Remember?"

"How can I forget? And I still don't think it was very funny."

"At the time, Howard, it wasn't, but you've got to see the humor in it now. Five supposedly intelligent adults actually thinking a ghost was ringing a dinner bell." Ken started laughing again and Mike joined in.

Howard looked at the two young men and smiled weakly. It was then that Ken noticed how tired and pale Howard looked. More like he had sat up all night than like a man who had just arisen from a comfortable bed. It was China House. This grand, cold, white palace was affecting Howard in a most adverse way. Ken checked himself. He had to stop thinking of the house as a living thing; a thing that could act and react. Look at what fools they had all made of themselves last night over a lousy stove timer.

They had been petrified, all of them, unable to move from where they sat or stood. All except Scott. Ken recalled how Scott had pushed away Mike's restraining hand and bounded across the room. In fact the scene in the salon last night was more vivid to Ken in retrospect than it had been while it was happening. Try as he might to push it from his mind the sights and sounds of the pathetic drama now ran through his mind like a strip of film.

"Scott, stay where you are," Howard had ordered. "Don't you dare leave this room."

Scott swung around, a wild look in his eyes and his voice once again on the point of hysteria. "Why, Doctor? What the fuck are you afraid of? You don't believe, remember? Or have you changed your mind?"

Howard's face was a tight mask. His lips a thin, rigid line. "There is obviously someone in the house besides us. Someone who was not invited."

"Not invited," Scott shouted back. "He lives here. He owns China House. We own China House."

"We'll all go," Howard answered. "Together. We'll all stay together until we find out who or what is in the other room."

Howard started for the door and Ken followed, then, very quickly, Alice joined them. "Come on, Mike," Howard called.

It was at this point that Mike delivered his humble confession and all hell broke loose. Ken had never seen Howard so furious but it was Scott who touched Ken's heart with his crestfallen face and the look of the betrayed in his clear eyes. Scott looked at Michael as Christ must have looked upon Judas. Scott wanted so much to believe and be believed. In his own bewildered mind he must have felt so close to discovering the truth at that moment, only to learn that it was all a joke; a joke prompted by the one he loved and trusted most.

Michael Armstrong looked as if he would gladly give his life if he could relive the past hour and undo the harm he had so unintentionally caused. His eyes never left Scott's face. They sought forgiveness but all they found was a void, for Scott was now so drained of all emotion and unable to cope that he simply withdrew.

Dinner was a nightmare. The roast was over-cooked, the potatoes not cooked enough and the salad, put together at the last minute, warm and limp. Thank God for the wine. A good red wine liberally poured by Michael acted as a tranquilizer for all of them, getting them through the meal and ready for bed as soon as it had been eaten.

Then, finally, came sleep.

Ken returned to the present with a feeling of guilt over the fact that only moments before he had actually thought the incident amusing. Immediately he blamed Mike Armstrong. The guy used his charm the way a magician plied his trade, distorting reality and turning black into white before his awed audience. "Would you like some breakfast?" Ken asked his father.

"Alice is getting me coffee," Howard told him.

"Alice? I didn't know she had come down."

"She came down with me." Howard walked to the window and looked out.

Ken stared at his father's back and when he turned his eyes he met Mike's gaze. Armstrong's lips curved into a meaningful smile. So he thinks there's something going on between Howard and Alice, too, Ken thought. He reminded himself once again never to underestimate Michael Armstrong.

"Do you think we can move the car?" Howard's voice broke the silent bond between Ken and Mike.

"I think so. That's a pretty powerful machine our boy's got parked out front. Why, did you want to go to town?"

"Not right now, but I might want to in the near future." Howard turned and was now looking directly at Mike. "Has it occurred to you that we are very isolated on top of this hill? And has anyone seen anything that even resembles a telephone in this opulent dwelling?"

Ken shook his head. "I never even thought of it till now, but no, I haven't. Mike?"

"No, and like Ken I never gave it a thought. But there is that inn about a half mile down the hill."

"Ken and I know about the inn. It contains one very old man who makes about as much sense—" He left the sentence unfinished but left no doubt as to who else among them made no sense to Howard Roth.

Mike sprang forward as Alice came into the room and relieved her of the breakfast tray she carried. "You should have called me," Ken commented. "I would have helped you prepare that."

"Just the standard," Alice answered. "Coffee, juice and toast. There's plenty for all, help yourself."

"I've had mine," Mike said, "but I could go for another cup of coffee."

"Did you all sleep well?" Alice asked.

She was answered by nods of the head and a mumbled yes as the others gathered around the tray and took what they wanted.

"And you?" Ken inquired.

"Me? Fine. Just fine," Alice answered.

Ken reached for a cigarette and lit it, keeping a steady eye on Alice Miller. Something was wrong, very wrong. Howard's complacent and always calm assistant was neither on this dreary morning.

"Scott not down yet?" Howard asked.

Well, Ken thought, someone finally spoke the magic name.

"Been down and went back up," Mike told them. "He always does that. Can't smoke till he has something in his stomach but can't put off that first cigarette till after he washes and dresses. So he has a bite, lights up, and goes back to his room."

"Habits," Howard groaned. "We're all slaves to our habits. We even form habits to facilitate our habits."

Ken looked at the cigarette he was holding. "My first today," and convinced no one, including himself, that he had struck a blow at his addiction to smoking.

"Did you speak to him?" Howard asked Mike.

"Scott? He woke me up. Brought me coffee as a matter of fact."

So they had made up. Good. Ken forced himself to be happy for Scott. Why not? He was a writer who demanded that all endings be happy ones. What about his own ending? That's a hell of a way to put it, Ken thought. My ending. It's this bloody house. Everything takes on a double meaning in this posh mausoleum. Mausoleum, indeed. A perfect synonym for China House.

"And how is he this morning?" Howard wanted to know.

"Fine. The same old Scotty." Mike avoided looking at Howard.

"He's a sick boy," Howard said, his voice lacking even a hint of sympathy.

"He has his moments," Mike shrugged. "We all do. Scott is

rich. Very rich. He's entitled to bigger and more elaborate moments."

"Bullshit," Howard hissed. "Stop trying to protect him, Mike. You're only hurting him."

Mike made no reply, instead he contemplated his coffee cup.

"You and I are going to have a talk, Michael. A long, long talk."

Mike was saved from answering Howard by the arrival of Scott Evans himself. They all looked at their young host, who appeared perfectly normal on this gray, overcast day. And they all greeted him too quickly and spoke too casually to fool him. Scott knew he had been the main topic of conversation and that his appearance had interrupted their discussion. But he gave no indication of this as he helped himself at the breakfast tray and joined Mike and Howard in speculating on whether or not they could move the car.

The minute Alice felt she could speak without being overheard she leaned toward Ken and asked, "Did you really sleep well last night?"

"I told you I did, but you, I take it, didn't."

"Hardly at all," Alice confessed.

Ken nodded. "I understand. The tension around the dinner table last night wasn't exactly conducive to a good night's sleep."

"It wasn't that, Ken. Last night didn't bother me at all once it was over. It was the noise. The noise kept me awake."

Ken looked uncertain. "Noise? What are you talking about?"

"Don't look at me like that, Ken. As if I had lost my mind. I was exhausted. I fell asleep as soon as I got into bed but I was awakened by. . . by the noise."

"I didn't hear a thing and I'm sure neither did Howard. Mike said nothing about it this morning. Are you sure? Maybe you were dreaming."

"I wasn't dreaming. I know when I'm dreaming. I'm one of those people who always do."

I'll bet you are, Ken thought, then was ashamed of himself as he looked at Alice's concerned face. Alice was truly afraid.

"Did you tell Howard?" Ken asked.

"No. I didn't think it would be wise. He's so upset by all this nonsense and I didn't want to add to it. Besides, I didn't think he would believe me."

"But you thought I would?"

"Howard is a scientist. You're a romantic," Alice replied.

A romantic in search of romance, Ken thought and said aloud, "You're a scientist, too. Remember?"

"Right now I don't know what I am."

Ken touched Alice's hand. "Get hold of yourself. I believe you. Right now I would believe anything. Tell me, what kind of noise was it? Voices? Banging? Maybe it was the wind. It was pretty rough outside as well as in."

"No. Nothing like that. It was... Oh, I feel so stupid."

"Tell me, Alice. It'll make you feel better."

"Crying," Alice said, her eyes avoiding Ken's. "A child crying. Loud at first and then softer and softer, a pathetic moan as if... as if he knew there was no one to answer his call. At first I thought it was the wind, you know how it can sound, and I tried to go back to sleep. Naturally, I couldn't. And when I heard it again I knew it wasn't the wind. It was human."

"Tom Evans, the twin." Ken shuddered as he whispered the name.

"Ken, is it possible?"

"I don't know, Alice, but you were right not to tell Howard. Last night was a bit much for him. He's got it into his head Scott and Mike are playing some sort of macabre joke with him as the target but now he thinks Scott is really sick and right now Howard isn't sure about anything... even himself."

"Scott is sick? What about me? I heard a child crying last night and until I came into this house I was perfectly sane."

"Alice, the mind can play tricks. Who knows better than you? The imagination...."

"It was not my imagination, Ken. I heard a child crying. It was very real."

"I'm sure it was," Ken said with compassion. "And before we leave here we'll find out just what it was you heard. I can promise you that."

"I don't want to find out what or who I heard, Ken. I just want to leave this house. The sooner the better."

· XIII ·

Ken had no chance to answer and, having no answer, was glad that his father, Scott and Mike had just then ended their parley and conversation was once again open to all. Ken knew that Howard was anxious to have his talk with Mike so he asked Scott for a tour of the house. Scott seemed more than happy to comply but Alice turned down the invitation saying she was going to wash her hair and then prepare lunch.

"Bloody Marys at one," Mike called out as the party began to break up. Ken assured him they would return at the appointed hour. He also realized that Mike had set a time limit on Howard's personal inquisition.

"I was going to ask you yesterday but forgot," Ken said as he and Scott climbed the broad staircase of China House. "About skis. Are there any in China House?"

"Skis?"

"Yes. The weather is perfect and the way it looks now it might be our best means of transportation."

Scott laughed. "You might just be right. I don't know, Ken, but I'll check on it. There's a storage room behind the kitchen where all sorts of paraphernalia was stored. I'll have a look."

Their first stop was the master bedroom at the end of the second floor hall, the side which now housed the Roths and Alice Miller.

"Perfect,' Ken exclaimed once inside the room. "What else can I say?"

The furniture, again a blending of oriental and early American, differed from the pieces in the salon in that here they were smaller and more delicate, and one was able to take in each detail unlike the room downstairs where the total effect was almost overwhelming. Ken spotted the portraits on the far wall of the room. They were mounted in huge gilt frames and hung on either side of the marble fireplace: the classic early American oils of the master and mistress of the house. He didn't have to be told who they were.

Scott saw where Ken's eyes rested. "Commodore Seaford. He built China House."

"I know," Ken said and continued to stare at the portrait. The Commodore was the exact image of the man Ken had created with his typewriter.

"You know?"

Ken was embarrassed. "To tell the truth, I did some research."

Scott folded his arms across his chest and looked amused. "Don't feel ashamed. I knew you would. Did you check it all out? Everything I told Howard?" Ken nodded.

"And it was all true?" Scott continued.

"Scott, you know it is. But it doesn't mean very much, you have to realize that."

Scott smiled. "Coincidences. My life abounds in them."

"You're not alone." Ken shrugged and shifted his weight. "I might as well tell you. When Howard and I first saw China House, weeks ago, it fascinated me so that I decided to use it as the locale for my next book. Highly fictionalized, naturally." He pointed to the portrait. "I called him Captain Jerome and would you believe the picture I drew of him with words is an exact replica of that."

"I would believe. Do you know about the Chinese mistresses and the daughter who all disappeared into thin air?"

"As much as I could find out. Is it all true?"

"Your guess is as good as mine. We're a very public family, Ken, with lots of skeletons in many closets and believe me, those stories are not the family's favorite topic of conversation."

"I can understand that." Ken waited for the next question and wondered how he would answer it.

"Do you know about the light? The light people have seen here, in China House."

"Mr. Billingsly, the innkeeper, told us about it." And then he blurted out, "Scott, I saw the light."

"You saw it?" Scott's voice rose an octave and Ken became afraid.

"Scott, I'm not sure, please believe that. At the inn, I got up during the night and went to the window. I looked up the hill at

China House and think, I said think, I saw a light in one of the upstairs windows."

Scott was now more excited than hysterical. "I've known about the light for a long time, Ken. My parents tried to keep me from hearing about it. They closed up the house right after the accident and never discussed what happened to Tom, either. Even when I asked about Tom and later about the light they refused to answer. They told me to forget about it and never to even think of it."

"But why, Scott?"

"To protect me, I guess. Children are very impressionable. Better to forget than to grow up with morbid memories."

"But you didn't forget."

"No, I couldn't. In spite of all the protection I couldn't forget."

"Do you remember anything at all about the accident? The one that killed Tom?"

"Nothing at all. I was here when it happened but I've blocked it all out. It's as if it never happened."

"Because you want it to have never happened. Do you understand that?"

"Ken, I'm not stupid. But suppose it didn't happen. No, I mean suppose Tom didn't die. We all left so fast. . . maybe he was still alive and crying. . . crying for us only we weren't here to hear him."

"Scott, stop that. You know what you're saying is impossible."

Impossible? And what Alice had heard last night was impossible. Ken felt cold. This damn house. He was always cold in it. The rooms were so big and the ceilings so high. The house reduced its occupants to insignificant specks whose wills were subservient to the giant. Like a big bully it ruled by the sheer force of its size. Ken had not wanted to talk about China House or the dead Tom Evans. He wanted to draw Scott out and learn what Scott Evans was all about when not preoccupied with the dead. But China House refused to be ignored.

Without thinking Ken's arm reached out and his fingers touched Scott's cheek. "Try to forget it, Scotty, please." He wanted so much to take Scott in his arms and protect him from China House and the memory of Tom and even, if necessary, from Mike and Howard.

They looked at each other, the moment as still as death and

then they were in each other's arms, their lips pressed together, their hard bodies seeking to become one. "I want you, Scotty, I want you so much," Ken moaned.

"I was sitting on that bench last week because I was afraid you would run right past the house."

"Then why did you throw me out?"

Their lips met again. "I didn't throw you out, you left."

"Bastard," Ken laughed.

Scott's hand moved between them and found Ken fully aroused. "You're fast," Scott whispered.

"Keep that up and I'll show you what fast really is."

"Let me take care of it." Scott's fingers began to open the buttons of Ken's jeans.

"Scott... Mike...."

"You and I are the only people in the whole world, Kenny."

Scott moved down Ken's body and allowed himself to be guided by the strong hand which now gripped his head. Ken moaned softly. He began to rotate his hips and the two were lost in a sea of pure eroticism. It didn't take very long. Ken's head lolled backward, his mouth hung open and as the explosion neared his eyes lighted on the portrait of Commodore Seaford and when the Commodore's lips curved into an evil smile Ken screamed out his release.

They were shy, embarassed and amazed. Scott shook as he lit a cigarette and Ken felt like a fool as he stuffed himself back into his tight jeans. "I didn't want it to be like this, Scott. I wanted—"

"Let's forget it, eh?"

"I don't want to forget it," Ken exclaimed.

"Neither do I but let's not analyze it to death either, okay?"

Ken looked at the master's portrait and was relieved to see the Commodore's lips once again set in a rigid straight line. Imagination....

"Look at this," Scott said. He was standing next to a tall lectern. "The family Bible."

Ken came to look as Scott opened the book and they both saw the inscription written on the first page in big bold script. Together they read it.

AN ANCIENT SAGE, UPON PASSING FROM THIS LIFE
AND ENTERING THE NEXT
FOUND HIMSELF BEFORE TWO DOORS
MARKED LIGHT AND DARK.

To dwell here, the first proclaimed, one need only knock
and answer when summoned.
To dwell here, the other stated
one need only enter.
The sage knocked boldly on the door of light.
"Who is there?" bellowed the voice of God.
"It is your faithful servant, my Lord." The old sage
answered.
"Be gone," God cried out. "There is no room for thee
within my house."
The sage, weeping, withdrew himself from the portal to
everlasting light and went where he could be alone to
meditate upon how he had sinned against the Lord. He
recalled all the days of his previous life: what he had done,
what he had seen and, above all else, what he had learned.
When he knew the answer he returned to the door marked
light and once again knocked upon it.
"Who is there?" bellowed the voice of God.
"It is thee, my Lord."
The door opened and the wise man entered into the light
of eternal bliss.

When they had finished neither Scott nor Mike spoke. The readers, as intended, were trying to grasp the meaning of the story the inscription told. Then Ken said, "I would like Howard to see this."

"So would I."

Ken laughed. "But for different reasons, I'm sure. Do you think he wrote this?" They both looked at the portrait. The handsome, fierce, yet somehow gentle Commodore Seaford returned their stare with a fixed gaze.

"I'm sure he did."

"It's very Eastern, if you know what I mean."

Scott nodded. "But Christian, too, if you think about it."

"Yes," Ken mused. "And in a way that's what China House is all about, isn't it? East meets west, not as opposites but rather as two sides of the same coin."

They left the room knowing, without stating it, that the tour of the master bedroom was over. "It's true, Ken, we are all the same," Scott said as he closed the door behind them. "We all look different and we all act different but we're all driven by the same motor."

"I've never heard it expressed exactly that way, Scotty, but I'm sure you're right."

"I like it when you call me Scotty."

Ken grinned. "I didn't realize I did."

"That's why I like it."

Scott pointed. "That's the nursery."

Ken noted it was the room next to Alice's and again China House made itself felt without flexing a muscle.

"Would you like to see it?" Scott asked.

Ken knew Scott had mixed feelings about entering the room and the question placed the decision on Ken's shoulders. "Only if you want to." Ken tossed the ball back to Scott.

Scott put his hand to the knob, twisted and pushed the door open. He didn't enter the room but stood in the doorway and looked in with Ken peering over his shoulder. It was another big room but this one was almost void of furniture, designed to give its occupants as much space and freedom as possible. Twin beds, dressers, a long, low table with small chairs that reminded one of a school room and a large assortment of toys now neatly stacked atop and around a mahogany toy chest.

Scott walked slowly into the room and Ken followed. Once inside Scott seemed to gather courage and appeared more at ease. He walked about, looking, touching and finally, remembering he was not alone he said to Ken, "It's remarkable how much I remember. Like a dream, you recall a fragment and the whole thing rushes back to your mind."

Scott was on his knees pushing a red fire truck back and forth across the floor. "I used to fit in this thing. One drove and one pushed. We would take turns."

"Which were you better at?" Ken was delighted to see Scott happy as he recalled the pleasant memories when for so long he must have dwelled only on the unpleasant ones.

"I think we were both relunctant pushers."

"But without a pusher—"

"There would be no driver."

"These are beautiful." Ken had opened a mesh bag filled with marbles. "The colors. They're more than just playing marbles, they're works of art. They must be very valuable." He looked at Scott and was shocked to see a deathly white face instead of the happy expression Scott had shown a moment before. "Scott, what's wrong?"

"I'm going to be sick."

It happened so quickly and Ken was so unprepared he could only stare in amazement as Scott rushed passed him and into the adjoining bath. Ken replaced the marbles and put them back on the toy chest. He looked anxiously at the bathroom door. He's been through a lot, Ken thought. Coming back to the house, now in the nursery itself, it was all too much and reacting with a sick stomach was as normal a reaction as any.

Scott came out of the bathroom looking pale but composed. "Forgive me. I don't know what came over me."

"Excitement. It happens to the best of us."

"Ken?" Scott touched Ken's arm. "A favor."

"Anything, Scotty, you know that."

"Don't mention this, please. I played the clown last night and I don't want to repeat the performance."

• XIV •

Howard and Michael talked and during the long conversation both smoked too many cigarettes and tried to wash away the taste of tobacco with the morning coffee which had turned bitter and cold. The effect of this only added to the tension between the two men. They were like animals out of their natural habitat and forced to share a common cage. Each kept up his guard, certain the other would attack when least expected. Howard probed and Michael acquiesced. But the younger man yielded only what was forced out of him, elaborating as little as possible and offering nothing that was not required.

Mike Armstrong and Scott Evans met when Mike's father went to work as chauffeur for Scott's family, some sixteen years ago. They were friends but in that odd way that so often happens between the classes in our classless society. Their friendship was an isolated factor in both their lives. They shared no common friends, no common school, no common ground. And for this very reason the bond between them was stronger and more intimate than is usual between boys of their age. They could confide in each other and be assured that their confidences would not be violated.

Mike told Scott of his ambitions. He would be a movie star, a champion skier, a racer of sports cars or whatever other exciting and always egotistical fancy caught his mind at the time. Scott believed Mike would be all those things. Who could doubt the boy with the raven black hair and blue eyes? Mike was aggressive, Scott was retiring, so it was only natural that when puberty made its appearance it was Mike who went out to meet it halfway.

It was Mike who taught the very interested Scott the facts of life and like all else Mike did, he went one step beyond and demonstrated his newly discovered pleasure. He encouraged Scott to experiment with him and a new, more intimate bond developed between prince and pauper. About this time Scott told Mike about his dead brother who was also his guardian angel. Mike listened and understood as only the very young can understand each other.

As they grew, Scott from time to time would refer to a mysterious "him" and Mike understood Scott's meaning. But what Mike did not understand was Scott's seriousness in the matter. He thought Scott's choice of words was just a carry over from their youth, Scott's particular way of explaining the unexplainable.

They later went their separate ways, always keeping in touch, but rejoined one another two years ago when Mike returned from an eventful but unfertile (his words) stay in Hollywood.

"And you found him no better when you returned?" Howard asked.

"No better than what? He was the same old Scotty. More preoccupied perhaps, but the same."

"More preoccupied with his dead brother?"

"Yes. He talked about Tom as if he were alive, and then this past summer he got it into his head that he had to come back here, to China House."

"After reading my work and misinterpreting it," Howard injected.

"Yes, after reading your stuff," was all Mike would concede.

"Because he thought he would find Tom here?"

Mike looked bored. "He never said so, but that was the general impression he gave."

"Did it ever occur to you that Scott needed help? That his family should have been told of all this and a good professional consulted?"

"Why? What harm was he doing? We all have our little idiosyncrasies don't we, Doctor? Except maybe good professionals, eh? But tell the truth, Doctor, don't you have fantasies about power or money or sex? What about sex, Howard? Beat your meat once in a while? Ever catch yourself looking at teen-age girls. . . or boys?"

Howard reached for a cigarette as his only means of defense, however futile. "We're not talking about me, Mike, or you. We're talking about Scott Evans. To have fantasies is one thing, to begin to believe them and act them out is quite another ballgame. And the harm that's being done is to Scott himself. He's half a person living half a life when at his age and in his position he should be at his peak."

"He's at his peak, believe me," Mike said lewdly.

"Can't you be serious?"

"I have never found anything in life to be serious about."

"Well I think you have now, so get with it. Your friend is exploding with guilt and he is very depressed. A perfect combination for suicide."

Howard's words did the trick. He never saw a more serious Michael Armstrong. The younger man's entire attitude changed as he sat up straight in his chair and looked directly at Howard. "Can you help him?"

Was it genuine concern? Or was it something else? A cover for Mike Armstrong's own diabolical plans? A most unpleasant feeling came over Howard. "Perhaps. But maybe he needs more intense care and medication. For that we'll need a psychiatrist. I'm a psychologist."

"I know the difference, Howard."

"I'm sure you do. Tell me something. On our way up here you said something to me about needing help. What did you mean?"

"I was afraid and I still am. I can handle Scotty, always could. But I thought here, in China House, he might go off the deep end and I wouldn't know what to do."

"Is that why I was invited?"

Mike shook his head. "No. I think you were invited to witness his revelation or to help him uncover it. It's just me that's glad you're here for more practical reasons."

Howard smiled. "I'm happy to know one of you is practical."

"I have my moments, Doctor."

"Now comes the jackpot question, Michael. The photo. You know the one I mean."

"I swear, Howard, I'm not sure. I might have taken it. I took a hell of a lot. . . ."

"Cut the crap, Mike."

The enemy had struck and, as always, when least expected. All the frustration the picture had caused Howard Roth seemed to reach its kindling point at this moment and Mike Armstrong was its target for more reasons than his availability.

"What—" Mike began.

"I don't care who the photographer was. I don't even care who it's a picture of. I want to know how you managed to take it from me the same night it was given to me and how you made it reappear, altered, in my office and then disappear again." Howard spoke without pausing for breath and when he was done he sat back in his chair looking like a man who had just dumped a heavy load carried for too long on shoulders about to break under its weight.

"Wait a minute," Mike said. "Are you telling me you lost the photograph?"

"I haven't lost anything, not even my good, common sense. I'm telling you that someone removed the photo from my jacket and my guess is it was done before I left Scott's house that night. It turned up in my office the next morning only the image of Scott had been replaced with one of a little boy framed exactly as Scott had been, standing on the jetty."

Mike looked at Howard as if the doctor had taken leave of the senses he had just proclaimed had never left him. "Howard, I don't know what the fuck you're talking about."

Howard's shoulders sagged as the load he thought he had gotten rid of was once again thrust upon him. Mike was either telling the truth or he was the consummate actor he insisted he was not. Howard looked closely into Mike's dark blue eyes and saw in them a look of bewilderment as genuine and void of guilt as the unblemished snow which surrounded China House. Howard had practice in reading the slightest nuance of human emotion, and looking at Mike he was convinced the young man was not lying. And if Mike knew nothing about the photo that left only Scott Evans.

Mike was still shaking his head as if trying to clear it. "I don't know what you're talking about," he repeated.

Howard stood up and began to pace, his thumb moving across his chin as he walked while Mike eyed Howard and ran his fingers through his straight black hair. Habits. Someone had once written that habits are second nature and nature is nothing more than habit.

"Someone conned me out of that photo, Mike." If Mike wasn't the culprit than Scott was. One thing was now clear to Howard. Scott must not know about the disappearing picture. If Scott had engineered the trick and learned it had scared Howard silly it would give Scott the confidence to continue his crazy game. And if Scott hadn't . . . well, there was no telling how he would react.

"I don't want Scott to know about this," Howard said.

"I agree," Mike answered as he continued to watch Howard amble about the room. "So the photo does a vanishing act and you immediately finger me as the villain without one iota of evidence. Why me, Howard?" The young man sensed Howard's consternation over the strange photo and knew it was time for a counter-attack.

"Because I think you encourage Scott in his illusions. Because a sick Scott Evans might just be to your advantage."

"Fuck you, Doctor."

"You would if you could," Howard shot back and felt better for it. Mike's obscene response told Howard that he had touched a sore spot and the doctor continued to probe. "Just what do you stand to gain if something happens to Scott Evans?"

"You are a bastard, Doctor, and a prick."

"How many more dirty words do you know?"

"Not enough to describe the level of your thinking."

"Very good, Mike. You are quick. But I'm just being practical."

"You're being small, Doctor. About knee high to a snake. I love Scott. I'm concerned for him and I want to protect him, even from himself. But because we happen to be of the same sex you find that difficult to believe so you look for a motive and the dirtier the motive the better you like it."

Howard made no reply Could he have so misjudged Michael Armstrong? Had he allowed his own prejudices and, God help him, his own fears, to color his evaluation of the man? Michael was fast becoming Salem's newest and most intriguing mystery.

"I'm sorry, Mike." Howard humbled himself with three words.

They were both saved from additional embarassment by Alice's arrival just seconds after Howard offered his meek apology Following Alice by a few minutes came Ken and Scott.

"Are we on time?" Ken asked.

"Not a moment too soon," Mike replied and Ken gathered that the meeting between Mike and Howard had not eased the strain between the two.

Bloody Marys were passed about for which each, for his own reasons, seemed in desperate need. The lunch Alice had promised and prepared was light, good and easy to take.

After lunch everyone settled in for a typical Sunday afternoon at home. Howard and Mike, strange as it may seem, went out to see if they could get the car started and to their surprise they did. Driving it to town would be another matter. They arrived back in the house shivering and announced that the temperature was surely at the zero point.

Ken and Alice and Scott explored the storage room behind the kitchen and delighted in discovering skis and boots in a variety of sizes. They each selected a pair and made plans to use them the next day.

Cocktails and dinner were calm and quiet affairs and a welcome relief. The wine once again put them in an easy mood and conversation was light and social. It was the get-acquainted type of evening that groups on sea voyages and tours usually experience their second night together. No one, hopefully, held any surprises and they could relax and cope with each other and themselves.

They all voted against coffee and for more wine to go with their after dinner cigarettes. It started to snow again just as they sat down and the warm room, good food and wine made them all feel comfortable and cozy. When the wine was poured Alice rummaged through her small evening purse and found that she had misplaced her gold lighter. "I must have left it in the salon."

"I'll get it," Scott offered.

"Thank you, but I think I know just where it is. It will only take a minute." Alice left the room.

Ken contemplated proposing a toast. He tried to recall one of those limericks they used to recite at college; everyone could join in with wittier and dirtier verses and the pleasant dinner would end on a joyful note. He began to recite to himself, "There was a young girl from Cape Cod—"

Alice's scream was so sharp, so clear, that it hit the four men around the table like a knife hurled at them from across the room with great force and perfect aim. They jerked backwards in their chairs as if hit from behind and then froze, waiting for the next blow or death. Ken dropped his wine glass and became hypnotized as he watched the purple liquid devour more and more of the white table cloth. Mike's chair tumbled to the floor as he pushed himself away from the table. Scott gasped.

And then they were all running from the room, trying to avoid each other, in a state of complete panic. When fear strikes, run. The subconscious alarm system works to protect the organism even if it has to kill it to do so.

Alice stood near the fireplace in the center of what had

become their gathering place for cocktails. She was staring at one of the large windows that faced the front of the house. As the others approached she pointed at the black glass. "Someone... out there... looking in. A face... in that window... watching me."

Scott and Mike raced for the hall and front door. "You'll freeze," Ken cried and then wondered at his own foolishness.

Alice melted into Howard's arms, sobbing, and he tried to comfort her with meaningless words. "Some brandy, Ken, quick," Howard ordered.

Ken moved to the bar and began to inspect the glasses. Brandy. What the hell did a brandy bottle look like?

"No, Howard. I don't want it. I don't want anything. Just get me out of here, now. Please, Howard, get me out of this house right now."

Ken found the brandy bottle and poured some into a shot glass. "Take it, Alice, it will make you feel better." He offered the glass to the sobbing woman.

Scott and Mike reentered the room, their faces red and their shoes wet. They looked at Howard and shook their heads. "Nothing out there. Not a living soul."

"Who the hell said it was living?" Alice screamed.

Howard, his arm still about Alice, urged her out of the room. "Come with me. I'm taking you to your room. I have a sedative in my bag and you need it." He turned to the others. "You all stay right here. Don't leave each other's sight for a second."

Ken watched his father and Alice depart until they had walked through the doorway and turned toward the stairs.

"If that son-of-a-bitch thinks that I...." Mike began.

"Shut up, Mike," Scott cautioned.

"I'm freezing and I need a drink." Mike went to the bar. "Scott? Ken?"

"I need a cigarette," Ken said heading out of the room.

"Where are you going?"

"The dining room. All the cigarettes are in there."

"I'll go with you," Scott said.

They looked at the dining room table as if it were the scene of the Last Supper. One chair on the floor, the others thrown back carelessly and an overturned glass of wine in the center of the table. They gathered up the cigarettes and Scott picked up Alice's purse. Without a word they carried all back to the salon.

"I made three," Mike said. "We can all use one, I'm sure." He handed a glass to Ken and casually asked, "Does your father know you're gay, Kenny?"

"Christ, Mike, shut the fuck up." Scott cautioned again.

"Why? We're all consenting adults and I think it's time we let down our hair, as the fags say." He looked at Ken.

"We never discussed it but Howard is not stupid," Ken answered.

"Which means he doesn't know or doesn't want to know."

"What's it to you?" There was a slight edge in Ken's voice.

Mike blew smoke in the air. "Because I think he has a thing against queers... or maybe he has a thing for them."

"I don't have to listen to this bullshit." Ken took a step toward Mike and Scott quickly came between them.

"We have enough trouble around here without you two adding to it. Knock it off, both of you." Scott took Ken's elbow and led him to the couch.

"No offense, Kenny," Mike grinned.

"Fuck you."

Ken sat and picked up Alice's purse. He opened it and began to go through its contents. "What are you doing?" Scott asked.

"Snooping."

"What the hell for?"

"This." Ken held up the gold cigarette lighter.

They all stared at the gleaming piece of metal and then Ken recited, "There was a young girl from Cape Cod, who thought all babies came from God, but it wasn't the Almighty who lifted her nighty, it was Weissman the iceman by God."

• XV •

Howard managed to get Alice to lie down, her head propped up by two pillows. He stood over her, a glass of water in one hand, a tiny pill in the other. Alice shook her head. "No, not now. It won't work. I'm too tense."

"That's what it's for. To make you untense and put you to sleep."

"Then I'll be alone."

"I won't leave you till you're asleep. I promise."

"Why must you leave me at all?"

Howard sighed. He seemed to be getting it from all ends. Scott, Mike and now Alice. He longed for his own home, his comfortable chair, the evening newspaper and, yes, even the honest bickering and exchange of wits between himself and Ken.

Alice patted the bed alongside her hip. "Sit down, Howard, please."

He put the glass and pill on the night table and sat. She put her hand in his lap and he held it there. "Feeling better now?"

Alice nodded. "Yes, a little. Do you think I really saw—" He put his finger to her lips. "I'm sorry. No, I won't talk about it." Her hand moved toward his crotch, found it and pressed into him.

"Howard, lie down with me."

"Downstairs," he protested, "they're waiting for me." But already he was beginning to tingle with the thought, the idea, the daring of it all. Her hand felt him respond and she held him, there, until he was fully aroused. "Alice, we can't."

"It's what I want. What I need. Then I'll go to sleep with or without your pill." Her hand found the tiny metal tab and slowly she began to tug it downward. She reached in and heard him moan, ever so softly, and she knew she had won.

His lips were suddenly on hers and his hands all over her body until finally they reached under her dress and tugged at her undergarment. When she reached for his belt he stopped her.

"No. Like this. With our clothes on."

"Yes," she giggled. "Oh, yes."

In the big, cold bedroom they performed like teenagers in the back seat of a car. They touched, felt, explored and each daring act was compounded in intensity by the possibility of discovery. He made her mount him and realized as he did so he was recreating his nightmare. He made her work and closed his eyes. He made Commodore Seaford appear, tall and straight and muscular, his penis in his fist. The master of China House watched and was pleased. He picked up their rhythm.

When Howard moaned out his climax he felt, with a mixture of horror and eroticism, the Commodore's blessing cover his face and throat.

They collapsed, exhausted, like rag dolls upon the bed. Howard's irregular breathing melted into a series of low, even sobs. Alice touched his hair and combed it back with her fingers.

"It's evil," he said. "This house is evil."

"No, my dearest. We're evil."

An hour had passed since Howard had taken Alice to her room. The three young men sat quietly and waited. Ken smoked and sipped at his drink. Mike made a second for himself and Scott. When they spoke it was of the most mundane things, stated in as few words as possible. Ken offered no excuse for having recited the limerick and none was expected. Odd behavior had become an accepted way of life inside China House.

Howard finally appeared looking drawn and haggard. Ken thought, "He's beginning to look his age even if he's not acting it."

"I waited for her to fall asleep." He shrugged his shoulders by way of an apology.

"We were getting tired of looking at each other," Mike said and when Howard gave him a questioning stare he added, "You told us not to let each other out of our sight. Well, we didn't."

"Yes," Howard answered. "I remember." He went to the bar and helped himself. "I'm going to take this upstairs. I'm ready for bed." He faced the other three. "I guess we all are."

"Did she calm down?" Ken asked.

Howard nodded. "I gave her something to put her to sleep.

Her imagination got the best of her, that's all. God knows this house can do that to the most stable of us."

"Do you think we should leave?" Scott asked.

"Let's talk about it tomorrow, Scott."

They rose and followed Howard out of the room. Scott and Mike turned off lamps as they passed them. They climbed the stairs and said their quiet goodnights. Ken refused to react when he saw Mike and Scott go into Scott's room. He was emotionally drained.

Howard began to undress, letting his clothes lay wherever they happened to fall. "Did you sleep with her?" Ken asked as if inquiring about the weather.

Howard grunted. "What a quaint way you have of phrasing things. The writer's art."

"Okay, did you fuck her? Is that macho enough for you?"

"It's neither macho nor very nice nor any of your business."

"It is my business. I'm your son and we live together and I'm interested in you. Since mom died you've never spoken to me about your sex life but I trust you do have one."

"And you, my son, have never spoken to me about yours and I trust you do have one, too." Howard pulled off the bed covers, sat and began to drink the whiskey he had carried up with him.

"I tried to once but you wouldn't listen."

"Are you talking about Kevin?" Howard sighed. "Ken, don't you think I knew what was going on? You were away from home for the first time, the anxiety of starting college, both of you in the same boat and the same room night after night, so you took your comfort from each other. It happens all the time, forget it."

"Did it ever happen to you?" Ken asked.

"As a matter of fact, no. But so what? It happens to enough young men to be considered perfectly normal." Howard watched Ken undress and when his son removed his shorts and walked to the night table for a cigarette Howard averted his eyes.

"Why didn't you ever say anything to me about it?"

"Because I knew you would get over it. In fact I was relieved when Kev got married. Had I known the incident would screw up your plans for medical school. . . well, that was my fault."

"I wish you would stop calling it an incident, it meant a great deal to me and it didn't screw up my plans for med school. It gave me time to think and when I had thought I knew I didn't want to be a doctor. That was your idea, never mine. I can't be what you or anyone else wants me to be, I can only be what I am and I'm happy with me."

"And you're a good writer and I lost. Now let's go to bed. I've had it." Howard wiggled under the sheets.

"I'm not talking about my writing, Dad."

"You're talking about an an adolescent attachment. It's been discussed. I knew all about it, it's not so unique so shake off the ghost and the guilt."

Ken wanted to scream. Instead he put out his cigarette and got into his bed. "Good night, Howard."

"Good night, son."

Howard put out the light and Ken listened to his father move about the bed until he found a comfortable position. He heard Howard's breathing grow fainter and fainter until it was barely audible. Ken lay on his back and stared into the darkness. Incident. Guilt. He had reduced Kev to those two words in two fucking minutes. To say nothing of Ken's own life. Ken kicked a long leg against the bed covers. He wondered what Scott and Mike were doing. Talking about him and laughing? He shut his eyes to stop the tears but they squeezed under his eyelids and rolled down his cheeks.

When Ken awoke his first thought was surprise at the fact that he had actually fallen asleep. He had no idea what time it was but knew it was still hours before dawn, the night at its apex and the bedroom cold and dark. What had awakened him? It wasn't the sound of Howard's steady, almost resonant breathing in the bed next to his. The anxiety he had taken to bed with him returned as he recalled his conversation with Howard and he didn't care now why he was awake. Then he heard it. A bell, coming from some distant place. He raised himself on one elbow and cocked his head forward. He heard it again. Ken pushed aside the blanket and got out of bed. He was naked and very cold. As cold as he had been the night he got out of bed at the Seaford Inn. Now why the hell did he think of that?

He was familiar with the room. Nothing blocked the way between the bed and the door but still he moved cautiously, slowly, one hand feeling the air in front of him and praying he would not touch something warm and breathing. Or cold and breathing. This last thought almost sent him flying back to bed but at that moment he did touch something. It was hard and solid. The door.

He felt for the knob and could hear his heart beat as he turned it. That's what had awakened him. The sound of a door being opened and closed. It seemed incredible that in a house of this size he could be disturbed by a sound so small and so ordinary. But the subconscience never sleeps; when programmed to listen, it does. Had Ken set his personal alarm to verify Alice's weird story of what she had heard the night before?

He opened the door a crack. The hall was black and silent. That's that, he thought and was about to close the door and return to his bed when he heard it again. A bell. Where had he heard that sound before? That dull, tinny clang. The fire truck! The big red fire truck in the nursery. Ken's scalp tingled and his body trembled with cold and fear. He clutched the door jamb. A child started to cry, the sound as clear and heartbreaking and frightening as a wail from the grave. Ken wanted desperately to flee but knew he would never forgive himself if he did.

The nursery door opened a crack causing a straight line of light to fall on the oriental carpet and outline the nursery door in a bright glow. Silence. The light went out and Ken looked into a black void. He couldn't see but he could hear something moving about in the hall. Now he didn't dare move even if he wanted to. If he could hear it, it could hear him.

It started to move up the hall, coming closer and closer to where Ken stood until he knew that if he stuck out his arm he would touch it. Ken held his breath in an effort to be as still as possible and hoped his paralyzed chest would silence his pounding heart which he imagined could be heard throughout the house.

It was directly in front of him now and for one brief moment he could see its shape. Not it. He. But not he, Christ Almighty, them. Two of them. Exactly the same height. Exactly the same— A door closed, the sound as final as the echo inside a tomb when its steel door is bolted for eternity.

The fingers which touched his bare shoulder were icy cold. He opened his mouth to yell but no sound came from it. The fingers dug into his flesh, he gasped and felt everything give way beneath him.

• XVI •

Morning. Never had there been a sun so brilliant, a sky so blue, an earth so white. Ken turned from the window and waited for his eyes to adjust to the light in the room before returning to sit on the bed.

The door opened and Howard entered carrying a tray. Ken smiled. "Thank you, but it wasn't necessary. I'm perfectly capable of coming down for breakfast."

"Just a device, Watson, to get you alone. I want to talk to you."

Howard seemed to be feeling his old self but was certainly not looking it. Ken was amazed at how Howard had aged — that was the only word for it — in the past three days. Not in a way that anyone else would notice. The change was subtle. The perennial sophomore air was gone and Howard suddenly looked like a man in his middle forties. Without a trace of bitchiness, for it was not in him to be so, Ken was happy that his father had become more man than boy.

"Do you want to talk about last night?" Howard began.

Ken sipped his juice and nodded, not sure what he was assenting to. His escapade or Howard's. "Do you know you almost scared me to death last night," Ken stated rather than asked.

"I realized that after the fact," Howard answered. "I woke up and noticed your bed empty, then I saw you, or someone, standing in the doorway and I thought you were walking in your sleep. All I wanted to do was gently guide you back to bed."

"Howard, I've never walked in my sleep in my life and don't bring up the Seaford Inn. I was fully awake then, too."

Howard nodded. "You've never fainted either."

"And I've never heard strange noises in the night or watched a ghost walk up a dark hallway."

"Tell me about last night," Howard said.

"Sit down, dad. First I'll tell you about the night before last night." Ken related Alice's story and Howard listened, making no comment, only nodding his head as Ken spoke. He's being damned professional, Ken thought. Next he told what he had seen and heard last night and ended with a recount of the tour of China House he had taken with Scott Evans, including the inscription they had read in the old family Bible.

"That is interesting," Howard commented. "I would like to see it."

"Just down the hall," Ken gestured. "I'll pass."

When Ken described the scene which had taken place in the nursery Howard was more than interested. He was elated. He made Ken repeat it, questioning his son to be sure nothing had been left out. "What was he doing when he became ill, Ken? Think."

"Why?"

"Don't you see, something in that room reminded Scott of what he's been suppressing all these years. But he fought against it. Fought so hard that he became physically ill. Now what was it?"

"The fire truck? He was playing with the fire truck."

Howard's hand moved across his chin. "No. When he was playing with the fire truck he was happy, that's what you said. It was after that. What was he doing?"

"Nothing. Nothing at all. We were looking at the toys, there are dozens of them in there, and then he became so ill he had to leave the room."

"The key is in the nursery and I wonder if we should explore it or leave it there."

"What would be best for Scott?"

Howard looked at his son as if seeing him for the first time. "You like that guy, don't you?"

"Yes. Very much."

Howard shook his head. "It could go either way. If he learns the truth it could kill him or cure him. If we allow it to remain buried he could get well or stay sick."

"What about last night, Howard? What I saw?"

"Could you have imagined it?"

Ken got up and hit his forehead with the palm of his hand. 'Could I have imagined it. Could Alice have imagined it. We are people who have never imagined anything in our lives and now, all of a sudden, everything is in our minds and nothing is real. It doesn't make any sense."

Howard sighed. "But tell me this, why didn't I hear any of it last night or the night before?"

"You're a very sound sleeper, Howard, however you're not the only person who seems to have heard nothing. Alice was too drugged to hear anything last night but Scott and Mike appear to be immune, too."

"I thought of that. You know, I all but accused Mike of promoting Scott's illness."

Ken was shocked. "Why the hell did you do that?"

"Because I believe it and after your experience last night I'm surer than ever. You say two people came out of the nursery. Both the same in physical appearance. Ken, think, those two young men are just about the same height and the same weight. In a dark hall, standing side by side, they would appear to be almost identical."

"Are you saying I saw Scott and Mike in the hall last night?"

"That's exactly what I'm saying."

"But why? If Scott was wandering around in the middle of the night wouldn't Mike tell you?"

"No," Howard stated without a moment's hesitation. "I don't think he would."

Ken shook his head. "I can't believe Mike is involved in a plot to harm Scott. He loves Scott. He really does."

Howard smiled reassuringly. "Love, Ken, means many things, even hate sometimes. Like the weather it's always with us but constantly in a state of flux. The emotion depends on the mood and more often on circumstance. Romantic love, the kind writers never tire of glorifying in song and story, just does not exist." Howard grinned at Ken but there was no malice in either his words or the gesture. "We want so much to believe in it," Howard continued, "because the idea is so pure, so simple and so all consuming it doesn't leave a minute to remind us of the multitude of drudgeries that are a necessary part of this thing we call living."

"So we escape," Ken offered. "Into novels and movies and daydreams."

"Right. But some of us work at looking for the real thing. It's about as rewarding as going through life looking for the Holy Grail. And you know why? Because every one of us, you and me and the group downstairs and every poor soul walking the earth, is pure ego. We fall in and out of love, make and lose friends, develop and cut off relationships of every kind for one reason and one reason only. To satisfy the ego. What's in it for me? What are my needs, my desires, my defenses? The sadist is as much a slave as the masochist only he doesn't know it. And we're all slaves to our egos and don't know it."

"Even the search for romantic love is ego driven," Ken said thoughtfully, "because the desire is to be loved the same way in return."

"I have a smart son, that was going to be my next point."

"I try, Pop," Ken kidded.

"You don't have to try, Kenny. You have the brains and talent in this family."

But not the common sense to commune with my father, Ken thought sadly, or the charm to find a lover. He thought of all the heroes he had placed in similar situations and what little thought he had given to their dilemmas. With a flick of his fingers over the typewriter keys he had solved all their problems that he himself had created. Now he was powerless to compose the words he wanted to speak to Howard.

"But it somehow all works," Ken, ever the optimist, got in. "People do fall in love and marry and raise children and—"

"Live happily ever after," Howard completed the thought.

"But they do," Ken insisted.

"I guess they do," Howard answered as if he doubted that happiness, true happiness, really existed in this world.

"So you think Mike encourages Scott. Promotes his illness to keep Scott securely under Mike's thumb" There is no balm like the problems of others to soothe our own cares.

Howard reached for a cigarette. "But I don't think Mike knows it," he struck a match and began to collect his thoughts. "If you told Mike that he would be offended and rightly so. I think he loves Scott as much as people like Mike Armstrong can ever love."

"Wait a minute, Howard." Ken held up his hand and spoke in a firm voice. "Are you talking about Mike personally or homosexuals in general?"

Howard's reply was just as firm and self-assured. "I'm talking about exceptionally egotistical people be they homosexual, heterosexual or non-sexual. I don't judge people, like or dislike them in groups, Ken... professionally or personally. It would be as stupid to do that as it would be to draw conclusions on the basis of one's skin color. Does that make you happy?"

Ken nodded. "Yes, Howard, it does."

"Good." Then Howard continued. "Mike believes that his love gives him the right to placate Scott's illness rather than help Scott get well. But what Mike is really doing is defending his own interests. As things stand Scott depends on Mike. He needs Mike. This makes Mike's position secure. A Scott free of his fears and guilt and depression might just decide he doesn't need or want Mike Armstrong."

"But Mike would never do anything to hurt Scott. Physically, I mean."

Howard shrugged. "Who knows? As I said, I don't think Mike is aware of his motives. Not consciously anyway. We act according to our needs and cover our actions with a blanket of martyrdom."

"Do you think Scott is capable of a relationship with... with someone based on mutual need rather than dependency?" Ken asked.

Howard avoided looking at his son. "Anything is possible, Ken, you know that."

"Are you going to help Scott, Dad?"

Howard looked at his watch. "Right now I'm going to go downstairs and Scott and Mike and I are going to attempt to drive the car into Salem, check the roads, fill up the tank and prepare to leave China House tomorrow morning."

"Does Scott know this?"

"He suggested it," Howard answered, "and I very quickly agreed to the plan." Howard started for the door. "Will you be down shortly?"

Ken nodded. "What excuse did you give for me not appearing this morning?"

"Just that you had a restless night and wanted to sleep in for awhile. No one raised an eyebrow. Get yourself together and come below," Howard finished and went out the door.

Ken looked up at the high ceiling, the large windows, the oriental and American antiques as perfectly formed and blended and placed as life was ill shapen, unmatched and haphazard. Again — or was it still? — China House made itself felt. Howard wanted to leave as soon as possible. Leave with all the loose ends untied. China House would never allow that to happen. It had called to Ken that cold dawn at the Seaford Inn. It had been calling to Scott Evans for twenty years. Perhaps the light in the window of China House was a beacon for all who cared to heed it.

Ken felt awed as he stood alone in the quiet room. They all now wanted to leave but China House would not let them go until its purpose was served. Of this, Kenneth Roth was certain.

• XVII •

The group in the sun room appeared as cheerful and bright as the sunlight that splashed through the windows and bathed the scene in its warm glow. One would never guess the undercurrents of fear and passion that hovered just beneath the surface of Scott Evans's house party.

"Ken, how do you feel?" Scott was the first to see him as Ken entered the room. There was genuine concern in his voice and even a hint of guilt.

"I'm fine. A sleepless night was all that kept me in bed so late," Ken reassured Scott. Poor Scotty, Ken thought, so many problems of his own and now he's beginning to feel guilty because he's involved his new friend in his own troubles.

"Ken, I was so worried." Alice walked up to Ken and kissed his cheek. Ken was startled by the gesture. It was so unlike Alice Miller. He could feel his father's eyes on them as he returned Alice's embrace with more enthusiasm than he felt.

"I'm flattered by all the attention but really it was just a restless night," Ken repeated.

Mike, looking as handsome in the bright light of day as he did in a softly lit room, waited for the fuss to die down before he asked, "Why didn't the Doctor give you one of his special sedatives?"

Ken winced inwardly and looked at Mike Armstrong. He could perceive, just barely, the slightest wink-like flutter in Mike's left eye and almost burst out laughing before the entire room. Armstrong was a bastard all right, but a delightful one.

"Special sedative?" Alice was wide eyed. "It's just the standard prescription, isn't it, Howard?"

Howard had not yet fully recovered from Mike's remark. So Mike knew, or suspected, about Howard's relationship with Alice. How? And was it Mike who had passed on the information to Ken? Those two, or rather three, young men had certainly gotten chummy very quickly.

Ken was not inclined to laugh off Alice's seemingly dumb remark. Her one-liners were beginning to pack the wallop of a bomb. Dr. Roth's assistant (and what a new meaning that title suddenly took on!) was not just an act; she was a complete package.

Howard spoke. "Let's forget about sedatives, mine and others," a quick look at Michael, "and make some plans. We're all watered and fed so what do we do now?"

"What about backgammon? Ken suggested.

"No way," Scott moaned. "Mike is unbeatable."

"It comes from years of practicing around Beverly Hills swimming pools." Howard was pleased that he was finally able to take a verbal punch at Armstrong.

Michael accepted Howard's remark with a grin and a shrug. It seemed none of them wanted to stir up any dust on this sunny day. To tread easily and survive another day and night in China House had become the party's unspoken policy. Even Alice had made no comment on her hysterical outburst of last night. Ken remembered this as he watched Alice light her cigarette with her small gold lighter. Had Alice forgotten that her supposedly misplaced lighter was the cause of ruining the one pleasant night they had spent in China House? Was she dumb or just plain brazen? Ken thought he knew the answer. Alice was tired of playing the closet lover and, having pushed open the door a crack, she was now about ready to step out. Well, Ken smiled, she wasn't alone.

"If we're getting off early tomorrow we had better drive the car to Salem." Scott, surprisingly, was taking command. "If we can make it to Salem we won't have any problems tomorrow. I'm sure the main highway is clear but I have no idea what the country roads are like. Better give it a try now rather than when we're all loaded up and ready to go."

"Should we all go?" Ken asked.

"Not necessary," Mike answered. "It's nice and warm in here and bitchy cold out there. Don't let that bright sun fool you, the air is like ice."

"But I don't mind," Ken spoke up again. "Some fresh air would do us all good." What he didn't add was that he didn't particularly want to spend a long morning alone with Alice Miller. Not right now, anyway.

"If you want some fresh air why don't you try out the skis we found the other day? You threatened to do it yesterday." Ken leaped upon Scott's suggestion.

"That's exactly what I'll do."

"What fun," Alice exclaimed. "It's been years since I've been on skis."

Ken's heart sank. He wasn't going to be stuck indoors with Alice but he was obviously going to be side by side with her on the snowy grounds of China House. But it was too late to renege now.

"They will ski and we," Mike looked at Scott and Howard, "will pioneer a safe path down the mountain and over the hill."

Wool slacks, sweaters and parkas were standard winter attire in Sea-Air and both Ken and Alice had wisely packed these items for their trip to New England. In the storage room behind the kitchen they found the boots they had tried on the day before and selected skis from the wide assortment lined neatly against one wall of the room.

"All these skis," Alice commented. "I wonder what they did with so many."

"House parties, I imagine," Ken said. "When Scott's parents were young they were very social. China House must have always been buzzing with guests and parties."

"I guess it was. And now it just sits here, empty and unused. What a waste."

Ken decided to make the best of the situation and not get involved, in any way, with Alice Miller. Her problem was between Howard and herself and Ken wanted no part of it. If Howard wanted to keep their affair a secret and she didn't... well, let them work it out. But he couldn't help taking a mild swipe at the lady. "I don't know how empty China House has been what with sounds in the night and faces in the windows."

"Ken, I did hear something crying in the night."

"I'm sure you did." Ken thought of what he had seen and heard last night and was almost sorry he had goaded Alice.

Alice looked at Ken closely. "Have you heard it, too, Ken?"

"I'm not sure what I've heard or seen around here. In fact I'm not sure of anything since we arrived here."

Alice nodded thoughtfully. "China House makes us see things that don't exist."

"Or that we don't want to exist," Ken added.

They found the others in the hall preparing for the trip to Salem. "I see you found what you needed," Scott said as Ken and Alice came from the hall passage dressed and carrying their skis. "I take it you'll try for a run down the hill."

"That's what I thought," Ken told him. "Down the hill to the inn. I'd like to say hello to Mr. Billingsly."

"Be careful, you two," Howard cautioned. "There's more ice than snow out there and it's downhill all the way."

"We will," Ken said and to Scott added, "Don't push too hard. If you can't make it to Salem we'll just sit it out for another day."

"We'll make it," Mike said. "If we don't Scotty will hire a 'copter to get us out of here."

"Stop at the inn on your way back," Alice requested. "If we make it that far we'll be in no condition to climb our way back."

"And that's the best suggestion I've heard all day," Ken said.

Once outside both Ken and Alice were elated by the clean, cold air. They breathed deeply, hardly feeling the cold in their joy at escaping from the confines of the overbearing house. Like pet dogs being let out the back door long past their usual airing time they marched across the wide portico without looking at their surroundings, only eager to experience their freedom. When they finally did look at the world about them all motion stopped as they were struck by the dazzling sight which met their eyes.

White and blue. Not another color or living thing obstructed the perfect, clear color combination. The ground and trees were covered with snow as pure and white as when it had fallen from the sky. Each flake appeared to stand out independently of the billions of others as it caught and held the light of the brilliant sun. The sky was ice blue and cloudless, a true winter sky. And the line between blue and white, heaven and earth, was etched with the steady hand of the Master Artist. China House, which should have been dwarfed by this awesome landscape, stood out bigger and bolder than ever, its white façade pasted, flat, against the blue backdrop.

When Ken had recovered from the sight and his eyes had adjusted to the dazzle of sun on snow he pointed to the limousine which appeared wheelless in the deep snow. "They'll have to dig before they can drive it an inch."

"Better them than us," Alice answered, already on the steps of the portico and bending to put on her skis.

Ken joined her and in a few minutes their boots were properly attached to the shiny black slats. They began to move cautiously from the house. The sun had warmed the earth enough to soften the top layer of snow but there were patches as slick and solid as a frozen pond. "Ken, look." Alice pointed to the north and Ken turned in the direction of Alice's outstretched arm.

It was a cemetery laid out along the ground on the side of China House that could not be seen from their bedroom windows. They had not seen it the day they arrived because its position made it impossible to be seen when approaching the house. "The family burial grounds," Ken said. "Not unusual, especially for this part of the country." But he knew that it was, like everything else about China House, unusual.

The grave sites were completely obliterated by snow and the narrow stone monuments that towered over them resembled the skeletal remains of an ancient structure. As Ken looked, the shape of the stones which at a glance seemed perfectly ordinary became very extraordinary before his amazed eyes. The monuments were crowned with inverted heart-shaped stones that resembled the phallic carvings of some primitive society. But these stones were smooth and beautifully worked by a master craftsman. Ken shivered for the first time since coming out into the cold air. Was this more of Commodore Seaford's work? His legacy along with China House? The man was diabolical, Ken thought, and he wondered if the Chinese mistresses had been laid to rest beneath those symbolic horrors.

"Do you think he's buried there?" Alice asked. "The little boy," she added when she saw the puzzled expression on Ken's face.

"I don't know and let's not mention it, please." Ken dug his ski poles into the ground and pushed himself away from the white blanketed cemetery with its stone erections pointing upward as if mocking God in His heaven.

Scott and Michael appeared, shovels in hand, their faces barely visible beneath the fur trimmed hoods of their parkas. Ken waved and shouted. "Where's Howard? Don't tell me he's going to let you two do all the work and then get carried off sitting in the back seat."

"He's not coming," Scott shouted back, each word made visible by the thin white puff of air he expelled as he spoke.

"Not coming?" Ken said in a voice audible only to himself as he eyed the huge façade of the white house. For the second time since his arrival at China House Ken knew panic.

"Five bucks says I'll be sitting in the inn when you arrive," Alice called from some distant world.

Ken forced himself to push forward on his skis. Howard alone in China House. Why? Howard was upset and China House tended to exaggerate fears buried deep within the soul and even to create new ones. Howard, especially now, should not be alone in China House. But how could Ken go back? What reason, what excuse would suffice? Then, suddenly, it was too late to retreat.

He felt the icy wind hit his face before he was aware of his quickening movement down the hill. His mind instantly drew away from China House and Howard as he concentrated on staying erect. He kept his eyes on the figure ahead of him as it swayed from left to right and then back again with great skill and certainty.

"Happy landings." The shout echoed over Ken's head.

· XVIII ·

Howard watched the big black car jerk forward and backward several times before the powerful motor exploded with a roar which thrust the heavy machine out of its icy bed, crushing the snow beneath it and leaving a wide U-shaped track on the white lawn as it headed down the hill.

He turned from the window and walked to the fireplace, lighting a cigarette as he moved, and finally came to rest before the marble hearth. The logs that had burned so cheerfully the night before were now cold gray ashes.

Howard had not driven to Salem because he wanted to be by himself for a while. He believed every human being needed to spend some time alone. Well, now he was alone. So what?

"So I don't have to look at them. All of them. What a day. What a bitch of a day and it's only just begun." At that moment the hall clock struck twelve times. Howard nodded mockingly toward the double doors which led from salon to hall. "Thank you, China House. God forbid anyone in your womb should have a private thought."

"So Ken knows about Alice." Just when Howard had decided to break it off with the lady Ken finds out. "And Alice. My God, Alice. She was hanging on for dear life and acting like a wife. Well screw them both." They weren't children and Howard was tired of playing father to the world.

He walked the short distance from fireplace to portable bar and poured a bourbon over ice with a splash of water. "If it's good enough for Scotty and Mike it's good enough for me." He toasted the empty room and drank.

"Good Christ, it's horrible."

Maybe one had to acquire a taste for it. "Did Mike Armstrong acquire a taste for bourbon and Scott Evans at the same time?" Howard grinned at his pun. "Maybe I envy them. All the needs, including sex, wrapped up in one neat, masculine package. No fuss, no frills, no clashing of personalities and, blessing of all blessings, no need to prove yourself over and over." Howard took another sip of the bourbon and it did indeed taste better.

What had Ken told him? A painting of the Commodore and something about a Bible. He quickly went to the bar for a refill then headed toward the master bedroom, happy to have a purpose to fill the solitude he had arranged for himself.

As he entered the hall the ticking of the grandfather clock filled the house and Howard thought of its sound as the one constant in China House. Mounting the stairs he heard other sounds. The heating system, which had been created to comfort, also serenaded those it warmed with a series of hums and crackles given off in fits and starts like an orchestra warming up before it erupts into one blended, harmonious sound. Wind rattled the windows and floor boards groaned. Did a door close? Open? Was that a laugh, a cry, a footstep? He concentrated on the cold glass in his hand. It was the only real and solid fact in what had become a nightmare world of imagination.

He paused halfway in his climb and looked down the long flight of steps. The ticking clock reminded him of the dream he had had so shortly after arriving in China House. That too had begun with the ticking of a clock. The passage of time. The link between past and present. Time. It was all that separated the living from the dead. Howard continued upward knowing that the door, the exit from China House, was growing smaller and only God knew what would separate him from it.

He pushed opened the door, glass in hand, and saw them as soon as he stepped into the room. She was smiling — or was it a grin? He moved in closer, looking up, his eyes as steady on her as hers were on him. It was a grin. Almost a smirk. Was she trying to imitate. . .? Howard laughed aloud, breaking the solemnity of the moment. And the Commodore? Howard's eyes moved across the wall and came to rest on the master of China House.

The Commodore eyed the intruder without a trace of a smile or grin on his face. His was a blank mask and written on it was the wisdom of all the sages who had ever lived. And suddenly Howard knew, in a way he could not explain even to himself, what the Commodore was saying.

"Everything is nothing."

The startling fact was as clear to Howard as if the canvas itself had actually spoken the words. For years Dr. Howard Roth had tried to explain to his patients the subtle difference between intellectual and emotional understanding and for years the Doctor had had a clear intellectual understanding of what he preached. Now, for the first time in his life, he experienced the emotion of understanding.

The realization of what had happened to him swept over him like a tidal wave, drowning his ability to think further as it flooded his being with pure, raw emotion. Wave after wave of naked feelings engulfed him, climaxed and receded only to rise again and repeat the cycle with an ever-increasing force. Joy, sorrow, fear, confidence, a sensuality that made him gasp and a cleansing that made him divine.

When he felt he could take no more he struggled to free himself from the eddy which threatened his very sanity. It mocked his pathetic effort. Intellect and emotion locked in mortal combat. Infant against giant. Howard knew he was doomed and gave up all hope of saving himself. He relaxed and accepted his fate and the moment he did the force freed him from its grip.

Howard turned, shaken and bent, and made his way to the door. He stopped before the lectern and saw the Bible. The book was opened, as Ken and Scott had left it, and when Howard saw the bold, painfully rigid writing he knew whose hand had written the inscription before he started to read the words.

AN ANCIENT SAGE, UPON PASSING FROM THIS LIFE
AND ENTERING THE NEXT
FOUND HIMSELF BEFORE TWO DOORS
MARKED LIGHT AND DARK.
TO DWELL HERE, THE FIRST PROCLAIMED, ONE NEED ONLY KNOCK
AND ANSWER WHEN SUMMONED.
TO DWELL HERE, THE OTHER STATED
ONE NEED ONLY ENTER.
THE SAGE KNOCKED BOLDLY ON THE DOOR OF LIGHT.
"WHO IS THERE?" BELLOWED THE VOICE OF GOD.
"IT IS YOUR FAITHFUL SERVANT, MY LORD " THE OLD SAGE
ANSWERED.
"BE GONE," GOD CRIED OUT. "THERE IS NO ROOM FOR THEE
WITHIN MY HOUSE."
THE SAGE, WEEPING, WITHDREW HIMSELF FROM THE PORTAL TO
EVERLASTING LIGHT AND WENT WHERE HE COULD BE ALONE TO

MEDITATE UPON HOW HE HAD SINNED AGAINST THE LORD. HE
RECALLED ALL THE DAYS OF HIS PREVIOUS LIFE: WHAT HE HAD DONE,
WHAT HE HAD SEEN AND, ABOVE ALL ELSE, WHAT HE HAD LEARNED.
WHEN HE KNEW THE ANSWER HE RETURNED TO THE DOOR MARKED
LIGHT AND ONCE AGAIN KNOCKED UPON IT.
"WHO IS THERE?" BELLOWED THE VOICE OF GOD.
"IT IS THEE, MY LORD."
THE DOOR OPENED AND THE WISE MAN ENTERED INTO THE LIGHT
OF ETERNAL BLISS.

Howard buried his face in his hands and wept. His own words
came back to haunt him. "When we dwell on something we begin
a series of actions, sometimes consciously, more often unconsciously, that cause the thought to become reality."

The salt of his tears became the salty air of that flawless afternoon in Salem. The comforting fire in their bedroom at the
Seaford Inn. China House in the pale light of dawn. Ken in his
arms. He knew then that what he felt for his son was wrong. He
knew it since he had discovered the thirteen-year-old boy comforting himself with his fist. And he knew Ken had loved Kevin
Roberts. Rather than acknowledge his feeling Howard had covered
it with the most common of disguises. Hatred for Kevin, jealousy
of Ken's success and a refusal to listen to his son's probing pleas for
love and understanding.

"If we face our fears, verbalize them and investigate their
source, more often than not we learn to see them for the
charlatans they are and in time they disappear or, at the very least,
we learn to live with them and not allow them to stop us from
functioning normally. But if we flee from fear we give it power
and, unchecked, fear grows all out of proportion to reality and
dominates our lives."

Howard had fled from the fear of love and the fear had infested
his ego until his masculine pride told him he could only triumph
if the threat to his masculinity was defeated.

Howard wanted to vomit but there was nothing left inside
him to come out. He was hollow.

"We thank Him for the good and damn Him for the bad when
it is we, and we alone, who are responsible for both."

He walked from the room and closed the door behind him
without a backward glance. In the hall he heard the sound of the
ticking clock downstairs. "God forgive me." He stopped walking
and smiled weakly at his childish words. He now knew that only
he could forgive himself

• XIX •

The aroma of freshly brewed coffee drifted pleasantly upward as
Mr. Billingsly lowered the tray of cups and coffee pot to the table
in front of the fire. Ken and Alice had enjoyed a good lunch with
their host, served to them not as customers but as guests. Mr.
Billingsly had been as talkative during the meal as it was possible
for the old brittle New Englander to be.

Ken suspected, and rightly so, that the old man was lonely.
The storm had cut him off from the town and the few neighbors
scattered along the road at the bottom of the hill. He was happy
for any company but especially for the company of the people who
were inhabiting China House for the first time in over twenty
years.

The innkeeper had recognized Ken at once and listened
intently as Ken told of his chance meeting with Scott Evans and
the subsequent invitation to China House. He made no mention
of the strange circumstances surrounding the invitation and
Billingsly, characteristically, did not pry. When the black
limousine had passed the inn and the car horn sounded Ken explained Scott's trip to Salem.

"The little boy, eh," Billingsly said.

"Not so little," Alice reminded him. "He's a young man now."

They took sherry before lunch in front of the roaring fire and
Ken recalled the wish he had made in this very room not six weeks
ago. He had wanted to come back to Salem in the cold beauty of
the New England winter and live within the picture-book surrounding of China House. He had gotten his wish but it had come
packaged with more than he had bargained for.

"Just like the old days," Billingsly said as he poured the coffee

"Ski parties and big black cars coming and going up an' down the hill."

"It must be very lonely for you here," Alice commented. "Your only neighbor is that big empty house on top of the hill."

"In the winter, yes." The old man stretched his long, skinny neck. "But in the summer the tourists crawl all over the place like ants at a picnic."

Ken smiled at Billingsly's typical Yankee dislike of strangers. And Ken was feeling better. The fire was comforting and the wine had warmed and relaxed his cold, tense body. In this frame of mind he decided to make the most of his visit with the innkeeper, especially as the old man seemed to be in such a talkative mood.

"Mr. Billingsly, did you happen to walk up to China House last night, or see anyone else walking up the hill?" Ken watched Alice put a cigarette in her mouth, reach for her purse, stop, and then pick up a book of matches from the table.

"Ain't been out of this place since the snow started. An' so far as I know Harry Blake, he oversees China House more or less, ain't been near it either. Would have stopped in here if he had." The old man looked at Ken questioningly. "What have you seen up there?" His head jerked in the direction of China House as it had done so often the evening Ken and Howard had questioned him about the house.

Alice spoke up before Ken had a chance to answer. "I'm afraid that it was my too-fertile imagination that prompted Ken's question. Last night I thought I saw a face looking into the house through one of the windows. I realize now that it was snow and the way it had formed on the dark pane that caused the illusion."

This was the first attempt at a logical explanation Ken had heard from Alice and he wondered when Alice had thought of it. Billingsly looked from Ken to Alice. "Always something funny going on at China House."

"Or with the people in it," Ken said softly, avoiding looking at Alice Miller. But now that the subject of China House and its mysteries had come up, however peripherally, Ken was determined to learn all he could. He remembered Howard's remarking how curious it was that Billingsly had not told them why Scott's family had so suddenly fled from their home.

"You didn't tell my father and me about the accident that occured in China House, Mr. Billingsly. The death of the little boy." Alice moved uncomfortably in her chair as Ken spoke.

"You never asked me," the old man said, not pausing in his attempt to light his pipe with a match that seemed to have no effect on the tobacco its flame touched.

"How could we ask you about something we knew nothing of?"

Billingsly struck another match and tried again. He puffed and shrugged at the same time. "Not a very pretty story. That's why. Did the boy tell you about it?"

"Yes. What he remembers. The rest I read in newspaper accounts of the accident," Ken said.

"So you know all about it," Billingsly responded.

"No, I'm afraid not. The newspaper was vague, to put it mildly, so I don't think even they knew exactly what happened."

"Ken," Alice spoke up. "Maybe Mr. Billingsly would rather not talk about it. After all it *has* been twenty years since the child died and there are some things best forgotten."

The old man had succeeded in igniting his pipe and he now puffed clouds of smoke out of his mouth as he waved his thin, wrinkled hand in the air. "I don't mind. But it's not a pretty story," he repeated, looking at Ken Roth.

"I would like to hear it, Mr. Billingsly."

The innkeeper leaned back in his chair, puffing on his pipe and spoke slowly more for effect, Ken thought, than because of a faulty memory. As Billingsly talked Ken looked at the fire burning before him and saw in its flickering yellow and red flames the huge staircase in China House.

A little boy, blond and handsome, is seated on the top step, a cloth bag in his hand. He opens the bag and its contents spill out across the oriental carpet. The beautifully colored marbles catch and reflect the shimmering glow of the fire. The smooth balls sparkle like gems and the boy is delighted as he watches them roll haphazardly over the floor. He picks one up, aims, and sends it crashing against another marble. He repeats the action again and again, sometimes hitting his target but more often missing the mark. A voice calls from below and the little boy looks down the long staircase. A smile lights up his face and, forgetting his game, he stands and races down the steps. He is hardly out of sight when another boy appears in the hall. He is identical, in every way, to the one who has just left the scene. He too is smiling as he takes one step forward and then, suddenly, his feet fly into the air, his head hits the top step, he lets out an ugly cry and begins to tumble down, the small blond head bouncing off each step until finally it crashes with a dull thud on the cold marble floor. Blood, red and warm, covers the white marble and splashes on the bare legs of the first boy at whose feet the limp body comes to rest. For a brief moment there is no sound but the ticking of the hall clock and then there is a scream. . . .

"Poor Scott," Ken cried. "Poor, poor Scotty. Living with that locked inside his head all these years."

"I told you it wasn't a pretty story," the old man said.

"Ken, it explains so much," Alice said.

Billingsly rose and started to clear the table. When he carried the tray away and Ken was sure he could not hear he turned to Alice. "Don't say anything about this, please."

"But why not? It's the key Howard needs to help Scott."

"I know," Ken nodded. "But let's wait until we're out of China House and back home. Scott looked fine this morning and he's acting perfectly normal. With any luck he'll stay that way until we leave. Alice, I don't want another scene in China House. I really don't think Howard could take it."

"I agree," Alice replied. "I really dread spending another night in that house."

"Alice, that noise you heard coming from the nursery, those crying sounds, Howard thinks—"

"You told him?"

"I told him," Ken said, "I told him because I heard those noises, too. Last night. Howard thinks it's Scott."

"My God. That's crazy. Is Howard sure?"

"No, just a hunch. But good Lord, the dead don't cry aloud and walk the halls. Not even in China House they don't."

Alice shivered. "No, they don't. But we'll never be sure, will we, Ken."

"What do you mean?"

"Just what I said. We'll never be sure. We will leave China House and if Scott continues to see Howard they will talk and Howard will work at drawing the full story out of Scott and if Scott resists, which he will, Howard will force him to remember."

"And make him well," Ken said hopefully.

"Perhaps. But suppose Scott refuses to remember? And suppose even after Howard tells him about the accident Scott still refuses to admit that out of guilt he resurrected his dead brother by periodically becoming Tom Evans?"

"Then he'll never get well."

"And we'll never know who, or what, was in the nursery."

Ken looked at Alice, beginning to understand what the other was hinting but hoping he was wrong in his assumption.

Alice confirmed Ken's fear. "Scott Evans is not a raving maniac. By all standards, legal and medical, he's as sane as you and me. If he refuses to ever admit that it was him who greeted us that godawful afternoon we arrived at the house and that it was him in the nursery at night how will we ever know, for certain, that he's not telling the truth?"

"We never will," Ken mumbled.

"Unless we prove it for ourselves," Alice said.

Ken shook his head. "Howard would never allow it. I won't ask him either. He's not been standing up too well under the strain of China House in case you haven't noticed."

"Ken, Howard doesn't have to know."

Ken was shocked, less by what Alice said than because it was Alice who said it. This was again the Alice Miller Ken did not know and he doubted if Howard did either. A determined lady who would not be deterred from her goal. There's a lot of passion in that charming lady was what Scott had said about Alice, and how right he was. Poor Howard, Ken thought for the second time.

"Alice, what are you thinking?"

"You want to know the truth, don't you?"

"I do," Ken admitted.

"Then we'll have to do it tonight. Tonight or never." Alice spoke as if she were making a decision that went far beyond the mystery of strange sounds coming from an empty room in China House.

"How?" Ken asked, catching Alice's excitement.

"Tonight, when they're all asleep, come to my room. If we hear anything, anything at all, we'll go to the nursery and see just who's there."

Ken did want to know who walked the halls of China House, as much for his own sake as for Scott's. And Alice was right. This was the only way to find out.

The sound of a car horn brought Alice and Ken to their feet.

"Tonight?" Alice whispered.

"Tonight," Ken agreed.

Mike was in the driver's seat so it was Scott who hurried around the car to help Ken and Alice carry their skis to the waiting vehicle. Mr. Billingsly stood in the doorway seeing his guests off and Scott, always polite, paused long enough to shake the old man's hand and say a few words to him before returning to the warmth of the car and his seat beside Michael.

Billingsly seemed oblivious to the cold as he stood in front of the open door with only a thin sweater to protect him from the freezing temperature. He watched the car make its slow way up the snow-covered hill but it was obvious from the look on his wrinkled face that he was seeing neither car nor snow. His mind, in fact was on a similar scene but the setting in his mind was not a cold winter afternoon; it was a warm sun-filled day.

The old man retreated back into the warmth of his inn and walked to the comforting fireplace where he began the joyless task of trying to relight his pipe. So the Roths had met the Evans boy and come to stay in China House. Quite a coincidence, that. Billingsly scratched his gray head. But the other lad? How the hell do you account for that?

"Always something funny going on around China House," he concluded aloud as the tobacco in his pipe finally reacted to the heat of the wooden match.

· XX ·

The sun was setting when the car came to an abrupt halt in the snow-cleared space from which it had been moved that afternoon. The blue sky was growing dark and gray clouds, low and heavy, moved inland from the ocean as if a giant shade were being drawn across the heavens. China House and its occupants would spend another night under a starless sky.

A strong evening wind picked up the snow and the white powder moved about in whirlpool fashion as the three young men and the woman struggled to get skis and poles out of the car and then hurried into the warmth of the house. "We'll be lucky if we don't get another storm," Scott said as he opened the front door and held it for the others.

"Christ, it's cold," Mike puffed as he entered the hall behind Ken and Alice, carrying Alice's skis in his arms. "Close the door, Scotty."

"Howard," Ken called, "we're back."

There was no answer. Except for the hall clock the house was deathly still. Ken walked to the salon and looked in. "Howard?"

"He must be upstairs," Alice said.

"If he's smart he's under a warm blanket, snoozing. Where do these skis go?" It was Mike who spoke.

"In the storage room behind the kitchen," Scott answered. "I'll give you a hand."

"I'll see if Howard's in our room." Ken's apprehension was now apparent. As he walked toward the stairs Mike reached out and touched Ken's arm. "I'm sure he's all right, Kenny."

"Sure? How can you be sure of anything around here?" Ken turned to leave and found himself face to face with Scott Evans. Scott had heard the remark and Ken now bit his lower lip as he saw the hurt look on Scott's face. "I'm sorry, Scott. I didn't mean—"

"No problem. I understand. Go check on Howard."

The scenario Mr. Billingsly had related to his lunch guests began to replay itself in Ken's mind as he mounted the wide staircase. He saw the small blond head tumbling downward and he gripped the banister tightly, his fingers white, as he thought that the child's head must have crushed long before it landed on the hall floor. The thick carpet which now cushioned Ken's feet had been laid after the fact.

From below he heard Alice's voice. "I'm going to light a fire in the salon."

"Is there enough wood? I know there's more in the kitchen. I'll get it." Was it Scott or Michael who had answered Alice? Ken was not sure. He moved quickly across the upstairs hall and to the bedroom door.

Howard was on the bed, sound asleep and, as Mike had predicted, covered with a quilt from feet to shoulders. Relief swept over Ken's body leaving him suddenly very tired and, as often happens when fear is banished, feeling a little foolish. What had he feared? What could possibly happen to a grown man inside an empty house? And it *was* an empty house. This nonsense of imaginations run wild had to stop. They all thought of Scott as being ill or confused but they were no better than their host. At least Scott had a reason for his vivid imaginings. They had none.

Ken moved to the bed and looked at Howard. His breathing was deep and even and there was a look of peaceful contentment on his face. Blissful sleep. Ken envied his father's unconscious state and was once again struck by the change which was now very evident in Howard's appearance. Howard had grown older. Perhaps mature would be a more apt word. It was not unbecoming. On the contrary, Ken liked what he saw. People, like fine wine, should age and grow more distinguished with the passing years. One's face should express the miraculous experience of life. Scott's did in the booding, boyish smile that said he was resigned to his fate, whatever that might be, and Mike's dark blue eyes, cynical and defensive, reflected what he had learned and what he felt deep within himself. Alice. . . .

Ken moved away from the bed and sat in one of the room's wing chairs. He felt as rigid and tense as the piece of furniture which held him. The back was too high, the arms too short and the seat too far from the ground. One should feel regal in such a chair, even powerful, like a king seated on his throne, but in this room one only felt awed and insignificant. China House always was and always would be, while those who were sheltered by it were transient and expendable. They would all be replaced and their passing would go unnoticed. Who was there to care? Only one's self. Ken bent to remove the heavy ski boots which were beginning to cramp his feet.

Alice? It was now obvious that what her small, delicate face showed the world did not reflect the nature of the person who exhibited it. Alice wore a mask. Perhaps several. Ken shrugged. "Don't we all?" Clever, quick, witty were the adjectives he would like ascribed to Kenneth Roth. And, on the surface, he was all that. But underneath the veneer he was one insecure son-of-a-bitch. He rose and began to undress. A hot tub followed by a nap was what he wanted and needed.

As the tub filled with hot water Ken emptied a tiny bottle of blue liquid into the flow and immediately the tub exploded with thousands of rainbow-colored bubbles and the scent of sandalwood filled the room. "I'm going to pamper myself and why the hell not?' Not coming up with a single reason not to he lifted his long masculine legs, stepped into the hot mixture and sat, sinking until the foamy water embraced him clear to his neck.

Outside it had grown dark and Ken could hear the icy wind moving the snow-laden branches of the trees which dotted the hill below China House. The thought of the cold landscape delighted him, making the warm womb he soaked in even more inviting and the effervescent water a liquid blanket that supported and comforted him at the same time. His body tingled with a myriad of sensations, some lingering, some fleeting and quite suddenly they seemed to join forces and rush, as if being summoned, to the center of his being. He did nothing to dispel this flush of pleasure, rather he invited it by parting his legs and allowing the warmth he felt there to be engulfed and lapped by the tepid tide.

His hand caressed himself and as he drifted, half asleep, into the erotic eddy he knew that he had awakened to the only reality. Imagination.

Howard was sitting up smoking a cigarette when Ken came

out of the bathroom, knotting the sash of his robe and looking clean and fresh and slightly flushed. "Did I wake you?"

Howard shook his head. "I didn't even know you were back until I was up and saw your clothes."

"You looked so peaceful when I came in. No bad dreams, I take it."

Howard smiled. "No bad dreams, just a beautiful void. How did the boys do?"

"To Salem and back with no trouble. Looks like all systems are go," Ken answered.

"I wish we were leaving tonight," Howard said. His fingers brushed back the fine blond hair which had fallen across his forehead. He looked tired and very vulnerable. Ken moved idly about the room looking and touching without seeing or feeling.

"Are you looking for these?" Howard offered Ken his pack of cigarettes.

"Actually I was trying to avoid them but if you insist...." He walked to Howard and reached for the cigarettes.

"But I don't insist," Howard said, withdrawing the pack.

"Now I really want one." He took a cigarette and Howard struck a match.

"How did the afternoon go?" Howard asked.

"For China House I would say about par."

"You saw Billingsly?" Ken nodded his response. "And how is the old goat?"

"Furious, I think, because of the snow. He's housebound and can't get out to snoop on us."

"Was he surprised to see you again?"

"I think so," Ken replied. "But you know how Billingsly is. You can never tell what he's thinking. He just sort of grunts."

"No more ghost stories, I hope?" Howard commented.

Ken got up and moved to the nearest ashtray. He answered without looking at Howard. "No more ghost stories." Ken hated to lie, especially about something he felt it was very important for Howard to know. Why had he promised Alice he would say nothing to Howard? Ken shook his head and then hoped Howard had not noticed the motion. It was Ken who had told Alice to keep the story of Tom Evans's death from Howard. Remembering Howard's peaceful look as he slept and seeing how calm he was now assured Ken that it was the right thing to do. He knew that Howard would be unable to resist probing Scott, and even

Michael, once he heard the true story of the young twin's death and the last thing Ken wanted was another scene between Howard and Scott or Mike Armstrong. Until they left China House they must all pretend they were the same people who had arrived there three days ago.

Three days. It seemed a lifetime.

But Ken had allowed Alice to talk him into the foolish business of sneaking about the house in the middle of the night when they both knew damn well it was poor Scott who made nocturnal visits to the nursery. Any other answer was not even in the realm of reality. But there, in that damn inn, it was possible to imagine anything. Those words again. . . reality and imagination. Ken touched his forehead. He felt a headache coming on. A very real headache.

"Why don't you rest a while," he heard Howard say.

"I think I'll do just that." Ken stretched out on his bed and Howard covered him with the quilt.

"Everything is going to be all right, son."

"I know it is."

"If you were sure you wouldn't be standing about shaking your head and mumbling to yourself."

Ken's laugh was a nervous reaction and not a joyous sound. "Was I doing that?"

"You were."

"Do you think it's old age?"

"I think it's anxiety."

"I'm not an anxious person, Howard."

"I didn't think I was either, until I came here for a relaxing week in the country." Howard sat on Ken's bed. "I did a little exploring while you were out." A flicker of fear clouded Ken's eyes.

"What are you afraid of, Kenny?" Howard suddenly asked.

"You. Me. This house and everyone in it."

"Hush. I won't hear you talking that way. It's not like you."

"What is like me, Howard?"

"Strong."

Ken laughed, again without joy. "We're only as strong as the people who support us."

"You have my support, Kenny."

Ken looked closely at his father, his heart swelling in his chest. Did Howard's words mean what Ken thought they did? As his mind raced for a response Howard spoke again. "I saw his portrait," he said, as if discussing a deity who cursed those who looked upon it.

"Do you think he's evil?" Ken saw the graveyard and the tall, erect monuments.

"I read the inscription in the Bible."

"Do you think he's evil?" Ken repeated.

"You read the inscription," Howard insisted.

"Yes, I read it."

"Don't you understand, Ken. He, this house and all of us in it are whatever we want him and it and us to be."

They were both silent. Howard's remark forcing them to withdraw and contemplate its meaning. Ken did not ask Howard to elaborate because he knew Howard could not. Somehow, it had all been said. "Christ told the same story in one simple sentence," Ken seemed surprised at his discovery.

"The kingdom of heaven, like the kingdom of hell, is within," Howard answered.

The sound of an icy rain being blown against the windows filled the dark room. It was an angry sound, pregnant with a rage that seemed directed at China House itself.

"God, Howard, another stormy night in this tomb."

"Promise me something, Kenny."

"What?"

"From now until the time we leave this house I don't want you doing anything foolish. I know how you feel about Scott Evans," Howard held up his hand, "Let me finish, please. Promise me you won't get any more involved in Scott's troubles than you already are." Howard's voice trembled as he spoke. It was unlike him to lose control of himself and Ken was as startled by the strange request as by the emotion of its delivery. The storm which raged outside the house seemed to rage within his father as well.

Were storms, too, a reflection of our thoughts? Did we cause them as we did wars and murders? Were we ignorant masters of the universe and therefore slaves to it?

"Why, Howard? What's going to happen?"

"I don't know, Ken, but there's an evil loose in this house and the house has nothing to do with it. It's our evil thoughts, all of us, that the house seems capable of turning into reality." Howard touched his son's arm and suddenly pleaded, "Forgive me, Kenny."

"For what?"

"For wanting you to be what you were not meant to be. . . and I don't mean a doctor." Howard managed a weak smile.

They stared at each other for a long minute. Without taking his eyes from Howard's Ken said, "I'm gay, Howard." In three simple words the frustration and anxiety of almost fifteen years melted into oblivion. No explosion, no scream, no protest. Everything is indeed nothing.

"I know," Howard answered. "I've always known but I refused to acknowledge it and my denial had nothing to do with you, son, it was my problem I refused to face."

"Your problem?"

Howard nodded. "When your mother died I refused to think about remarrying because I thought it would upset you. And, at first, it was true. But when you had gotten over the loss I still used you as an excuse because I didn't want to share you with anyone else."

"Don't, Howard," Ken cut in. "It's not necessary, not now. Let's forget about it."

"But it is necessary, Kenny. Understand that. No more running from our emotions." Howard reached for a cigarette. "My reaction was perfectly normal. I had lost someone I loved and I wanted to replace her with someone we both loved, someone who was a part of her and me. That day I caught you masturbating. . . do you remember that?"

"I've never forgotten it," Ken said.

"If I had been a lesser person," Howard laughed sarcastically, "I would have had you physically that afternoon." He stood up and turned on the bedside lamp. His face looked peaceful in the warm glow of the light.

"I thought about that, Howard. . . a lot." Ken whispered.

"What we should have done. . . no, what I should have done was discuss it with you. We had both suffered a loss and we both needed someone to touch in our grief. It was all perfectly normal but I ran from it and allowed it to become a monster. I was afraid to love you because I thought I would love you too much and I didn't want anyone else to love you. . . especially not another man."

"Why are we so afraid of love, Dad?"

"Because civilization, bless it, has taken the verb to love and broken it down into a hundred non-existent parts. Mother love, father love, brother love, wife love ad nauseam. Bullshit. There's only one verb to love and it means the same thing regardless of its recipient. We must know where and when to draw the line into the physical but certainly we should never be ashamed of what lies beyond the line. That shame that we suppress when we say we are rising above nature is exactly what reduces us to the status of animals. Ugly animals. It caused me to be jealous of a very brilliant and beautiful son."

Ken did nothing to stop the tears from rolling down his face. "I love you."

Howard once again sat on Ken's bed and kissed his son's wet cheek, his hand trying to make some order of the blond hair that fell limply over Ken's head. "You see, I can do that now with no shame or fear or guilt. I'm more of a man than I've ever been."

"I feel so... so relieved, Howard. Free. It's like meeting yourself for the first time and actually liking you. And all it took was a little honest talk."

"I've been telling my patients that for twenty years and I finally followed my own advice. I'm one hell of a psychologist."

They laughed and the tension was broken. They were both back on a normal footing but they knew that a bond now existed between them that was as solid as steel and as pliable as a feather.

"Howard. You and Alice... if that's what you want..."

"No, Kenny, it's not what I want. It was just another excuse to prove myself. More bullshit. But I didn't use her, Ken. She's not a child and I never promised her more than I was willing to give."

"I'm sure you didn't. But I think she's hung up on you."

"That'll straighten itself out. No, Kenny, if I remarry, and I just might, it will be to a woman closer to my own age and one who doesn't know the meaning of the word psychology." They laughed again, then Howard looked at Ken and asked, "What about you?"

"What about me?" Ken turned away; Howard took hold of Ken's chin and forced him to look at his father.

"You're stuck on the rich kid, eh?"

Ken shrugged. "It's a one-way street. In case you haven't noticed, Scott's fully occupied by Mr. Beautiful."

"Kenny, my boy, if your hair would stay in place and if your legs were a little shorter and if your nose was a little less tilted upward you would be just as handsome as Mike Armstrong."

"Fuck you, Howard."

"Scott has a lot of problems, Kenny."

"My first got married and my second is headed for a padded cell. Maybe I should get my nose fixed, eh?"

Howard stood up. "That's my boy. Never lose your sense of humor and life will never defeat you." He started to unbutton his shirt. "Just remember what I told you. No matter how you feel about Scott, don't get involved until we're out of this house." He turned and walked into the bathroom. A minute later Ken heard the sound of the shower as he pulled the quilt over his head.

The icy rain beat madly on the glass panes and Ken thought about his clandestine meeting with Alice Miller set for that very night. "Well, it's not really getting involved. It's just having a look."

• XXI •

They assembled in the salon, as usual, on their last night in China House. A fire blazed in the hearth, its dancing flames the only cheerful note in the huge, opulent room. These five people who had come to the majestic dwelling in the middle of a snow storm, not knowing what they would find, were now in a mild state of shock because they had discovered themselves. Ken's eyes were on Michael Armstrong.

The young man with the raven black hair and blue eyes and the face of a god mixed their cocktails. He did that well, as he did other things well, like playing backgammon and amusing those about him and performing well in bed, especially when what he gave was so amply rewarded. Michael took life as he found it, only twisting it here and there, as he would alter a pair of jeans, to suit his taste. Had he, or would he one day, twist too hard and cause genuine harm? Michael looked upon the world the only way he knew how to look at anything: in the light of his own needs.

He loved Scott. Or did he love the Evans name? No, it was Scott. That's why Michael had left; to prove himself and return to his friend as an equal. But things had not turned out as he planned they would. When Scott called for him, Mike had returned and found his boyhood friend a bewildered and despondent young man. So Michael had given up his quest for fame and fortune and had remained with Scott because he loved him and Scott so desperately needed Michael Armstrong.

It was a pretty story, a story of self-sacrifice and nobility, and it appealed to the writer in Kenneth Roth. "Life, Ken, is not a romantic novel." Was Howard right? Could Michael Armstrong never love anyone but himself? Ken hoped not for the sake of. . . .

Scott Evans accepted his drink with a smile and a thank you that formed on his lips but never became audible. Had he ever failed to say thank you? Had he always been grateful, even humble, to any kind gesture shown him? In fact he was always amazed that anyone would want to be kind to him. He didn't deserve it. But why? He always went out of his way to be good so that he would be deserving, but the harder he tried the more unworthy he felt.

He was a tragic figure and tragedy surrounded him and engulfed those he touched — especially those he loved. John Summers was dead and all Scott had done was what the teacher wanted him to do. Scott had given himself freely and happily. It was later that the boy had felt remorse, then guilt. It had all been so easy, so daring, when it was happening. But when the school term ended and Scott had time to reflect upon the situation he had felt uneasy and undaring and cheap. He never wanted to see John Summers again and he never did.

When Scott learned of the teacher's death he remembered, very vividly, the death of his tutor. Why had he disliked the man? Scott had no idea but thought it was because his parents had replaced Tom with the stern guardian. "Take him away, Tom, and then you can come back," the child had thought. And then the tragedy occurred. Scott knew it was a tragedy because that's what his mother had called it.

And then Scott knew, although he did try to suppress the idea, that it was Tom who had caused both deaths. Tom, the one who had died while Scott had been allowed to live. Tom, who was not protective but envious of Scott. Tom, who would never allow anyone to take his place in Scott's life. So Scott had not tried to stop Mike when Mike left to try his luck on the west coast. Scott knew that away from him Michael would be safe. But how lonely he had been those years when Michael was not with him. So he asked Mike to come back so together they could confront Tom, implore him, do battle if necessary and end, once and for all this hell on earth.

To do this Scott knew he would have to return to China House. But he would need help. He would need someone who would understand. Someone who was trained in the strange and little-known world of the human mind and its awesome powers. And then he had come upon the writings of. . . .

Howard Roth sipped his drink as if he were taking medication. He had no desire for the liquor but thought it would do him

good. Lift his spirits or drown them, he didn't really care which.
He only wanted to escape, to get out of China House and away
from these people. He wanted to be with Ken, safe, in their own
home. For so long he had harbored the thought that Ken was a
threat to his misplaced sense of masculinity that he had actually
been trying to thwart his son's growth as a person and an artist.
What other thoughts had he allowed to fester in his mind? "When
we dwell upon something we begin a series of actions, consciously
or unconsciously, that cause the thought to become reality."
Howard was certain of his theory but uncertain as to when the
thought began to act of its own volition, without the aid or
consent of the thinker. "This house has a way of making our
thoughts become a reality." He had to get Ken out of China
House. And after he did that he had to start thinking about. . . .

Alice Miller was being the life of the party on this particular
evening which, all things considered, was an easy title to claim
among the solemn group gathered in the grand salon of China
House. The others thought carefully before they spoke and then
measured each word carefully lest it cause a jarring note or, worse,
force the subject of China House itself to rise to the surface of
their mundane conversation.

But not Alice. She was as carefree and gay this evening as she
was usually shy and retiring. When conversation lagged Alice
came right to the fore, jibbering away and moving about like an
actress performing on an elaborate set made especially for her
talents. And, for a few embarrassing moments, she even flirted
with Michael and Scott.

Alice had indeed come into her own. She was no longer going
to be the small town girl with the mousy appearance whose name
people forgot and more often than not referred to as Dr. Roth's
assistant. It was time they all knew that she was a person in her
own right and one to contend with. She was more than Howard
Roth's assistant, much more. And why shouldn't everyone, including Howard's son, know that? She was tired of being taken for
granted, especially by Howard. Did he think she would always be
at his beck and call in the office, in the car, minutes snatched like
thieves in her apartment? She had come to China House as a fifth
wheel but had every intention of leaving as one of a pair.

Dinner was over, a fact for which everyone but Alice offered
up a silent prayer of thanksgiving. All that remained was to clear
the table and do the dishes, then they could each politely feign

tiredness and retire for the evening. Tomorrow they would leave China House and no one wanted to think beyond that. Like prisoners counting the minutes to freedom they thought only of getting out. They would cope with their future when it presented itself and not a moment sooner.

Ken had come to a firm decision. He would not keep his appointment with Alice and he intended to tell her so as soon as he could get her alone for a minute. He pushed himself away from the table, announcing that the meal was over, and was in the middle of volunteering himself and Alice for clean-up detail when China House made it known that it was by no means finished with its visitors.

At first they thought the loud pounding sounds were caused by a sudden intensity in the wind that had been blowing steadily all evening.

"A shutter must have come loose," Mike said, looking at Scott.

Everyone was now looking at Scott Evans. Was that young man to be blamed for every disquieting moment in China House?

When the pounding sound continued all heads turned to the yawning expanse of the dining room doorway. The sound was not that of a loose shutter but an insistent throbbing that seemed concentrated on one particular spot of the house.

"I think someone is at the front door." It was a perfectly ordinary and logical statement and Alice tried to deliver the line in a perfectly ordinary manner which, in China House, made it sound like the most extraordinary explanation possible.

"At this time of night and in the middle of an ice storm?" Howard's eyes were on Kenneth.

"It *is* the front door," Mike said, standing, "and I think someone should answer it."

"I'll go." Scott now stood up and placed a restraining hand on Mike's shoulder.

"We'll all go," Howard ordered.

They all walked out of the room together. It was Michael who saw the humorous picture they made as they crowded the doorway at the same time. "Maybe we should take this show to Broadway and call it Four Jacks and A Jill."

By now there was no mistaking the sound. Someone was pounding on the front door of China House late in the night and in the middle of an ice storm. Mike pressed forward and undid the heavy bolt. All eyes were on the door as it swung open and what they beheld was no more exotic than two men dressed like Eskimos, their red and wet faces surrounded by the fur trim of their hooded coats.

"I'm Detective Parker," the taller of the two shouted. "This is Sergeant Smith. Can we come in?"

Mike stepped aside and the two men, along with a cold gust of wind, entered the hall of China House. Mike pushed the door closed and pressed his back against it as if afraid the strong wind would blow it open once again. His blue eyes contemplated the backs of the two hooded men who now stood facing Scott Evans and his three guests.

"Sorry to bother you but we got trouble," the one who had introduced himself as Parker spoke.

"I'm Scott Evans. What's the problem?"

"How do you do, Mr. Evans." The man looked at the others.

"This is Dr. Roth and his son, Kenneth, and Miss Alice Miller and Mr. Armstrong. They're my guests."

Parker and Smith nodded at each introduction, even turning to acknowledge Michael. "Did you know Harvey Billingsly?"

"Mr. Billingsly," Ken exclaimed. "Has something happened to Mr. Billingsly?"

Smith, for the first time, spoke. "Yes sir, you might say that. He's dead."

· XXII ·

Ken felt Howard's fingers dig into his shoulders.

"But we saw him just this afternoon," Scott answered. "Has there been an accident?"

"Depends on what you call an accident. The old man was strangled by a very powerful pair of hands."

If Smith's crude pronouncement was meant to draw a meaningful response from his audience he was disappointed. Five blank and immobile faces stared at the intruders in silence.

Ken did not know how or when they all moved from the front hall to the salon. He only knew that when he was once again aware of his surroundings they were all in the main room, the two policemen warming themselves by the fire as Scott poured a generous amount of Scotch into two glasses and gave the drinks to Parker and Smith. Ken's only thought at the moment was that in all the detective fiction he had ever read the police always declined an offer of liquor when on duty. But in fiction how often did the police call on an isolated mansion in sub-freezing weather? Parker tossed down his drink in one quick motion, licked his lips and proceeded to answer a question Ken had not heard Scott ask.

"It was Harry Blake who put us on to it, Mr. Evans. You know Blake?"

"Only by name," Scott said. "He keeps an eye on China House for us."

Parker nodded. "So I've heard." He made the comment in a tone that implied that Harry Blake would be the last person the detective would employ in such a capacity. "He and Billingsly were old buddies. Both about the same age, I guess. They generally saw each other every day, weather permitting, and when it didn't permit they'd keep up by phone. Seems Blake called Billingsly about seven this evening and when he didn't get an answer he figured the other was sleeping or had stepped out for some fresh air. He called a half hour later and still didn't get an answer. When the same thing happened right up to nine o'clock Blake called us and asked us to go take a look. Nothing unusual. Old man, all alone, toting too much firewood in this here weather can go just like that." Parker looked at Smith who quickly nodded his agreement.

How unaffected they are by murder, Ken thought, or are they just imitating the dozens of television detectives they undoubtedly watch weekly? When were they going to tell who did it?

"Who did it?" Mike asked to Ken's relief.

Both policemen looked at Mike Armstrong and Smith answered the question. "Ain't got no idea. Do you?"

"A tramp. Some crazy kids high on pot. How the hell should I know? I only saw the man once in my life and never even spoke to him."

"Was anything taken?" Howard asked, unable to hide the note of hope in his question.

"Nope." Parker again. "An' no sign of a forced entry either. The old man opened his door to whoever did him in." It was now obvious that Parker's rank entitled him to answer questions that required more than a one sentence answer. He was also the better speaker of the pair, a fact he seemed to know, and was careful to direct himself almost exclusively to Scott Evans. In rural America the concept of the country squire was not a thing of the past.

"An' you can forget about tramps an' crazy kids," Parker continued. "In the first place there ain't nobody, sane or crazy, walking around in this weather. In the second place, far as we can tell this time of night there ain't but one set of tracks coming up the hill an' from the size of 'em I would say they were made by that big caddy you got parked out front. If someone came up the hill to murder the old man he floated up like a ghost."

The listeners, painfully, avoided looking at Scott. Clearly the police did not know who had murdered Mr. Billingsly and were in China House to question its inhabitants. Ken felt sick to his stomach and again panic, the irrational desire to flee, assaulted his chest. The feeling seemed to be a specialty of China House.

It was unthinkable. He, Kenneth Roth, was a murder suspect. They were all murder suspects. Until that moment the house had only made them question their lifelong beliefs. Now it threatened to expose one of them as a brutal murderer. But Ken had seen Mr. Billingsly alive not seven hours ago, they had all seen him and none of them had left the house since returning from the inn. It couldn't possibly be one of them. Ken was so relieved by his deduction that he quickly, and a little hysterically, blurted out the fact to the two men who stood politely with their backs to the fire.

"That's why we're here, Mr. Roth," Parker answered Ken's outburst. "What we want is a timetable of events. Doc figures the old man's been dead about four or five hours, making the time of death say six or seven this evening."

"We were with Mr. Billingsly—"

"Excuse me, Ken," Scott broke in, "I think if one of us gives Mr. Parker an account of the day it would be easier for him to get all the facts straight." And, he didn't add, Mr. Parker would not dare refute or try to cross examine the master of China House.

"It would," Parker agreed. "Go ahead, Mr. Evans."

Scott looked pale but his voice was surprisingly calm and strong as he detailed the events of the day for Detective Parker and Sergeant Smith.

"Shortly after noon Mr. Armstrong and I drove the car to Salem to fill the tank and test the roads. We intend to leave China House tomorrow morning. Mr. Ken Roth and Miss Miller skied down the hill to the inn and had lunch with Mr. Billingsly. On our way back from town we picked them up from the inn and I even spoke briefly to Mr. Billingsly before we came back here. Mr. Billingsly was fine when we left him and none of us has been out of the house since then."

Ken felt better when Scott restated that final fact. He looked at the detective apprehensively but Parker was looking at Howard Roth. "I've not left the house all day," Howard volunteered before Parker had a chance to ask.

Smith had taken a notebook from the pocket of his coat and was laboriously taking notes. The husky, red-faced man made an incongruous secretary.

"What time did you leave the inn?" Parker asked.

"About four," Ken spoke up. "I'm very sure of that."

"And what did you all do when you got back here?"

Alice, who seemed to have lost the vitality she had flaunted so generously that evening, spoke for the first time since the arrival of the police. "I made a fire, in here, and read for a while. Then

I went upstairs to rest and later washed and dressed for dinner. I came out of my room just as Ken and Howard were leaving theirs. We came down together."

"Yes, that's right," Ken said. "I went directly to my room where Howard, my father, was sleeping. I bathed and rested and we both came down here for cocktails, with Miss Miller, at about seven-thirty."

There was a pause, all eyes on Sergeant Smith, as if none of them wanted to get too far ahead of the unlikely scribe.

"I went to my room," Scott said, "and Mike came with me. We talked for a while and when Mike left I slept for an hour or so before showering and coming downstairs."

"When I left Scott I did the same thing," Mike quickly added.

Smith closed his notebook and with a sinking feeling Ken realized exactly what Smith and Parker were thinking. They had been out of each other's sight for an hour or more after returning from the inn. He and Howard had been together but who would believe a father and son testifying for each other? None of them had an alibi for the time Harvey Billingsly was murdered. But none of them had a motive either, Ken quickly reasoned. Surely one needed a reason, and a strong one, to willfully commit murder. Only a madman would. . . . Again the sick feeling came to the pit of Ken's stomach and again he felt the compulsion to look at Scott Evans.

Scott had walked about China House, talking to all of them, the day of their arrival and later swore he did no such thing. And it had to be Scott who walked about at night, too, making strange noises, and he didn't know he did that either. What else did Scott do that they, or he, knew nothing of? Howard had realized almost immediately that Scott Evans was extremely neurotic, obsessed by the idea of the dead returning to haunt the living. But how long had the young man been having these black-outs, or whatever they might be called, and what was he capable of during these episodes?

Had the teacher from Ryder Prep been alone when his boat, for no apparent reason, tossed him to his death? Long Island Sound. The Evanses had a house in Southampton. Surely they owned a boat. Perhaps several. Did the tutor just step in front of a taxi while crossing Fifth Avenue? Accidents? Coincidences?

When we dwell upon a thought we often begin a series of actions, sometimes consciously, more often unconsciously, that cause the thought to become reality. Not by magic but by very real human effort.

And Ken knew how the murder could have been committed. In fact it was amateurishly simple. The inn was about a mile, downhill, from the house. It had taken him and Alice less than five minutes to reach it on skis. It would take a strong young man less than half an hour to walk back up the hill, especially if he were properly outfitted with skis and poles. Forty minutes, at most, there and back, and Scott, all of them actually, had been by themselves for well over an hour.

If Ken realized all of this so did the police. No doubt they had figured it out the minute they saw the ski tracks in the snow leading from China House to the inn.

"That's it for now," Parker was saying. "I take it you folks won't be leaving tomorrow."

Very subtly put and, they all knew, because of Scott Evans and all the Evans name implied. Were Scott not with them they would have just been told, in no uncertain terms, not to leave China House until the police had finished with them.

"No, we won't be leaving until this is all cleared up," Scott assured the two men as he followed them to the door.

"You've all been very helpful," Parker said with a slight bow to his audience. Smith nodded his agreement with a backward glance as the two left the room.

"Those bastards think one of us—"

"Shut up, Mike, they can hear you," Howard cautioned.

"So what? I'm not afraid. We have nothing to be afraid of."

"Don't we?" Howard began but cut himself short when he saw Scott reenter the room.

"They'll be back tomorrow," Scott announced. "They should know more by then and they'll want formal statements from us about our moves this afternoon. Anyone for a drink?"

Every eye in the room was on Scott but none answered his invitation. He could have been an actor in a play, speaking on an empty stage before an interested but uninvolved audience.

"I think we've all had enough and I see no reason to sit up half the night rehashing something we all know nothing about. We've all been shocked by this and the best thing we can do is try to get some rest and discuss it among ourselves in the morning. And I'm sure the police will have it all solved by then."

"Amen," Ken sighed to himself when Howard had spoken.

Scott, who had been perfectly calm since the news of the murder, suddenly turned from the bar and addressed all of them in a voice that betrayed his true feelings. "Everything I touch turns to shit. Everyone who comes near me dies."

"Take it easy, Scotty."

"Let me handle this, Mike. Scott, come with me." Howard extended his hand toward Scott Evans.

"All I did was talk to him." Scott was sobbing now. "All I did was say a few words to an old man and now he's dead. Murdered."

Howard walked directly to Scott and put his arm around the younger man. "Come with me, Scott. We'll go to your room and talk for a while and then you're going to sleep. It'll all look better in the morning, I promise you it will." He led the crying Scott from the room as the others silently stared at the departing pair.

"Did I do it, Dr. Roth? Am I responsible for this, too? Or is it just another coincidence in the life of Scott Evans. Help me, Howard. . . Oh, Christ, somebody please help me."

Ken buried his face in his hands and Mike quickly stepped forward and shook Ken by the shoulders. "Come on, Kenny, that's not going to help anything. What we have to do now, all of us, is try to help Scotty."

"What do you mean?" Alice asked. Of all of them Alice looked the most uncomfortable but whether this was due to the old man's murder, Scott's pathetic departure from the salon or something completely unrelated to either remained a mystery to Ken.

"You know damn well what I mean," Mike all but hissed at Alice and Ken was shocked to discover a side of Mike Armstrong he had never seen before. "Scotty has been acting crazy ever since we got here and if he left the house after we got back from the inn—"

"But we don't know that he did," Ken objected.

"What odds would you give me?" Mike shot back.

"Well I think we should learn the truth," Alice said, "and we shouldn't leave here until we do." Alice looked directly at Ken as she spoke.

Ken avoided Alice's gaze. "Let's let the police discover the truth." Ken knew exactly what Alice had meant by learning the truth. The truth concerning the nursery, not the murder. But the two were now intrinsically linked and knowing who kept a nightly vigil in the nursery of China House was no longer a matter of curiosity or of trying to help Scott Evans, but an essential step in solving a senseless crime.

As if in answer to Ken's silent thoughts Alice again reiterated her ideas on the subject. "A murder has been committed and like it or not we're all implicated in the crime. I have no intention of leaving the discovery of the truth to those two so-called policemen. Why, they'll keep us locked up here all winter while they play Hercule Poirot."

Michael smiled his best condescending smile. "I don't think, Alice, that the misters Parker and Smith have ever read Agatha Christie. Elliot Ness and Columbo, yes, Hercule Poirot, no."

So Michael was once again his old self, Ken thought. It irritated him. He was beginning to notice that Michael was always at his best when confronting other people's woes. And Alice was right. Another irritating fact. "I think we should discuss it among ourselves in the morning as Howard suggested and I'm sure my father will have some suggestions on what to do at this point."

"I second that motion," Mike put in, "so let's follow the good doctor's advice and call it a night."

"I'll never be able to sleep tonight," Alice said.

That's it, Ken thought. The final confirmation of tonight's escapade. Alice must actually devour Agatha Christie novels.

"We'll just leave the dishes and stuff till the morning," Mike said, ushering them from the room. As they walked past him Ken caught Alice's eye. Alice nodded almost without moving her head. The meeting was on.

Tonight or never.

• XXIII •

They stood as still as statues, the room a silent tomb. Even the fire
which blazed steadily in the hearth made no sound as it caressed
the logs it devoured, taking their life to sustain its own until both
would cease to exist because there was nothing left to give or take.
The winter wind which had made itself heard all evening was now
hushed as if it dared not disturb the drama that was about to
unfold in the grand salon of China House.

Ken wanted to speak but knew no sound would come from his
throat if he tried. Howard's face was a white mask. Alice's red lips
were parted, stuck somewhere between a smile and a cry of agony.
Scott stood facing the double doors of the salon as Michael's hand
held his friend's arm in a firm grip.

It was a scene from a film frozen on a single frame.

The first one landed on the marble floor in the center hall.
They could not see it but they all heard it. The sound was sharp
and clear and unmistakable. Marble striking marble. The little
ball bounced twice and then rolled.

Still no one moved. They knew there were more to come.
Even now the balls advanced like a silent army down the carpeted
steps. Then they struck, one after the other, then two and three at
a time, echoing in the high vaulted hall and filling the house with
a timbre that was out of all proportion to the size of the tiny balls.

Ken covered his ears with his hands.

Scott shook Mike's arm from his elbow and, with an air of
confidence, marched to the sliding doors which he pulled apart,
then he turned to his guests, a look of triumph on his face as he
pointed to the hall floor which was now covered with the small,
iridescent balls.

"We know you're up there, Tom," Scott shouted, his voice ringing with an authority the others had never before heard.

They clustered together and then advanced as a group to a few feet from where Scott was standing.

"Come down here, Tom," Scott demanded. "Stop playing games. We're not children anymore. Come down, Tom, and stand beside me. Side by side for the benefit of Dr. Roth."

Howard was the only one among them who did not seem to have any idea of what was happening. He looked at Scott and then at the marbles which still moved about the floor, their bright hues flashing and dying as they rolled.

An upstairs door slammed shut. They moved closer together except for Michael who took a step forward. "No, Mike," Scott held up his hand. "It's me he wants and I have to face him alone. I've waited twenty years for this. Twenty long years."

It began moving down the steps. From where they stood only the lower half of the staircase was visible and they stared at it, breathing as one, waiting for it to appear. The marbles came to rest and the hall clock began to chime.

Scott moaned as the two small feet, clad in white shoes, appeared above their heads; then the little legs, bare, only able to descend the high treads by taking them one at a time. Slowly it came. The short pants and the child's hand gripping the rail.

"Not you," Scott whispered. "Not you," he repeated, louder, and then again and again and louder and louder as the little boy's shirt and arms and torso materialized and the short legs quickened their pace until finally the head, bashed and battered and covered with blood, one eye hanging form its socket and grotesque beyond all recognition, looked down at the horrified faces in the hall below.

Alice screamed and the child fled back up the steps as Scott darted after it. Now they all followed Scott, running in place, their feet slipping and sliding over the marble balls, their arms waving in the air and their legs as useless as rubber stilts.

"Wait," Scott screamed. "Please wait." And they all joined in, chanting, as they tried in vain to cross the moving floor.

"Wait. . . Wait. . . Wait. . . ."

Ken opened his eyes, his body drenched in sweat, his arms extended upward, the word 'wait' echoing in his head. "Christ," he mumbled, as every horrific detail of his dream flashed before his eyes. He brought his arms slowly down to his sides, his breathing gradually returning to normal. Damn Alice, he thought. Her stupid midnight caper was the cause of the worst nightmare he had ever had. And then he was fully awake, remembering that on this particular night he wasn't supposed to have fallen asleep at all. He pushed the dream from his mind as his fingers felt for the book of matches he had left, along with his watch, on the small night table. He had planned well, if somewhat reluctantly, for his adventure.

He struck a match. Eleven-fifty. Alice was expecting him one hour after they had all gone to bed and that had been about eleven, just after the police had left. The police. He had forgotten all about that and the thought descended upon him like a weight crashing against his chest. He eased himself out of bed, shivering, and struggled into his robe in the dark. It was amazing how cold the house became at night. The icy, numbing cold somehow seemed inhuman.

None of that, Ken thought. Not now. I'm going out there and getting this over and done with as fast as possible. A straight line would take him to the door. How well he remembered that. There, that was something else not to think about. He must just do what he had to do. Act. Not think. His hand touched the heavy oak. He felt for the knob. It was cold as ice. He twisted and opened the door a crack.

First came a rush of even colder air than that which engulfed the bedroom. He pushed the door closed, tightened the sash of his robe and brought the collar closer about his throat. He knew he was procrastinating but indulged himself nonetheless. When he opened the door again he was fully prepared for the blast of frigid air that greeted him but not for the black silence that met his gaze. Only the ticking of the hall clock, louder than ever in the still house, was audible.

Doesn't that thing ever unwind, he thought. And why the hell hadn't Alice left her door open a crack, with a light on, to guide him across the hall. God, Alice was stupid.

Well, again it was a straight line across the wide hall. The staircase was to the right of Alice's door as Ken faced it and the nursery to the left. Scott's and Mike's bedrooms were on the other side of the stairs so he had no fear of disturbing them and he had just left Howard sound asleep and knew that his father could remain in that state through a war. Ken took a deep breath, shivered slightly, then sticking both arms straight out he began to cross the hall.

Suppose he should touch something? His skin crawled. Stupid. There was nothing to fear but fear itself. Great, what other uplifting and meaningless phrases did he know? It was so cold and that damn clock so loud it could wake the dead. Ken froze. Why the hell had he thought of that? He imagined the Commodore's stern face. No, not him. Please, God, not him. Did the Commodore walk the halls of China House, placing a light in the window from time to time, keeping guard over his priceless possessions and scaring off those who tried to break the sanctity of his home? No, he was happily at rest under one of his hard-ons. Ken smiled at the thought and felt better.

Screw this. He would return to his room and the warmth of his bed and the comforting sound of Howard's snores. In one quick motion he would retrace his steps and rid himself, once and for all, of this foolish nightmare. In the morning they would tell the police everything and let them deal with the whole bloody mess. End the final chapter, cover the typewriter and go back to whatever awaited Howard and him in Sea-Air.

But in the morning he would also have to face Scott.

Ken continued. Step by step. The hall was wide but certainly not this wide. Would he never come to Alice's door? Was he destined to walk for eternity, his arms stretched out before him like a sleepwalker, seeking and never finding his goal? Was he dead and this his hell?

The tips of his fingers touched a hard, wood surface. Quickly he reached for the knob and turned, anticipating the light and warmth within. He pushed and nothing happened. He twisted and pushed and still nothing happened.

The door was locked. Alice had locked her door. That just wasn't possible. Alice was stupid but surely she wasn't mad. Or was it Ken who was mad? Or perhaps all of them were mad and China House their asylum.

He couldn't knock and wake the entire house. How would he explain himself if someone heard? What he wanted was to pound on the heavy door and yell at the foolish woman behind it. Knowing he could do neither he shrugged in despair and turned to begin the dark trip back to his own room. He took one step and paused. Had he heard something or was it his imagination? Maybe it was Alice, coming to open the door. He waited. It came again, this time stronger and in his stomach he knew what it was.

A child, crying. The sound forlorn and pathetic; it was not deep enough to possibly come from Scott

Ken cringed, falling back against the door, one hand scratching its smooth surface, the other twisting the big brass knob.

Now it was sobbing, the sound that of a lost soul adrift in a black void wailing and moaning its misery, pleading for someone to comfort it.

Ken tried to pray but what prayers he knew had fled from his head. His mind was filled with but one thought, to make it across the hall and into his own room. But Alice was closer. Just on the other side of the door. Why didn't Alice hear him? Why was the door locked? "Alice," Ken hit the door with his fist. "Open the goddamn door."

The sobbing grew louder. No, not louder, it was coming closer. It wasn't in the nursery, it was in the hall, walking up the passage, coming directly toward Ken. In a moment it would be between him and his bedroom. It on one side of him and a locked door on the other side. He had to cross the hall before it took another step.

His heart pounded in his chest. "Wait. . . Wait. . . Wait. . . ." His nightmare returned to haunt him, the child's feet on the steps and then the horrid, bloody head looking over the banister.

Now Ken wanted to shout and wake the entire household, to wake the world if necessary, but panic gripped his chest, squeezing it until he had to gasp for air. His throat was paralyzed. "Flee." It was the only thought in his head now. "Flee."

He began to move, the only way he could, down the hall and away from the approaching sobbing little boy. He clung to the wall until there was no wall to cling to. Back and back and back, his arms flayed the air. His foot touched something small and round.

His scream, loud and terrifying, pierced the cold black night. His legs flew upward, the long robe he wore became a straitjacket for his body. He screamed again. His shoulder hit the top step and then, miraculously, his mind went as black as the void which surrounded him.

· XXIV ·

For almost a full half-minute the upstairs hall remained dark and silent. Then a door opened, sending a shaft of light across the oriental carpet. Michael, tall and straight, stood in the flood of light fastening his robe.

"Who's there?" he called. "What's going on?"

Another door opened and more light filled the hall. Howard, his face swollen with sleep, struggled to get into his robe. "Ken?"

"Howard?" Michael stepped into the hall. "Did you hear a scream?"

"Ken is missing. Is he out here? Have you seen him?"

"Take it easy, Howard, there's no one out here. I'll get the lights."

Michael found the panel of switches and flicked them all on. "Holy shit," he exclaimed. "Marbles. The floor is covered with them. What the hell is going on?" Howard started for the stairs. "Don't try to walk, Howard. I'll go down and see if Ken is there." He carefully made his way to the stairs and started down. "Oh, no," he cried.

"What do you see? Is it Ken? Where is he?"

Michael was halfway down the staircase when Howard tore past him, pushing the younger man aside as he lunged down the steps. "Christ, Howard, take it easy. You'll end up in the same heap down there and what the hell good would that do Kenny?"

Howard jumped the last few steps, hitting the floor and falling to his knees in one motion. "Ken? Ken? Can you hear me?"

"Is he—" Michael was standing over them.

"No. Thank God, no. He's breathing and I don't see any blood, but who knows what's going on inside." Howard picked up Ken's hand. "He's freezing. Mike, get a blanket, quick."

"Should we carry him to the couch?"

"No. I want to make sure nothing is broken."

Michael looked up the long flight of steps. "The carpet saved his life. If it wasn't for the carpet—"

"I know. Ken... Ken... can you hear me?"

Another cry, distinctly female, drew their attention and both men looked up. "Howard, what happened? The floor is filled with little balls." Alice held fast to the banister post at the top of the staircase. "I thought I heard someone scream. Is it Ken?"

At that moment Scott appeared at the head of the staircase. Clad in his brief undershorts and T-shirt he looked like a little boy grown out of proportion to his clothes. He seemed oblivious to Alice who stood a few feet from him, but stared down the steps at the limp body being attended to by Howard and Michael. He took one step down and then sat, his elbows on his knees, his trance-like gaze never leaving the body stretched out on the floor below. Then he began to whimper softly.

"Scotty," Mike whispered.

"I did it," Scott was sobbing. "I did it and they never told me. And I did it again. Look, I did it again."

Scott, still sobbing, began to play with the marbles that surrounded him.

Howard thought he would go mad. His only concern was for Ken but he was finding it impossible to tend to his son as the others began to fall apart around him. And something else was wrong. As his mind raced between the hurt man on the floor beside him and the grown man who now acted like a little boy on the landing above him, Howard realized that something had happened inside China House which had nothing to do with Ken's accident or Scott Evans. What was it?

"Howard, what should we do?" Alice moaned.

"Scotty... he's gone off the deep end, Howard. What should we do?" Mike joined in.

It was a circus and Howard felt like the star attraction. It took all his strength to take control, first of himself and then the others.

"Alice, get a blanket from your bedroom and bring it down here at once." He turned to the gawking man who knelt beside him. "Go to Scott, now. Get something warm to cover him with and put him to bed. And pick up those goddamn marbles. Now! Move!"

Alice disappeared from the landing and Mike raced silently up the carpeted steps. The only sound came from Scott, still sobbing as Mike led him away. Then the house was still.

"That's it," Howard mumbled.

He raised his eyes slowly from Ken to the base of the big clock inches from where Ken lay. He looked up at the round face with its delicate inlaid design. From Howard's kneeling position the clock towered over him. The hands stood, one atop the other, straight up. The pendulum was at rest. The heart of China House had stopped beating.

"Howard." The sound was barely audible.

"I'm here, Kenny." Howard squeezed his son's hand.

"I'm so afraid, Howard."

"There's nothing to be afraid of, Kenny. Not any more. It's all over."

Ken's eyes closed and he slipped back into unconsciousness.

Alice came down the steps carrying a blanket. Silently she knelt opposite Howard and covered Ken's body with the quilt but to Howard's horror she pulled the cover up and over Ken's face.

"Christ, Alice, he's not dead." Howard tore the quilt from his son's face.

"I'm sorry," Alice mumbled.

"Sorry that he's not dead." Howard's tone was cruel and accusing.

"No, sorry that I covered him... like that." They knelt, staring at each other over Ken's body, their faces not one foot apart. "You know what I meant," Alice whispered. "Why did you say that?"

Howard shook his head. "I'm sorry. I don't know what's wrong with me. This house. The old man murdered. And now Kenny. Alice, I can't take any more of this."

"Maybe you said it because you want him dead."

He stared at the woman he had made love to on countless occasions. The woman he delighted in seducing in his office, his car and even under the roof of this cursed house. "Damn you, Alice. Damn you for saying that." Howard's face was distorted with anger.

"It's true, Howard, isn't it?"

"Shut up," his throat ached from straining to keep his voice above a whisper.

"I won't shut up."

"You will, and right now. It's over between us, Alice. And after we leave this house I never want to see you again."

Alice began to sob and Ken again regained consciousness. The whispered shouts had not aroused him but Alice's low, moaning sobs had. There was a look of terror in Ken's eyes as he tried to raise his body from the floor. "Howard."

"Don't move, Ken, just try to flex your muscles, as many of them as you can." Howard spoke rapidly, fearing that Ken would once again drift off to sleep. "Can you do it?" Ken nodded. "Good. Do you feel any pain, any place?"

Ken shook his head. "No, Howard, but I can't keep my eyes opened."

"Don't," Howard answered. "I'm going to lift you and carry you up to our room."

"Why is Alice crying?"

"She's upset," Howard said. "Now be quiet and don't even try to think."

Howard didn't know if he was more furious at himself or Alice. The little scene that had just been enacted beneath the stilled clock of China House had left him confused to the point of actually being disoriented as to time and place. He was unable to feel; he could only act, instinctively, and wait for his two selves to blend into a thinking, feeling, cohesive one.

The interminable ascent up the staircase began. Michael met them in the upstairs hall. "Let me help you, Howard."

Howard shook his head. "I'm okay. Just open the door for me, please." He carried Ken into the bedroom and carefully placed him on the bed.

"Do you want me to stay and help, Howard?" Alice asked.

Howard stiffened as Alice spoke. A kind offer from one we have just rejected is the most cutting of retorts. "No, thank you. I'll be fine. I think we should all try to get some rest." He looked at the two standing in the doorway and wondered vaguely how he had become so intimately involved with what were now two strangers.

"Scott is sleeping, Howard, but he's in a bad way," Mike offered, showing no sign of intending to leave the room. "He put those marbles on the floor and... and he said he killed old Billingsly."

Howard looked with total disinterest at Michael Armstrong. "Scott doesn't know what he's saying."

"Mr. Billingsly told us about the marbles. It was how the little boy was killed. Scott must have—" Alice's voice came to Howard from a million miles away. He pressed thumb and forefinger into his eyes until he could feel the pain deep within his head. "No more. Not now. Just go, please. Ken has to rest and so do I."

Either Howard's tone or the realization that he was in no condition to discuss anything finally moved Alice and Mike from the doorway and out of the Roth's bedroom. When the door closed Ken opened his eyes. "I heard them. It was Scott." The pained look on his son's face went straight to Howard's heart.

Damn them both, Howard thought. "I told you not to think," he said, touching Ken's head. "Just try to sleep, Kenny, for my sake if not your own." Howard sat on the bed and took Ken's hand into his own. He felt a weak response. "We'll talk in the morning." Suddenly he wanted to giggle at his own words. In the morning. There would be a talking marathon all over China House in the morning.

Ken closed his eyes and as Howard studied the now-peaceful face he thought of all the questions he wanted to ask his son. What was Ken doing out in the hall at midnight? What did Billingsly know and what did he tell his lunch guests? But all he could do was sit and hold Ken's hand until the boy fell asleep. Howard knew that Ken would remember nothing after falling down the steps. These moments of consciousness were nothing more than nervous reflexes, a response by rote rather than thought, and not a true awakening. Howard guessed that Ken had suffered a mild concussion, compounded by shock. Aside from a bad headache he would be fine in the morning.

When he was sure the boy was asleep he disengaged his hand and stood up. His back ached. He reached behind himself and rubbed, with both hands, just below the spine, then reached into his robe pocket for a cigarette. Just as he realized his cigarettes would not be there his hand touched what he thought was a piece of cardboard. He pulled the object from his pocket and even as he walked toward the lamp he knew what he was holding. With a steady hand he placed the picture under the light.

The beach at Sea-Air. The rocky jetty. The ocean lapping the feet of the little boy who once again grinned up at Howard Roth.

Howard studied the photo carefully but this time not a trace of nausea or fear or confusion accompanied the act. All he felt was numb. He put the photo back in his pocket and walked to Ken's bed. In the dim light, Ken's body stretched out before him Howard looked like a man praying at the bier of a loved one. And, for the second time since coming to China House he wept.

Then he felt Ken's hand, like a feather, touch the hem of his robe. "Howard... what's wrong?"

"I know, Kenny. God help me, I know everything."

• XXV •

Ken was sitting up in bed when Howard came out of the bathroom. "Alive and kicking," Howard said.

Ken looked at his father without moving his head. "Alive, pop, but not kicking. I tried to get out of bed but the floor kept climbing the wall."

"Just stay right where you are and you'll be doing fine in a few hours. Can I get you something to eat?"

Ken grimaced. "Please, don't even mention food."

"Sorry." Howard sat on his bed and faced his son. "Now, do you want to tell me just what the hell you were up to last night?"

"I feel like a fool."

"You are a fool."

"Don't rub it in, Howard, it hurts."

"I won't rub if you talk. And start from the beginning which, I suspect, goes back to something Mr. Billingsly told you and Alice yesterday afternoon."

Ken nodded and closed his eyes. "It hurts when I move my head."

"You don't have to move your head to talk, son, so start talking."

"My father is a monster."

"And my son is an ass."

Ken sighed, rolling his eyes upward, and began to relate everything, from lunch with Harvey Billingsly to his tumble down the majestic staircase of China House. When he was done he looked at his father sheepishly. "I'm sorry, Howard, I should have told you."

"Yes, you should have." Howard stood up. "So the mystery of

the marbles is solved... among other things. You realize it was the bag of marbles you were holding in the nursery the other day that caused Scott to become ill."

, "You don't have to be a psychologist to know that now. Had we known it two days ago my head would now be in one piece."

"I wouldn't be too sure of that, Kenneth," Howard answered.

"It's Scott, isn't it, Howard? He's behind everything. Crying in the nursery, the marbles on the floor... even old Billingsly." Ken closed his eyes as if in pain. When he opened them he saw his father standing by the window, rubbing his chin with his thumb. "Scott is sick, Dad, and he shouldn't be made to stand trial. You'll testify to that, won't you?"

Howard turned from the window as if he had not heard his son speak. "The police are swarming all over the inn and the hill. They should be here very shortly." Howard reached for his jacket. "I'm going downstairs, Kenny, and I want you to do nothing but rest. Understand?"

Ken nodded slowly.

"And, Ken, don't worry. Just trust your old man. Okay?"

Ken managed a smile. "I trust you, pop."

Mike Armstrong jumped out of his chair when Howard walked into the sun room. "How's Kenny?"

"A bad headache, but aside from that he'll live."

Mike smiled and Howard was awed, as intended, by the young man's beauty. "Alice was down and had some coffee, then she went back up to rest." Mike made a sound that was halfway between a grunt and a laugh. "This is the only place in the world where people have to rest five minutes after getting up in the morning."

"And Scott?" Howard asked.

"Still in his room. Howard, Scotty is... he's different."

"In what way?"

Mike shook his head. "I don't know if I can explain it. He's very quiet, withdrawn and he acts as if... well, as if he doesn't know me."

Howard touched the coffee pot which stood on the sideboard. "Good, it's still hot," he mumbled as he poured himself a cup. Mike watched him with a questioning look on his Adonis face.

"What do you think, Howard?"

"What do I think of what?"

"Scotty." There was a slight edge to Michael's tone.

Howard sipped from his cup. "I think, Michael, like everything else in China House, it's remarkable."

"What's remarkable, Doctor?" All trace of politeness was now gone from Mike Armstrong's voice.

"The fact," Howard began slowly, "that your lifelong friend, who knows you so well, suddenly doesn't know you at all and I, who hardly know you, suddenly know you very well." Howard drank more coffee. "That's what's remarkable, Michael."

"What the fuck are you talking about?"

"When in doubt use a four letter word," Howard smiled. He pulled the photograph out of his pocket and shoved it at Michael. "This is what the fuck I'm talking about."

Mike pushed Howard's hand away as he stared at the photo. "So, you found it."

Howard began to laugh. "You are a sensational actor, Mike. Truly sensational. Had you spent more time in Hollywood auditioning your acting talent instead of your sexual prowess a new star would have risen in the west."

It was once again open warfare between them and when Mike answered he made no attempt to hide his hostility. "You've been pussy-footing around since you walked into this room, Doctor, so if you have anything to say just say it and cut the bullshit."

"That's just what I intend to do. Why don't you sit down."

"I don't want to sit down."

Howard shrugged. "Then stand." Instead of looking at Mike he looked at the picture he still held in his hand. "I wasn't supposed to see this until last night. It turned up in my office by mistake, or by a bit of poor coordination, right?"

"I don't know what the fuck you're talking about." Mike reached for a cigarette, trying to act disinterested but failing miserably. A thin film of sweat appeared on his smooth forehead.

"You don't? Then I'll fill you in." Howard helped himself to more coffee. "Having seen the picture before, and then seeing it again last night, I realized at once it was the same little boy who greeted us on our arrival in China House. Who are they? An actor friend and his son?"

"I never saw them before in my life," Mike replied calmly.

"Now you cut the bullshit, young man. You posed Scott on that jetty in Sea-Air and then you posed the boy in the same position. You planted the photo in my robe pocket yesterday and I was supposed to find it after Scott Evans, not Kenny, lay dead at the foot of the staircase."

Mike Armstrong started out of the room.

"There's no place to run, Mike. The police are all over the hill."

"I don't want to listen to any more of your crap, Howard."

"You should. It might be a good thing for you to know exactly what I intend telling the police." Mike paused at the door and then reluctantly returned, still not sitting but staring at Howard with a look of pure hatred on his face.

"When I told you about seeing the little boy's photograph in my office I watched you closely and I could have sworn you were completely unaware of what I was talking about. And I was right, you were, because I wasn't supposed to see it until last night. You're a good actor, Michael, but not that good. Now let's go back to the beginning. The chauffeur's son. You knew how Scott's brother died. What is it called? Backstairs gossip. Servants know everything. I suppose, when you were a boy, you were cautioned never to mention the accident to Scott Evans and you didn't. But you never forgot it either.

"When you saw Scott again, two years ago, both adults, you realized how the memory of the accident he had blocked was festering in his mind. You didn't try to help him, rather you encouraged his illness. It gave you a strong hold over Scott but you wanted more, and last summer, when Scott started to take an interest in my work, you knew just how you were going to get more.

"Telling Scott he had taken a picture of a seascape and then substituting one you had taken of him on the jetty was child's play. It was what Scott wanted to believe. Giving me the picture and then having it alter itself was just a con, a con meant to confuse and mislead the players from the true purpose of your game. And I was the perfect patsy. Interested in the extra-sensory and given a chance to explore it first hand, you thought I would believe anything. And, God help me, I almost did. That little boy in the hall passage scared the hell out of all of us, and especially Scott who was now in the perfect frame of mind for his stay in China House and for the pill you somehow got into him a few hours later. What was it, Mike, secobarbital? You have a wide choice these days. Given Scott's state of mind and a hypnotic drug it was so easy for you to suggest to him that he was Tom and send him on his rounds to welcome his guests to China House. And when the drug wore off he wouldn't recall a thing. I should have known he was in a drug induced hypnotic state the moment he entered my bedroom. He looked at me as if he had never seen me before in his life and, believing he was Tom, he never had.

"And you led him to the nursery every night and encouraged him to play with the fire truck and the marbles and you made enough noise to be damn sure we all heard. More secobarbital, Mike, or was the poor bastard so mentally deteriorated you could now lead him around without the help of a drug? Each time you played down Scott's illness all you were really doing was drawing attention to it. You wanted me here for more practical purposes, as you so aptly put it. I was to be your star witness. I was to confirm that Scott was depressed and irrational. I was to state that Scott had killed himself in the same way he believed he had killed his brother.

"But you got fucked up along the way, Mike, eh? The picture of the kid turning up in my office was mistake number one. It gave me a lot of time to think about it and make the connection when I saw it again."

"You can't prove a thing," Mike said when Howard paused to drink more of his coffee.

"That remains to be seen. But error number two, that was the big one, correct, Michael? Namely, Harvey Billingsly."

"I never saw the old man in my life. Never."

"No, you didn't. But he saw you. He saw you last summer when you came to China House. The old man saw everyone who passed his inn. He even told Ken and me the mysterious light suddenly appeared again early last summer. That must have been you, Mike, putting in a little overtime. Oh, it was simple for you to get a key and call the overseer. Any excuse would do. You came to China House to set your stage, to go over every inch of the place so that you could manipulate your actors, us, from day one. The dark passage beside the stairs was perfect for the appearance of your little ghost. And the stove timer; you brought that with you. It's a very modern one that could not possibly be in a house closed and locked for over twenty years. We allowed our imaginations to run amuck and when you do that you start to swear that what isn't is.

"Billingsly saw you yesterday afternoon. You could feel his eyes on you, Mike, couldn't you? Scott's suicide would mean an inquest and an inquest would start the old man talking and the first thing he would talk about was seeing you in China House last summer. Then I would start getting ideas, and so would the police, and more questions would be asked that you would have no answers for. And I would be in possession of the picture, the con, and I might start questioning the tradesmen who supplied China House last week and learn that among them there was no young man with a son named Billy.

"It was a big risk but you had to do it. You had to silence Billingsly. Once we were all out of sight you went to the store room, got a pair of skis and returned to the inn."

"Anyone could have done the same thing, Doctor. Even you." In spite of himself Howard admired Mike Armstrong's courage.

"I could have, but I didn't. You did. Doing it was risky but resolving it was simple. As soon as the police had left us you began pointing the finger at Scott Evans. You even told me Scott had confessed to the crime. Scott killed Billingsly because the old man knew that Scott had caused his brother's accident and then Scott kills himself. You are a bastard, Michael, you are one despicable bastard."

Mike began to laugh, a note of hysteria in the sound. "You should have been the writer, Howard, not your son. By the way, do you know your little boy is as queer as a three dollar bill?"

Howard's clenched fists were the only outward sign that Mike had finally aroused his anger. "Error number three," Howard pushed on "was completely thanks to me and how happy that makes me, except for the fact that it almost killed Ken. After we had gone to bed you set the stage for Scott's suicide. You covered the hall floor with marbles and then went to rouse your star actor. What a shock it must have been when you found you couldn't wake him. It must have taken you ten seconds to realize I had given him a pill when I took him up to his room. You would have gladly carried him into the hall and tossed him down those steps but you couldn't do that, could you? I would have testified that Scott Evans was not capable of leaving his bed under his own steam until long after midnight. So you had to wait for the effect of the pill to wear off naturally and meanwhile Kenny—"

"You can't prove a thing, you stupid asshole," Mike cried. "Not a fucking thing."

"The police are going to find three sets of ski tracks in the snow, Mike."

"Let the stupid bastards find a hundred sets of tracks So what?" Michael Armstrong turned ugly. His mouth twisted into an insolent grin, his dark blue eyes turned black with rage and fear and the perspiration which had first appeared as dew on his forehead now covered his face like a greasy mask. "You, the police and all the ski tracks on the Alps can't prove a fucking thing," he ranted.

"But I can."

Both Howard and Michael jerked spasmodically at the sound of the gentle voice which answered Armstrong's outburst. Scott Evans stood in the doorway, his back erect and his unclouded eyes riveted on Mike. "I saw you, Michael. When you left my room yesterday afternoon I couldn't sleep so I went to your room but you weren't there. I walked to the window and saw you skiing down the hill."

The silence was audible. The two young men looked at each other, terror on the face of one and a sadness on the face of the other of an intensity that no human being should be made to suffer. Howard knew better than to intrude upon the moment.

"Why, Mike? Why?" Scott whispered. "For the money I provided for you in my will? I would have given you anything you wanted, Mike... anything."

Mike was panting; tears rolled down his face and mingled with sweat. "Look at me you bastard... look at me and tell me what you see."

"I see a beautiful guy, my friend, someone I loved and trusted," Scott answered.

"Do you know what I see when I look in the mirror?" Mike shouted. "Do you want to know? Well let me tell you. I see the chauffeur's son, that's what I see. The chauffeur's son. A fucking servant. Scotty's friend?" He began to laugh hysterically. "What a joke. What a fucking joke. I was Scotty's plaything. His toy. A jack-in-the-box, made to pop up when needed and then shoved back in when Scotty went to the parties and fancy balls and good schools." He took a step forward and began to punch the air with his fist. "Do you know you never introduced me to a single one of your friends... do you know your mother still looks down her nose at me... at the fucking chauffeur's son... and I don't want what you give me... I want my own... you hear me you little prick... my own."

Scott shook his head in disbelief. "No, Mike. No. You never

wanted to meet my friends from school. You refused, time after time, and no one ever treated you with anything but respect and even awe but you never lived up to your expectations so you blamed the world in general and me in particular for your self-inflicted failure."

Mike fell into a chair and began to sob. He buried his face in his arms and his shoulders heaved as he tried to contain his contorted body. Howard heard the pounding sound but there was now no mistaking where it came from or what it was. As he went to answer the door he saw Scott kneel and put his arm around Mike's shoulders.

Detective Parker greeted Howard with one loud bark. "There are three sets of tracks in that snow, mister, an' I ain't talking about the car."

"I know, Mr. Parker. I think you had better come in and meet the man who made the third set."

· XXVI ·

"I'm perfectly all right," Scott Evans reassured Howard for the third time. "I just feel a little disoriented, like waking up after a long sleep."

"In a way you have," Howard answered. "I don't want to scare you but when this business — I mean Michael — sinks in you might need help coping with it, especially after what you've just been through. Don't be afraid to ask for it."

Scott smiled and nodded. "I think I can handle it but if I find I can't I know where to come. Thank you, Howard."

They were in the sun room, Michael's absence a constant reminder of what had happened to all of them since coming to China House and what still lay ahead of them after they left. The handsome young man who had been led away by the police had taken all the mystery of the mansion with him. What remained was a somewhat big and overwhelming museum. An interesting place to visit but certainly not to be lived in.

Alice, who had come downstairs as soon as the police had left, sat in a corner chair, pale and trembling, her eyes red from crying. She twisted a wet, limp handkerchief between her fingers as she stared at Howard Roth.

"It's funny," Scott was saying. "I always envied Mike. His good looks, his intelligence, that magnetic personality and those big dreams. I thought Mike Armstrong was what life is all about and now I discover he hated life almost as much as he hated himself."

"Egotistical people often suffer from gross insecurity. It's all veneer on top and rot underneath." Howard looked at Alice and she managed a weak smile that made her appear even more pathetic and afraid.

"But Mike had everything going for him," Scott insisted.

"That's true," Howard said thoughtfully, "and his self-image was completely false. But imagination, Scotty, true or false, is the only reality and that's what wins all the time."

"You mean what I am doesn't make any difference, but what I think I am does?" Scott asked.

"Not always as simple as all that," Howard responded, "but you're close enough. And, by the way, the fact works both ways, for good or evil. I mean it creates villains as well as heroes."

"I never thought of Mike as a servant's son," Scott said. "If anything I felt he was superior to me in many ways. And I did want him to be a part of my crowd but he never wanted any part of them. He wouldn't even come to a ball game or movie with us."

"I believe you," Howard told him. "He was afraid of the competition. He had you hooked but feared he would be shown up in front of your peers. And don't you start getting any ideas about who's to blame for this bloody mess. Armstrong dug his own grave and you had nothing to do with it. Am I getting through?"

Scott laughed. "I hear you, Howard. I think I'm finished with blaming me for everything that happens around me. Including coincidences. That's what they were, weren't they? The teacher at Ryder and my old tutor."

"They were, but mixed with a little imagination they became as lethal as an atom bomb." Howard, who had been watching Alice from the corners of his eyes, now turned to her and casually asked, "Are you feeling better?"

"A little," she answered. "I just can't seem to accept what happened. It's like a nightmare."

"Something to eat might help," Scott quickly said. "It's way past lunch time and I don't think any of us have had anything but coffee all day." Scott's new-found confidence and his ability to play the part of host seemed to startle both Alice and Howard. They looked at Scott, Alice with astonishment and Howard with admiration, as he spoke. "And I'm sure poor Ken is starved. I'll go to the kitchen and put something togehter."

"Let me help you," Alice said, standing.

"It's not necessary."

"But I want to. It will give me something to do besides think."

Howard watched them leave and then he walked to the window, his thumb moving slowly across his chin. He looked out on yet another gray day in China House. When Alice returned she said Scott was taking a tray up to Kenny and then he would bring something into the sun room for them.

"I'm going to resign from the Institute as soon as we get back," Alice announced.

"I think that would be best."

"Like a piece of garbage, I'm out," she spat at him.

"I didn't say that, you did." There was no sympathy in Howard's voice.

Alice began pacing the room like a caged panther, moving as far as she could go and then turning to retrace the path that had led her nowhere. They could have been strangers in a depot, one knowing exactly where he was going, the other uncertain the train would even arrive or where it would take her if it did. The fear Alice had displayed earlier was now replaced with a nervous energy Howard had never seen her exhibit beore. She was seething with anger and he knew his aloofness was a major part of her consternation. Howard Roth smiled, hardly aware that he had done so.

"What do you find so amusing?" Alice snapped.

"Everything. Nothing. What difference does it make?"

"To you, obviously none." She had stopped in the center of the room, her hands buried deep in the pockets of her loose fitting jacket. "You're so damn smug, Howard. So secure. You think you can just walk out on me and go back to your precious son without a backward glance."

"Ken has nothing to do with this," Howard calmly answered.

"On the contrary, Ken has everything to do with this. Don't think I'm going to be the only one made to suffer—"

"We get what we deserve," Howard cut her short and the confrontation ended as abruptly as it had begun with Scott's arrival on the scene.

"I've got sandwiches and wine and your son was as hungry as a wolf." Scott's smiling face and bubbling conversation were in sharp contrast to the atmosphere in the sun room, but the young man, engrossed in his own thoughts, hardly noticed the others as he emptied the tray he carried on the sideboard. "Except for a slight headache he's feeling himself again," Scott continued. "In fact he wanted to come down and eat with us."

"He should rest until the headache is completely gone," Howard said.

"That's what I told him. Come on, help yourselves."

Alice hardly touched her food, seeming to prefer a lunch of wine and cigarettes. Howard made an effort to eat while Scott kept a conversation going which neither Alice nor Howard paid the slightest attention to. What a reversal of roles their visit to China House had brought about. Howard thought.

When they were done Scott said he was going back upstairs to keep Ken company and disappeared as soon as the words were spoken. Alice quickly began to follow him out of the room.

"I take it we'll be leaving as soon as Ken feels able."

"If the police are finished with us for now, and I think they are," Howard replied.

"I'll wait in my room."

"Not afraid of strange noises coming from the nursery?" Howard asked.

Alice, halfway to the door, stopped. Her shoulders tensed and rose slightly. "What did you say?" She kept her back to Howard.

"Those strange sounds you heard in the nurserry and told Ken about, knowing damn well he would tell me. Mike had no idea what rooms Scott would assign to us and as luck would have it you got the one next to the nursery. I couldn't hear what was going on in there so you had to tell us."

Now she turned to face him. "I had nothing to do with—"

"The old man's murder? No, you didn't. But you're as guilty as Armstrong and if there were any justice in this world you would hang with him."

"You would like that, wouldn't you?"

"I would love it."

"Well, at least you're honest." Alice didn't move from her position near the door. "It was a silly game. Mike said he wanted to play haunted house and he asked me to help."

"Stop it, Alice." Howard said with disgust. "Christ, stop it. Don't you know when to quit?"

"I did quit. I told you that a while ago."

"You are a brazen bitch, aren't you? So brazen that you almost got away with it. When the photo disappeared I did some research and learned that in magic acts and con games an accomplice was necessary to pull off the vanishing trick. And there were two of them; Scott and Michael. One obviously the accomplice to the other. But the obvious proved false so I tried the probable. Mike worked it all by himself, but that didn't add up either. So when the obvious and the probable don't work look to the impossible. I did, and there you were.

"I didn't get a travelogue of New England in the mail that week before the convention. You showed it to me and told me it had come in the mail and you pointed out the Seaford Inn, knowing that if I stayed there I would be sure to see China House. And you were waiting for me in my car that night I left Scott's in Sea-Air, so anxious to make love . . . so anxious to remove the photo from my pocket.

"But I wasn't supposed to see the substituted photo of the kid in my office. I wasn't supposed to see it till last night. I bet Mike gave you hell when I told him about the picture. Why did you do it, Alice? Your own diabolical turn of the screw?"

"I thought it would amuse you." She seemed very confident now that the calm had erupted into a storm.

"Well it didn't. I asked the receptionist if she had seen any strangers near my office and of course she hadn't. She had seen you and she saw you in my office every day. What a fool I was. What a bloody fool. I've been manipulated like a puppet on a string for the past five months and I know just where it started. On the beach at Sea-Air. Mike picked you up on the beach. Did you really think that handsome bastard was interested in you?" Howard began to laugh.

"Stop it!" Alice shouted. "Stop it!"

"I won't stop it, you pathetic fool. He was interested in Dr. Roth's assistant. He needed you and he got just what he wanted from you. I can just hear the two of you. The would-be movie star, broke and down on his luck while Scott Evans was so rich, and the misunderstood girlfriend who had to compete with my son. Scott and Ken had everything while you and Mike had nothing and Mike told you exactly how to load the dice. What did he promise you Alice? Money, I'm sure, but something even more. Me. I was the big prize. You would force my hand in front of Kenny and so we were treated to mysterious faces in the window. But that didn't work, did it?"

Howard was on his feet now, walking toward Alice. She held her ground, not retreating as he advanced.

"You knew what Mike had planned last night so you made that ridiculous pact with Kenny to get him out into the hall knowing damn well. . . ."

"Yes," Alice screamed. "Yes! I would do anything to get him out of my way."

"The only thing ever in your way was yourself."

She tried desperately to control herself but her voice rose and her head shook as she answered. "I'm not going to be the only one to suffer. You are, too, and I don't care what happens to me. I don't care, Howard."

"What the hell are you talking about?"

"This." She pulled a small bottle from her jacket pocket. "This is what I'm talking about. Your sedatives. The bottle is empty, Howard. Empty. If you want the rest of your pills you'll find them in Kenny's stomach."

Howard stared at the ranting woman. "You're crazy. You haven't been near Kenny all day."

"Guess, Doctor. Try the impossible."

He had her by the shoulders, shaking her. "What the fuck do you mean?"

She laughed wildly. "I emptied the bottle in the glass of wine Scott brought to Ken with his lunch. How long will it take, Howard? Twenty minutes. . . thirty. . . ."

He shoved her aside and began to run, only one thought in his head as he mounted the stairs two and three at a time. "When does the thought begin to act of its own volition, without the aid or consent of the thinker?"

The tranquil scene that Howard encountered in the upstairs bedroom seemed as insane as the reason for him breaking into the room. Ken was sitting up in bed and Scott lounged on a chair beside him. They looked at Howard, startled, when he burst through the door.

"The wine," Howard shouted.

"Dad, what's wrong?"

"Howard, what is it?"

"The wine. The wine Scott brought up with your tray. How much of it did you drink?"

Scott and Ken looked at each other, then at Howard. "What's the matter, Howard?"

"For God's sake just tell me how much wine you drank."

"None," Ken said.

"None?"

"He didn't want it," Scott said, still having no idea what Howard was after.

"I thought it would make my headache worse." Ken explained.

Howard, calmer now, looked at Scott Evans. "What did you do with the glass, Scott?"

"I brought it back downstairs and then... I remember, I only had to pour two more for us."

"And what did you do with Ken's glass?"

Scott shrugged. "I gave it to Alice."

· XXVII ·

The white lawn of China House was gorged with tire tracks and pitted with bootprints turned to icy craters. The Seaford Inn, gray and lifeless without the familiar spiral of smoke rising from its chimney, resembled a deserted fort routed by the invaders who had stormed it in search of justice. The house observed the battlefield, disinterested, assured that a thaw or a new dusting of snow would erase all traces of the war between good and evil. The Commodore had known that good and evil exists only in the minds of those who had invented the words and assigned them meaning. That the creation of one automatically gave birth to the other has not yet occurred to the inventors whose penance for their ignorance is eternal conflict between their humanity and their false sense of Godliness.

Howard turned from the window, arms folded across his chest, and watched Ken pack. "Are you sure you're well enough to make this trip?"

Ken paused momentarily and looked at his father. "I've never been surer of anything in my life." He tossed a sweater into one of the bags without bothering to fold it. "Scott wants to leave now and so do I."

Scott Evans had been functioning in a state of delayed shock since Mike had been taken away by the police. It would not last long, Howard knew. Alice's crisis had served to precipitate the inevitable. Howard and Scott had carried the unconscious woman to the car and then drove to the inn where the police were still at work. Acting quickly they had radioed ahead and an ambulance had intercepted the police van on the main road taking Alice, Howard and Scott to a hospital. Once they were assured that Alice would recover one of the officers offered the two men a ride back to the Seaford Inn and their car.

"Let's go, Scott," Howard had said. "The last thing she wants to see when she comes to is us."

Driving back to China House Scott had lapsed into a morbid silence and Howard knew shock had been replaced with reality. Scott Evans was about to take his first step on the road to recovery; it would be a long and lonely journey. Once back at the house Scott announced that he wanted to leave immediately and Ken had agreed. Together they had packed Mike's gear, to be dropped at the police station and Alice's, to be deposited at the hospital. "This is one hell of a job," Scott had said.

"It's the least we can do," Ken answered.

The road to recovery is long, Howard had thought as he watched the two young men, but perhaps, for Scott Evans, it wouldn't be lonely.

Now Howard helped his son with the packing. "It's going to be a while before Scott is completely well. He's just beginning to realize that Mike Armstrong fully intended to kill him."

"And I almost got in on the act. Christ... Alice... I still can't believe it."

Howard held down the lid of an over-stuffed bag as Ken closed and strapped it. "It's what comes from blaming others for our own inadequacies." He looked at his son. "And I'm not completely blameless, Ken."

"None of us are blameless, Dad. Even Scott knows that. He told me he was going to arrange for Mike's defense. Lawyers and whatever else Mike is going to need."

"Noblesse oblige?"

"You know better. He loved Mike for a long time and you don't turn it off like a cold shower. I admire Scott for the decision."

"So do I," Howard said. "Are you still going to write your China House book?"

Ken laughed. "Yes, and I'm going to be very kind to the Commodore. He wasn't really a bastard, you know. Weird, yes — but who isn't? His only crime was that he told it like it is."

"In our society, Ken, that's the greatest crime of all."

"Fuck our society."

"Now you sound like the Commodore," Howard answered with a broad grin.

"I hope I do." Ken helped his father close the other valise. "Did I ever tell you I keep a small apartment in New York?"

"No, but I long suspected you did."

Ken shook his head. "A fine pair we are. Suspected... thought... imagined.... No more, Dad. From now on we speak up loud and clear."

"Speak, I'm listening."

Ken took a deep breath. "I thought I would settle into my place on a more permanent basis and work on my book there."

Howard rubbed his chin with his thumb. "So," he began, "I take it Scott is going to close the house in Sea-Air and move back to New York."

Ken flushed. "It's been mentioned."

"So you got the rich kid, eh?"

"I don't know what I have, Dad. I only know that I want you to wish me well."

Howard put his hand on his son's shoulder. "I do wish you well, Kenny, and more. But remember, only you can make the dream come true."

"'Who is there? bellowed the voice of God. It is thee, my Lord,'" Ken recited.

"And don't ever forget it."

"After this," Ken said, stretching his arms wide, "how can I forget? But there's one mystery that's still unsolved."

"What's that?"

"The hall clock. Why did it stop ticking?"

Howard began to laugh. "That, Watson, is no mystery at all. Do you remember that headache you woke up with this morning?"

"Do I ever."

"Well, that's what stopped the clock. Your hard head. When it struck the base of the clock it jarred the mechanism and halted the pendulum."

Ken touched his blond head. "We really are responsible for everything, aren't we."

"I'm afraid, my son, we are."

The three survivors, bundled against the cold, closed the door to China House and walked quickly to the waiting car. Scott took the wheel with Ken beside him as Howard made himself at home in the back seat. "Do you think you'll ever come back?" Ken asked.

Scott thought before he answered. "I might. Would you like to come with me if I do?"

"I'm wide open, Scotty."

"Stay that way for a while, okay?"

'Okay."

As the black car turned to head down the hill Ken caught a glimpse of the cemetery. The erect monuments were boldly silhouetted against the fast darkening winter sky. They were now candlesticks crowned with petrified flames that almost glowed as they caught the reflection of the setting sun. Ken smiled and quickly rolled down the car window, turning his head for a final look at China House.

A light was shining in a second floor window of the mansion. It wasn't beckoning. . . it was saying goodbye.